The Rockstar's BODYGUARD

INTERNATIONAL BESTSELLING AUTHOR
PEBBLES LACASSE

FIRST EDITION 2025
Paperback 978-1-989979-60-0

EDITED BY:
Partners In Crime Book Services – Lily Luchesi

COVER DESIGN © 2025 PEBBLES LACASSE
PUBLISHED BY PEBBLES LACASSE
WWW.PEBBLESLACASSE.COM

CHAPTER ONE

Fifty-thousand people scream and pump their fists as they rock to the beat of the music. Having all those eyes staring at me will never cease to thrill me. They love me! They love my voice. They love the steady, heavy beat of Venus's drums, the screams from Lacey's guitar, the deep thrums from Pony's bass, Dex's thunderous trombone, and the high and low notes from the voice that got me to where I am today: a rock star making millions of dollars every year and touring the world.

Not all of my adoring fans are good people. I've had stalkers threaten to kidnap, rape, or kill me. Any of these people looking at me now could be one of them. I don't fear them. When I'm alone, the memories of those who've already hurt me are what have me shaking with fear.

Clearing that thought from my mind, the last note tears from my body followed by a gasp to fill my emptied lungs as the last few beats of the song come to an end.

My screamed words rip through the humongous speakers. "Thank you, Calgary, Alberta!"

The roar of the crowd explodes through every cell in my body. Is my pride making it difficult to catch my breath or the exhaustion from the efforts of the high-adrenaline performance of an amazing concert?

I set the microphone back on its stand, step back, and wave with both arms. The crowd screams for an encore at a deafening level and the urge to perform yet another song has my adrenaline pumping enough to make me want to begin the entire playlist again, but my band is striding off the stage as they too wave and smile.

In the wings, Venus and Lacey hug and kiss, as they were married in secret two years ago. Lacey's reputation is that of a loose woman with a need for dominance, which doesn't draw in a crowd if they knew she wasn't available for their fantasies of owning her. Venus is stunningly gorgeous with deep, brown skin, and she's known as the good wild woman with an adventurous reputation. Following tradition, they'll head up to their room and make love all night to take advantage of the adrenaline spike.

Pony and Dex will likely party in one of their rooms with some of the set-up crew until late into tomorrow morning. The hangover they'll bear will last for hours, but it's their way of celebrating a great concert.

Me, I'll go back to my room and drink alone to drown my sorrows while I cry in a bathtub of bubbles. Coming off the high isn't as easy for me as it is for the band. I have trouble leaving it all behind; the excitement of knowing how much they want me. When, in reality, I'm lonely.

Millions of people love my music and claim to love me, but I have nobody to call my own who truly knows me. My band and manager know the real me well and not just my rock and roll persona.

For twenty-six years, the girl who lived next door to the Frewns, Rachel Hanover, has tried to understand the shitty attitude I earned from the torment I suffered as a child. She knows me about as well as anyone could. We basically grew up together, but I can only handle her clinginess for short amounts of time before I need my space. I still call her my bestie, but we're not as close as we used to be. Maybe we were never close as young children, and I put her in my circle simply because she was the only person my age I could trust. We live completely different lives as adults, but I'll always give her extra financial support whenever she needs it. Not that she asks all that often.

My career has been my life. It's cluttered up every moment of my days, weeks, months, and years. At thirty-two years old, I'm coming to realize how much I wish a man knew *me*, the real me and not the vixen my career has driven my reputation to carry.

Each time I meet someone who may be a great prospect, his true colours show through, proving he doesn't value me as much as my financial success or my status which could boost his own claim to fame. Where are all the trustworthy men? Can a life in the limelight allow for an honest love story or will my music be the only true love of my life?

We're ushered by two members of our hotel's security team plus one of our longstanding guards, Brick, through the back halls of the stadium to the private elevator. The sounds of excited fans continue to hum through the air until the metal doors slide closed. My bandmates excitedly recall their favored moments through the performance as I quietly watch the lighted numbers ascend. A low ding signifies we've reached the exclusive twenty-eight floor where only the elite can afford to lay their heads.

We pile out while Lacey's steps mimic a child's enthusiasm. She leads the group down the wide hall. Her and Venus disappear past the open door to their room before Venus kicks it closed with the three-inch heel of her thigh-high leather boots. Nobody will see them for the rest of the night.

Pony's calm as he hugs me and tells Dex he'll shower and see him soon. He pulls off his leather vest before disappearing through a door in his room I assume is the bathroom.

When we come to Dex's room, he reaches for my hand to stop me from continuing to my presidential suite.

Knowing how difficult it is for me to ease myself back to reality, the sadness in his sexy blue eyes forces me to fake a smile to ease his concerns. Although I treasure all of them, Dex is my closest friend among the bandmates. If he weren't strictly a lover of the penis, we'd be years into a marriage.

"Do you want me to come in? We can drink all the booze in your stocked bar, order everything on the menu, and eat until our stomachs explode." Seeing that I'm unconvinced, his eyes stop halfway through a roll. "Fine. You drive a hard bargain. We can watch whatever sappy, tearjerker movie you want, and you can cry yourself into a puddle." The humor in his tone was mixed with honest concern.

My brows nearly ascend to my hairline. "Who's going to cry themselves into a puddle?"

Dex's eyes dart down and to the right. "Okay. I'll be the one crying, but I'll let you laugh at me." He scoffs teasingly at my chuckle. "It's not my fault you're dead inside."

"It's true; I am, but no, thank you. I'll be fine. Really, I will." My head tips as a weary grown escapes me. "I'm going to take off the layers of make-up clouding my pores, pour myself a giant glass of wine, and slide my tired body into the tub."

He takes my hands in his as the bodyguards talk quietly among themselves. "Jade, I can join you. We'll leave our panties on, so none of our bits mistakenly brush past each other." Feigning disgust, his lips pinch and brows lower as a cringing shiver lifts his shoulders.

I pat a gentle kiss to his cheek before my palm presses to the sweaty skin over his heart aside the leather harness criss-crossing his chest. "Dex, we can bathe together when you decide to give vagina a go. Until then, this girl soaks alone."

Defeated, he pouts with a twist of his mouth. "All right. If you need me, I'm only a phone call away. Well, for the next hour anyway. After that, I plan to be deep in someone's ass or a slurring, drunken fool. If you need me…"

My green eyes squint. "Maybe I'll wait until you're drunk so I can sway you into a night of passion with my feminine wiles."

Dex saunters away from me backward and says, "Girlfriend, I'm looking for a hairy chest and a deep voice begging me to go deeper into his tight ass."

"Maybe if your equipment were longer, they wouldn't have to beg for more." I tease as my long legs stride further down the hall. "But I suppose we're out of luck: I have a tight ass but no hairy chest. Looks like I'm going to do it solo again tonight."

"Call if you need me," he says as he winks at the second security guard who doesn't seem flattered by the wink.

The mirror reflects a beautiful brunette with dark, heavy make-up a mess from sweat. Dancing, singing, and simply standing before those bright, hot lights had me sweating beneath my leather shorts and barely-there bra and harness. It's damn near impossible to see the crowd gleaming at me from meters away, but their excitement could be felt in spades.

The rockstar behind the reflection is a simple woman whose professional dreams have come true. She has almost everything she's ever wanted. Almost.

Hidden behind the façade called Jade is a broken child who barely survived being raised by a physically abusive alcoholic mother until fostered by a diddler at the age of four. His secret was exposed when I was seven and finally sent to live with Mike and Feona Frewn.

Living with them was like I'd struck gold. Mike and Leona Frewn were the perfect couple for a shattered little girl who needed space and time to heal her emotional scars.

They did their best to show me how to love, and that I could be loved, but it was too late. I was damaged goods. For that reason, I make sure to call them once a week to check in with them because I know how much they worry about me.

Do I love them? I suppose, but what is love? How can it be measured? Do I want them to die? No, but I don't want to see the people at my concerts die either, so do I love them, too? Do I want to talk to the Frewns every day and hug them at every greeting? No. So, the question remains; what the fuck is love?

My heart bears an impenetrable armour built from years of pushing down the anger and pain associated with those memories, and that's not going to change.

As the gauze pads and witch hazel remove layer after layer of the rockstar make-up, tears drip down my cheeks. As the black mascara smears from the oil, the image mirrors the person I am today: broken but strong.

With a snap of the latch, the black harness criss-crossed below my breasts that feeds down to the leather bands encircling my upper thighs falls to the floor. The black push-up bra goes next, freeing my C-cup breast from the leather prison. I unzip the leather shorts, and they fall to the floor, followed by the soft beige panties I never remove during costume changes on the wings of the stage. I kick them aside and bend at my hips to unzip the knee-length leather boots and toss them onto the costume pile.

My cell phone rings from the bedroom, but I won't answer it. Anyone who knows me well enough to have that phone number is well-aware that I need time to let the adrenaline rush subside and my mood to level out.

I dry off using the softest white towels I have ever touched and consider going to Pony's room to join him and Dex and the selected crowd of groupies to party like—well, like a rockstar.

A knock at the door has me peeking through the peephole. I sce Dex walking down the hall in his jeans and t-shirt. Curious as to why he knocked, I opened the door to confront him. A bouquet of bright red roses—my favourite flower rests at my feet. An envelope with the word *Love* written on the front is tucked between the flowers.

"Someone has a Valentine." Dex sings before he slips through the open door to Pony's room where the music, voices, and laughter spill into the hall. How does Pony manage to get so many groupies past security in such a short time?

I yell even though Dex won't hear me. "Not likely. They're probably from Alex."

Alex has been my manager for twelve years. He's like a father to me. As such, he isn't afraid to give me orders if he thinks it'll benefit me, even if I disagree. He's almost always right, so I often do as he says under protest.

My heart pounds because I know the roses aren't from Alex. If he sends anything, it's a bottle of champagne and a high-priced male prostitute. "*Only the best for his girl,*" he always says. A night of physical pampering always brings up my spirits.

A quick scan of the hall proves I'm alone, so I pick up the envelope and slide the paper free. Only one crease folds the mauve paper. They always write on mauve paper.

A whisper or a whistle could draw your ear. I'm never far away. When will you realize that you belong to me? We are destined, after all.

My slippered foot kicks over the vase. The roses float as the water washes over the blue and burgundy carpet. The note falls from my fingers as they go numb. Has all the air around me been sucked away?

Brick, our main security guy, rushes from down the hall toward me as his eyes jolt from the shattered vase to me, and I shoot him an infuriated glare.

"Where were you?" Not giving him a chance to respond, I point my finger at the huge man with apologetic eyes, and scold him from behind clenched teeth, "Not acceptable!"

My fingers span across my towel covered chest and force myself to breathe through the rage. I step back and allow the door to slam closed. Nearly tripping, I rush to the bedroom to find my phone and dial Alex.

His voice is low so as to not disturb the muffled voices creeping over the speaker around him. "Jade, how did the concert go?"

"There's another note."

Seconds pass as his breathing grows louder. "I'll be there in a minute. Don't touch anything."

"Too late!" I toss the phone onto the fluffy white duvet and quickly slip into leggings and a sleeveless t-shirt.

The lock clicks and the door swings open as I rush from the bedroom. Alex strolls into the suite with trepidation narrowing his chocolate eyes. The letter is pinched between his forefinger and thumb as he reads, careful not to rub off any DNA or fingerprints.

He drops it onto the glass table by the door and runs his hand over his bald head before scratching his fingers through his salt & pepper beard.

"Okay. Enough of this. Whoever this is has gotten too close."

"You're goddamn right they're getting too fucking close. What the fuck, Alex? This security team isn't doing their fucking job."

His head shakes in defeat. "I know. We're trying to find a replacement for Jackson."

My hands rest on my hips as my weight rests on my left leg. "Yeah. What's with that? He shouldn't have fucking split with a day's notice. Fucking asshole!"

Alex slowly turns to face me and takes a deep breath as his stature and glare try to put me in my place, but fail, as always. "His mother died. He's grieving. I told him to go and care for his elderly father. What was I going to do; tell him he couldn't attend his mother's funeral because he had obligations to protect your spoiled ass?"

We lock eyes, and his lips bear a shadow of a quirk. My arms rise at my sides, palms up, and I nod. "Duh! I'm the fucking queen."

"And you're just as spoiled." His palm cups my cheek as his smile proves his 52 years on this earth haven't always been kind.

As his hand drops away, I step away to get some distance and grunt when my fingers fail to brush through my wet hair. "Are the key card swipes recorded to know who came and went?"

His head shakes as he stands poised in his tailored grey suit. "We're looking into it. The hotel staff key usage is recorded, and security will question them. Maybe they saw something out of the ordinary."

My arms cross my chest, and the pressure of tears threaten to make their appearance. Although Alex has seen me at my worst, crying in front of people isn't something I do. A long time ago I learned that tears bring on sympathy and often hugs come with a catch. I don't like to be touched, including hugs. My band is the exception and only on rare occasions. Alex always keeps his distance, and I treasure him for it.

He leans against the pale-yellow wall as his hand brushes down his coffee-coloured face. His finger punches at his phone's screen before he lifts it to his ear. Seconds later, his fatherly voice breaks through the silence in the room.

I continue to pace as he speaks.

"How are you, Fixer?" Alex nods and picks a fuzz from his grey dress pants. "I'm fine. I'm calling because I have a job for you, if you're interested." He unbuttons his suit coat and sits on the white sofa with his left foot at rest on his right knee. "Protection. My client has a stalker and they're getting too close. She needs constant guarding. Nothing but the best of the best for her." He snickers and sniggers at me.

Alex's arm lays along the backrest as his eyes look at nothing in particular. I sit on the white leather armchair across from the sofa and stare at Alex as my head shakes. "Yeah. She needs a babysitter."

"I don't need a fucking babysitter." Alex ignores my statement, so I toss one of the silver packaged chocolate candies I'll never eat from the bowl on the table. "Alex, I don't need a fucking babysitter!"

The phone parts from his ear. "You're getting a bodyguard whether you want one or not."

I flop back on the chair and cross my arms over my chest like a spoiled child on the verge of a tantrum.

"And you trust him?" Alex asks into the phone and tosses the chocolate up and catches it several times before tucking it into the pocket of his lapel. "I'll get you that information. I look forward to hearing from you."

He slips his phone in the same pocket and laces his fingers together on his lap. That look proves I'm in for a scolding.

"I need a drink. Join me?" I ask, and he shakes his head, but his thoughts are miles away.

I stand to pour myself another glass of wine, take a long swig, and sigh as the red liquid swirls inside the crystal glass. I've come a long way from sipping cheap red wine from plastic cups. Now I guzzle expensive wine in crystalware and rarely take the time to savour it.

"I'll have someone here tomorrow before we leave for Vancouver. You'll be nice to him?" he demands in the form of a question as he glares at me like a father to a petulant daughter.

"Do you know this guy?" Another mouthful of wine eases down my throat.

"Not personally, but if Fixer recommends him, he'll be the best." Alex stands with a low grunt only someone into their fifties can afford. "Don't stay up all night; you have the talk show interview in the morning. Costume, make-up, and hair will be here at six. Please, eat and shower before they get here. Time is limited. You have to be there by 8:30 AM and it's a fifteen-minute drive."

He takes my hands in his and smiles at me. At 5'10", the same height as him, meeting his falsely happy expression is easy. My smile is just as unconvincing as his.

Alex leaves and closes the door behind him. I'm alone again.

CHAPTER TWO

The sprawl of green in the valley is vast before me as I lounge in my Adirondack chair with my feet perched on a log cut to the perfect height. The air is almost chilli enough to warrant steam from my breath because the day has merely awoken and isn't yet in full bloom.

Birds sing their songs as they seek breakfast and stretch out their wings from being snuggled against their small bodies through the dark hours. The range from the tiny voices from yellow finches to the cackle from the Jaybirds, the silence of the night is no longer.

Steam rises from my coffee mug in a sensual dance, reminding me of how long it's been since I've had a sensual moment with anyone. How long has it been since the incident?

Just as I'm about to take another sip from my mug, a deep voice startles me and I jolt upright, spilling coffee down the front of my shirt.

"What the fuck, man? You scared the shit out of me. Give a guy a little warning next time." My palm rubs the front of my shirt to no avail as I set the mug on the chair's armrest.

"Sorry, Arrow. I should have called first but wasn't sure if you'd answer this early in the morning."

"If I knew it was your sorry ass calling, I wouldn't have." Giving up on the shirt, I grimace and reach up to shake what's left of my best friend's hand. "Want a coffee?"

"No. No. I've had my fill. Kim asked me to cut back on my caffeine, so to appease her, I only have one cup in the morning."

I lean back and sip from my half-empty mug. "She sure has you by the balls."

Not skipping a beat as he sits in the chair beside me, he snaps, "And I love the way her soft hands cradle them."

We chuckle and sit in silence to take in the stunning scenery.

Fixer lives in town which is a forty-five-minute drive from here. He used to live closer but moved to town when his wife was having a troublesome pregnancy with their twin girls. They decided living closer to the school, church, hospital, and basically everything would be a better place to raise the girls.

"What brings you here this early, Fixer, if not to sneak a caffeine fix?"

"I have a proposal." He holds his hand up and tips his head. "Before you say no, let me give you the details. All right?"

Fixer's real name is Emmett Reckset. We grew up together and did almost everything in life together. We attended the same grade school and high school, went to the same church before I decided God is an asshole and he won't miss one person's prayers, and joined the Navy on the same day. Who knew that when we signed our names at the exact same time that our destinies were sealed to suffer more pain than any man should.

"Make it quick," I mumble and clench my jaw.

We've both been given honorable discharges due to medical issues from *the incident*. We don't talk about it even though the memory awakens when we see each other. It's obvious in the way our eyes carry more gloom when we look at each other. I love him. I'll always love him, but the ache his presence carries cuts deep. That memory is too painful for both of us.

"A singer has been getting death threats from a stalker. Guess who it is?"

I cut in quickly. "No."

He sighs in frustration. "Listen, I worked for Alex DaVinette years ago, after our first tour and before we did the second. He's the guy you hire to make you famous, but the man has no clue how to hire qualified security to keep his client safe.

This stalker is getting too close, and he needs our help. She's in danger."

"And? What does this have to do with me?" My tone carries the indignation of a man with an icy heart. "I'm done watching the back of others. This is my life now." My palm raises toward the vast wilderness.

"What life?" Fixer stands and leans against the railing facing me. "I worry about you. You're up here all alone with only the demons that haunt you to keep you company. I'm surprised they haven't taken over and drove you to insanity."

The way his deformed hand grips the railing using only two long fingers and three short stumps has me turning my head so the memory of how he got that way doesn't assault me. It comes and goes but seeing the way he looks now— because of what I did—is almost too much to bear.

"I'm fine up here, and I like being alone. How many times have you wanted to have a moment of quiet, but the wife and kids are there to stay?"

Fixer's deformed pink lips twist as his head nods.

I sip my cool coffee and grimace. "I can sit on my deck, wrap my fingers around my shaft, and jack off all day if the mood hits. *You* can't do that." As soon as the words leave my mouth, I'd give my left arm to take them back. "Fuck, I didn't mean it the way it came out."

"Nah, it's okay." Fixer lifts his arms to hold what's left of his hands to look at them. "Maybe that's why I keep the wife around; she'll gladly jerk me off whenever I ask her to."

After the incident, Fixer spent months in hospitals. They saved what they could of his hands and facial features; the rest was amputated. His face is nothing like it was growing up and it eats at me. He had so many surgeries, so much physio, and more pain than any man should experience. There's still pain today, but he never complains. He suffered physical scars while mine ached deep and haven't healed over.

My hand rubs down my face as a heavy sigh escapes me. I lean forward on the chair as I stare into the nearly empty mug. "Why are you asking me to do this job and not someone else; someone who's looking for the work?"

"I don't know." His shrug is in my peripheral vision. "Do you want the job or not? If nothing else, it'll get you a front row seat to some rock concerts."

With my mug in hand, I rise and stretch my legs. "I don't listen to rock. I'm a country music boy. You know that."

Fixer follows me through the eight paneled glass door and into the house. As he does each time he comes over, he admires the impressive woodwork I put into the redesign of my kitchen. It may not be huge, but I outdid myself when I updated certain areas of the house. Every cupboard, countertop, stool, and cabinet I made from wood harvested on my property. I cut the trees, milled them, dried them, and worked until my fingers bled—literally. This kitchen is my pride and joy. A lot of the furniture in this house was built by either myself or my grandfather.

He passed away when I was overseas. There was no way to get home in time for the funeral, so I had to mourn him while watching my back for stray bullets or bombs.

Gramps was a kind-hearted man. He built this cabin and added onto it as the years passed. He raised my father here, but at the age of eighteen, my father left and never came back. My Gramps buried my Grams at the top of the hill about two hundred meters from the house. She loved to sit there in the shade from the horse chestnut tree that once stood tall and proud, and read. It was her favourite place, so putting her to rest there only made sense. I had to cut the old tree down last year after lightning hit it and split it down the center, killing it. To appease her, I planted another horse chestnut seedling in its place.

Gramps willed the property deed to me, not my father—his son. Dear old Dad disappeared when I was three-years-old. He left my mother to raise me on her own. Having no family of her own after her parents passed away in a freak boating accident, she was truly alone. He took us under his wing. Thanks to him, we didn't have to struggle to pay for food or rent. He helped out when he could.

It was Gramps who taught me the woodworking skill. He loved wood like nobody I've ever met and was damn talented. I loved him so much and his death hit me hard. After being informed of his death through my mother's letter, I broke down and cried like a baby. My troop didn't tease me as we'd all cracked at some point. That's when Fixer sat beside me and offered me one of the cookies his mother sent him. No words were spoken, but his company was better than anything he could have said.

"I haven't forgotten how you love the wallowing songs of men and women complaining about their partner leaving them and taking their dog with them, and how they took their revenge on their truck. No thanks."

He isn't entirely wrong. "Angry music brings out the anger in me, and that's what rock music is all about."

Fixer shrugs because he knows I'm not far off the mark. "So, what do you think? Do you want to do this or not?"

"Let me think about it." I lift the coffee pot to offer him some but again he refuses.

"No, thanks." He sits on the oak stool with the spindled legs my grandfather made many years ago and still stands sturdy today. "There's no time to think; you'd fly out today."

My head rolls as I turn to glare at him. "I can't just get up and leave."

Fixer turns on his chair as he looks around the place. "Why not? You don't have animals relying on you, there's no kids you have to explain your absence to, and you don't have a woman to beg forgiveness. So, yeah, you can just up and leave."

He's right. I'm always prepared to leave at a moment's notice. The packed rucksack in my bedroom closet proves it. Nobody knows what can happen from one moment to the next, and as someone who's seen the worst in people, I wouldn't stick around if something came down the wire.

After a sip of coffee and a wince at how hot it is, I sigh and rub my thumb along my bottom lip to wipe away a stray drip. "Where at?"

Fixer straightens his spine and clears his throat. "Calgary. She's doing a talk show and then leaving later in the day to fly to Vancouver. They want you there before the flight."

"Today?" My glance at my naked wrist reminds me I haven't put my watch on yet. The clock on the stove reads 7:30 AM. "I'd have to call for a flight and likely won't make it there in time."

Fixer reaches into his pocket and slides a few folded papers my way. I reluctantly pick them up and recognize one page as a boarding pass. The flight time reads 8:22AM.

"Cutting it a bit short, aren't you?" I ask through a smile and a scoff. "And what would you have done if I said no?"

"I suppose I'd have gotten back in my car and driven home while I begged the booker for a refund."

After one last gulp from my mug, I dump it and rinse the mug before setting it upside down in the sink. "Fine. Let me get dressed and you can drive me to the fucking airport."

"It's the least I can do." Fixer turns on the stool before he stands headed toward the door. "I'll wait outside."

"You're a fucking asshole," I say, and he laughs as he closes the door behind him.

Dressed in my blue jeans, a black t-shirt, my leather jacket, and the black boots I always wear when on the job – a habit brought on by my time in service – I lock up and toss my ruck sack over my shoulder. My boots thump the dirt and sporadic sprigs of green grass toward Fixer's pick-up.

I toss my sack in the back and climb in. "Let's go, fucker."

His head tilts as he slips the truck into reverse. "It's *Fixer,* not fucker. You continue to get them confused no matter how many times I correct you."

"Just drive."

CHAPTER THREE

No matter how much coffee I guzzled, the haze of sleepiness can't be shaken away. The make-up artist did what she could to hide the bags beneath my eyes.

Waiting just off stage to be introduced by the host, my head bobs side to side as I shake out my hands. Doing live interviews should come natural to me by now, but it's a task I'll never be comfortable with. The deep-rooted fear I'll say something inappropriate or give away too much of my private life or that of my band has my stomach in knots.

Alex is chattering about some last-minute instructions on what I can and can't discuss. He's adamant I don't say anything about the stalker because it may taunt them to take the next step. It's not something I want to discuss with anyone let alone tell the entire world how vulnerable I feel. I'm a rockstar, and that means I'm supposed to be tough and afraid of nothing. Right?

The host greets the audience and applause erupts. She yaps on about something she did last night, but I'm not listening to her words. How can I when Alex won't shut up.

A tap on my shoulder draws my attention.

"You're on. Go." A tiny man with grey hair and more wrinkles than a sherpa is pointing to the stage.

How did I miss my name being introduced?

My stomach feels light as air as my legs carry me onto the stage without me willing them to move. As if programmed to do so, my smile grows wide to show my bleached white teeth. The screams and claps drown out the three-inch high heeled black knee-high boots that surely clack on the two steps up to the platform.

I'm greeted by the host with a quick hug like we're old friends even though we've never met. Welcome to the world of show business where everything is fake for ratings.

"How have you been, Jade?" Kelly takes my hand and leads me to the two white sofas.

Not a sound comes when I sit on one of the stiff sofas. It's harder than it looks, which leads me to think they're made with little cushion to prevent the sound of fabric from being picked up by the tiny microphones attached to our shirts.

The soft shush from my leather pants as I cross my legs is barely noticed, so why the shitty sofas?

Like the professional I am, my voice is calm and my smile wide. "I'm well. How about you? What's new with you, Kelly?"

Should I have asked that question? It leads to the fact that I don't watch this show. Who has the time? Not me. But I'm not supposed to let the show know that, even though they must know people with busy careers in the business of *show* don't have much free time for television, especially if they're on tour.

If the question bothered her, she isn't showing it. "I was just about to tell everyone that my daughter has gotten her black belt. We're so proud of her."

A name is whispered through my earpiece, but I don't use it. "Give her my congratulations, will you?"

"Sure thing. She'd love to see you, but we all know how busy you are lately." Her eyes widen as she picks up the mug of water on the low glass table separating the two small sofas. "Tell us about the tour? How's that going?"

My hands rest on my thigh as I glance between the crowd in the stands and a wide-eyed Kelly. "The tour is going very well. This time I wanted to make it to every province in Canada. The only one left is British Columbia, and I'll be heading there soon. The Vancouver concert is set in three days and we're all so excited to play for the Vancouverans – Vancouverers?

"I think it's Vancouverites, but I could be wrong." Kelly glances past the crowd but I'm not sure who she's trying to get the answer from. "I'm sure you'll find out before you get there. If not, they aren't going to care as long as you play your heart out for them."

"That's the intention. We always give everything we have on stage. Concert goers spend a lot of money on tickets just to see us play, so we do our best to never disappoint."

Kelly's eyes widen and she sets her mug in front of her. "And pay for tickets they do. Concert tickets go for so much these days. It's not like it was when I was a teenager. But everything is so expensive, especially after Covid."

"We can't blame price hikes on Covid alone. There are money grabbers everywhere who'll take advantage of situations for their own greed. My tickets sell for fifty dollars, but my fans pay so much more because of the greedy companies selling them and government taxes." My head shakes as my hand waves between us. "Let's not get into politics because that's where this conversation is heading."

Our silent eye rolls and scoffs show our disapproval of our political situation.

Her hands raise between us as excitement widens her eyes. "Tell us about the new album? There are rumours something is in the works. So, tell us the nitty gritty of it all. What's the theme of this one?"

Well, Kelly. The theme of this one is my own personal hell, my anger and anxiety caused by the person stalking me, the dreadful thought of never feeling safe, and the exhaustion caused by having to wear the veil of a fake personality whenever I go into public.

Knowing I can't say all of that, I repeat the statement given to me for just such a question. "The new album's theme will be revealed at a later date, but that was a great attempt at pulling that information from me. You're good, but not sly enough for me." We both chuckle. "I can say that these songs are a bit different from my usual style, but I think you're all going to love this album."

"I heard through the grapevine that something special will come with the purchase of a CD or vinyl record. Is that true?"

My body shifts to face the crowd a bit more. "Yes. One-hundred CDs and one-hundred vinyl records will be randomly chosen to have a picture of the band with all of our signatures on them. Anyone who purchases a hardcopy version of the album could get a surprise inside.

"It's like Charley and the Chocolate Factory with the winning ticket. I love it!"

My fingers play with the hem of my leather vest that doesn't cover my belly button.

The crowd screams their applause and Kelly yells over them as she speaks to the camera with the red light. "We'll be right back. Don't go anywhere because we're going to take calls from some of our viewers."

Suddenly someone yells, "We're in commercial. Two-minutes."

Kelly smiles at me before she leans toward me and I to her. Waving off the make-up woman about to touch-up her lipstick, she covers her mic with her phone and whispers, "I heard you have a stalker?"

That information wasn't made public. I wonder who her sources are because they're damn good investigators.

"Imagine that; a rockstar with a crazy fan. It's not unheard of." My tone was snarkier than I'd intended but her question took me off guard.

Her eyelids flutter as her mouth opens and closes twice before she speaks. "I didn't mean anything by it. I had a stalker break into my home in Tuscany. Thankfully, my family wasn't there at the time."

My brows lift in their center and my lips pull into a stiff line as my shoulders sag. "Sorry. It's a touchy subject. I didn't mean to snap at you. It's just been really hard and—"

"And you're afraid. It's okay to be afraid. There are scary people out there. To some people, a public figure belongs to them. They forget we're human with real emotions and lives that aren't anything like we portray to them." Her hand reaches for mine, which I give to her. "I just want to let you know how sorry I am that this is happening to you. If there's anything I can do, please don't hesitate to call me. My manager will give you my personal cell number. Use it. Okay?"

I swallow down my weakness and prepare to toughen up for the camera. Rockstars aren't weak!

The deep voice counts down before the red light on the camera beams.

Kelly releases my hand, and we sit back, both wearing wide smiles as fake as my tits, but they'll never see through them because we are well-practiced at creating a great façade.

"Welcome back. As promised, we're going to take some calls from fans of Jade. Here's the first caller. Andrea, what's your question?"

A female voice squeals from excitement, and it pierces our ears. Her quivering voice speaks with difficulty. "Oh, my god! I can't believe I'm talking to Jade! Well, and you, Kelly. I can't forget you. You're great! But, Jade! Oh, my god! This is so—"

Kelly nods to the audience to share the caller's enthusiasm. "What's your question, Andrea?"

The woman's voice calms but still reeks of awe. "Jade, first of all, let me tell you how much I love you."

Love me? She doesn't love me. She might love my music but not me, Phoebe Moore.

"Who do you think of when you write songs about being in love?"

Kelly's mouth forms an O as she sits up straighter. "That's a good question. Is there someone special in your life or is there one that got away?"

Why do people always ask the same questions? Can't they come up with something new? Why does the love life of famous people interest them so much?

Clearing my throat sounds loud when picked up by the microphone. My fingers comb through my long dark hair to pull the wave off my cheek and away from my eye.

"If there were someone—and that's only an if—I wouldn't give their name on live television."

Kelly bites her perfectly painted pink bottom lip before she looks at the camera. "That's not a no! The suspense will drive us mad, but we won't push."

Good because I'm not going to tell everyone how this rock star who can have any number of partners any day of the week goes to bed alone every night and cries herself to sleep.

Instead, I smirk and wave my brows as my palms lift at my sides to add to the mystery.

She turns her body as she switches her crossed legs. "Next caller, Michael. What's your question?"

"Jade, I love you. You love me, too. We're destined, after all." The voice well masked through artificial intelligence sounded almost human.

A cold shiver rushes down my spine. My face pales and a moment passes before the spinning in my head stops. "Michael, is it? If I did love you, you'd have no reason to disguise your voice. Therefore, you're a fan, not my lover. Why don't you drop the AI and talk to me like a real man would."

Ignoring my request, their next question makes it difficult to maintain my composure. "Did you enjoy my note? I love that mauve paper. Mauve is your favourite colour."

They aren't wrong. "Yes, but everyone knows that."

Kelly's squinting her eyes prove she hasn't realized this is my stalker and I need her to cut them off. Shock suddenly erupts onto her face as she spins to look at someone behind the scenes and waves her hand at her throat to suggest they cut them off.

The voice says one more thing before hanging up. "I'll see you in Vancouver."

Kelly spins to look at the camera as her fingers pull a lock of hair from her cheek. "We're going to take a quick break and we'll be right back."

The red light on the camera dies out and the male voice alerting everyone to the break rings through the room.

Kelly leans toward me as she stands. I rise on shaky legs and fake my smile, as I've been trained to do like a monkey at a circus. She takes my hand and rounds the table to pull me into a hug which brings immediate discomfort.

I copy her action when she covers her microphone, and she whispers, "I'm so sorry. They never should've gotten through the vetting process. Someone's head is going to be lopped off for this." She leads me off the stage, and I wave to the clapping audience as if that call hasn't shaken me to my core.

"It's okay," I tell her as we stop just out of view of audience members.

"No, it isn't." She sighs and snuffs her nose and closes her eyes for several seconds. "I know how hard this is, and if you need anything, call me. Please. Maybe I can help. I have numbers to some great bodyguards, if that's the route you choose to go. I recommend never being alone."

My smile is sad but genuine. "I'm always alone, even when I'm not."

After an understanding nod, she takes my hand in hers, as a deep voice calls out, "We're on in twenty."

A man reaches in front of me to take the tiny microphone from my shirt as Kelly rushes back to her seat on the sofa.

A woman insistently brushes another layer of lipstick on Kelly while she sits still. She's trained like a monkey to do what she's told, as am I.

Being the protective father-type he is, Alex places his arm around my back as we walk toward the dressing room. No words are spoken as a big man with an earpiece and a radio follows us. As soon as the door closes, we part and I sit on the fur-topped stool in front of the lighted mirror with decorative packages comped for me from the show. The watch, perfume, and bottles of wine are great, but it's the roasted almonds in a ceramic bowl that catch my attention.

Out of earshot from anyone, my tone is low but harsh as my eyes burn into his. "What the fuck was that, Alex?"

His fingers scratch through his salt and pepper beard as his chestnut eyes hold my glare. "The callers were supposed to be vetted. Security had someone trace the number, but it was a burner phone."

A deep breath fills my lungs, but it doesn't feel like enough air is inside me. Tears threaten to fall but I clench my jaw and jolt to my feet to pace. My arms cross over my chest to hug myself. Alex knows better than to try to hug me when I'm angry. I'd only push him away if he did. Instead, he taps his finger to his phone then holds it to his ear.

"When will he arrive?" There's a pause. "Good. We'll be back at the hotel shortly."

The instant he hangs up my hands go to my waist to prepare for an argument. "Who's here?"

His brows rise before he speaks to me matter-of-fact. "The bodyguard."

My head jolts back as I huff. "Don't you mean the babysitter?"

His hand rises between us to stop me from going off like a top. "We need him, and you know it. This person is too close. Someone assigned especially to you and you alone is essential, and mandatory. He'll be your Siamese twin until we catch this pervert. I'm putting my foot down on this one, Phoebe."

Alex's the only person other than my best friend I'll allow to use my first name, but not in public—to keep up the persona for my popularity and keep away anyone wanting to dig into my history.

"A fucking babysitter…" I want to scream but our quarters call for hushed voices. "The last thing I need is for someone to be stuck to me like glue. When will I be able to really let my hair down and be myself? I like my privacy. I can't do this."

Alex's voice rises to almost yelling. "You're getting a bodyguard whether you want one or not. I'm not going to risk your life because you're afraid of someone getting close to you."

My voice rises. "Afraid? I am not afraid of letting someone get close to me. I don't want my personal business splashed all over the fucking rags."

"He's already signed an NDA."

I scoff and feed my fingers into my hair and pull just slightly. "You and I both know an NDA doesn't prevent someone from talking. They do it through friend of a friend for plausible deniability. All it takes is one slip of the tongue and I'll be splashed on the damn tabloids."

Alex's brows rise as if an idea has struck him but before he can say anything, my finger points at his face.

"Don't get any ideas. Bad press is *not* better than no press." My hand drops and I take in a breath so quickly my nostrils flare. "Fine. But if this asshole steps out of line, I'm going to pop him in the nose."

Alex chuckles and crosses his hands at belly button level. "I accept your conditions."

"So, this guy's flying here only to get on a plane later tonight to fly to another province? He should have just met us there tomorrow. Where's he coming from?"

He cracks open a bottle of water and hands it to me. "I'm not sure; somewhere in northern Ontario."

I take it and thank him before my ass meets the fuzzy stool. "What do you know about him?"

Alex scratches his beard as he often does and sits on the armrest of the leather sofa across from me. "Not much. He served in the Navy—overseas. That's all I know. I'll get more information later, or you could be polite and have a conversation with the man. If you smile and pretend to be interested, he might be forthcoming."

"What's his name?"

Alex fumbles through his phone. "Arrow. His name is Arrow."

"Weird name."

Like a father, he scolds me with a glare. "Stop it. You'll be polite. Right?"

"When am I ever polite?"

"I know it's out of character for you, but can you try?"

I shrug him off and mumble under my breath, "Why *Arrow*, I wonder?"

"Again, you could ask him. Be polite." His finger points at me.

"I'm polite," I say with a voice unconvincing and roll my eyes as my shoulders twist. "Well, I can fake it."

The way Alex's lips pursed and his head tips forward to look at me from below his perfectly trimmed brows has me grimacing.

"I'll try to not hate him. That's all I can promise. He might prove to be an asshole. You don't know!"

Alex's smirk is interrupted by a knock on the door. He opens it and a woman's voice leaks into the room. "Your car's here. If you'd like to follow me."

There's no need for me to take the gifts as someone will immediately come for them and put them in the trunk of the car. When we get to the hotel, someone will bring them up to the room and set them on the glass and brass table just inside the entrance to my suite. But the almonds are coming with me.

As the car begins to drive, Alex takes my hand without saying a word. We meet eyes and understand the bond we share is strong. We exchange smiles before resuming our distant stares through the side windows and lose ourselves to our deepest thoughts.

On to the next recorded interview with yet another television host.

CHAPTER FOUR

It's quiet, too quiet. We're moving forward but something feels wrong. Why can't I tell them to stop? I have to stop walking. Now! Stop now! No! Fire so orange it's red hot. It's too hot. I can't find them. I can't find—

My eyes burst open as cool air fills my lungs. There's no fire. Nobody is lost. I'm safe, but not okay. My fingertips brush the beads of sweat from my upper lip before wiping it onto my jeans. After my palm does the same to my forehead, I close my eyes and fill my lungs with the recycled airplane air and hold it before easing it out.

A soft voice pulls my attention across the aisle to an elderly woman in business attire wearing genuine concern in her eyes. "Are you okay?"

I force a smile and nod sharply.

She whispers, "Thank you for your service."

Without looking back at her, I ask, "How did you know?"

"My grandson served three tours. The first was fine, and the second had him riddled with nightmares and PTSD. They didn't make a big deal about it in 2004 like they do now."

"He went back for a third tour?" I meet her eyes and see the torment of a heart no longer whole. "Derek didn't come home. We buried him in 2005. Well, most of him." She stares straight ahead but sees her memory, not the seat before her.

"I'm sorry for your loss." The words sounded empty and common, but those five words I've heard more times than I can remember and sound so foreign coming from my own lips.

Not another word or glance is shared between us as we deboard the plane and go about our lives.

A short, chubby man holding up a cardboard sign with *Arrow* written in red marker seems to pick me out of the crowd flooding the baggage area.

"I'm Arrow," I say and offer him my hand. We shake and I hold up a finger to ask him to wait. After retrieving my bag from the conveyer, I toss it over my shoulder, not allowing the smaller man to carry it. It's my bag; I'll carry it myself.

He offers to lift it from the trunk when we arrive at the hotel, but I'm quick to scoop it up as if it weighs nothing. The man looks relieved because it may have been too heavy for him.

At the counter, a short woman with perfectly straight blonde hair hanging down her shapely ass smiles and asks for my name. The only name I give her is Arrow. Not asking for another name, she types it in and smiles at the computer before lifting her face to meet my gaze. She seems more flirtatious as she hands me a key card and explains the hotel amenities.

Neither the swimming pool nor her interest me. Although, bending her onto her hands and knees on a bed while I fist her beautiful hair and pound into her cunt like I hate her does make my cock stir awake.

I regret taking on this fucking case, which puts me in a shit-disturbing mood. Unfortunately, I'm about to overstep with this ever-so-polite woman. My eyes drop unabashedly to her cleavage and assault the round breasts squeezed into the neatly pressed white button-down. She remains professional as she directs me to the private elevator to my right. She falls quiet when I interrupt her by rudely tapping my key card on the counter. Flashing her a wink, I turn and walk away with my sack over my shoulder.

I press my key card to the elevator's screen and wait only a few seconds before the doors open to welcome me. I lift to the private floor at the top of the hotel. The door opens and I step out.

Knowing nobody has access to the floor without a traceable card to scan is reassuring. There were no cameras in the elevator that I could see, and none in the hallway, which concerns me. What hotel doesn't have cameras in their elevators? I saw four at the entrance and eight in the lobby but none anywhere else.

The hall was wide and dimly lit. The carpeted floor would enable anyone to make their way unheard to any of these rooms. Six doors line this lengthy hall, growing further apart until the double-wide door at the end faces the elevator. That must be the rockstar's suite. The door to my right just off the elevator is partially open and the sounds from a television seep through.

My bag makes a thud as it's dropped to the floor. It's a test, so I wait with my hands folded together. Forty-seven seconds pass from the time I exited the elevator until a tall, thick man eating a sandwich from a folded napkin graces me with his presence.

If this man is their security, it's no wonder a stalker is getting too close. Besides, he's a bit too chubby to be an effective defender if it came down to stamina in a fight. If he had to grab the client and run, he wouldn't make it far without being winded.

He scowls as he scans me from bald head to military boots. While chewing, he asks, "Who are you and why are you on this floor?"

"The question is, why did it take you forty-seven seconds to question me? You're a danger to the client. You're fired."

He stops chewing and glares at me with a dumb expression. "Who the fuck are you?"

"I'm the new head of security, and you're fired. Pack your shit and get out."

With my sack hanging at my side, I pay him no attention despite him spitting questions and insults my way. He shuts up when my key card held to the room across from his opens the door. I set my bag at the door to hold it open and turn to stare at the shocked man.

"You're the new guy." He groans knowing he needs to suck up to me to keep his job. "Sorry about not getting out here fast enough. Eric was supposed to be back to relieve me but… There's nobody here. The floor's empty. They aren't expected back for a while yet, so I thought—"

"You failed at performing the job you were hired for. For that reason, you're fired. It's not personal. I'm sure you're a charming man beneath all of this…" My eyes scan his shirt to see what looks like mustard on his white dress shirt. "You've got a little—" I don't finish. Instead, my finger points to my chest and wiggles.

He looks down and curses.

"You have five minutes to get your things, hand me your key card, and get on the elevator."

My eyes glance at my watch before returning to him while no expression cuts into my face.

Again, he curses and lets the door close as he retreats into his room.

Six minutes later my sack is on the bed, the man is gone, and I've left the floor to survey the hotel. For being a hotel famous for their stays by the elite, their security is lax. A door to the kitchen beside the staff room is held open by a large stone. Anyone could walk in with no one the wiser. When questioned about it, I'm told that's where the staff sneak out to have their cigarettes when they get a few moments.

I say nothing to them but will mention it to the hotel's manager before we leave here in a few hours. Not sure of what door my charges will enter through, I decide to go back to the floor to await their return. My door remains wide to keep an eye on who comes and goes.

Not two minutes after I get to the floor, the elevator door opens and three people exit. A big man with arms the size of tree trunks follows a well-dressed black man and a sexy woman in leather pants, three-inch pin-sharp-heeled knee-length boots, and a leather vest barely able to maintain her huge breasts. Long chestnut hair flows in waves over her tanned, bare shoulders. She's fit, having spent many hours in a gym.

So, working out is something we have in common.

All three stop to look me up and down. The gentleman in the suit speaks first. "You must be Arrow."

"And you must be Mr. DaVinette."

"Mr. DaVinette was my father, and he was a mean son of a bitch. So, please, call me Alex."

We shake hands and he turns to introduce the security guy as Brick—a name well suiting. I shake his hand which is the size of a baseball mitt, but he's gentler than I thought he'd be. Some men try to prove themselves by squeezing another's hand and acting as if it's unintentional because they're too strong to know any difference. Not Brick who seems humble. He and I will get along well.

"This is Jade. She's being stalked by someone, and the threats are getting closer. We can discuss the details later." Alex's head turns to look at the closed door to the room of the man I fired. Did he just suppress a smile?

She doesn't offer me her hand. Offering her mine seems pointless since she hasn't uncrossed her arms. She's scanned over me and wears no expression as she drinks in my facial features.

"Jade, it's nice to meet you. There's no need to worry. Leave the worrying to me."

Her voice has grit when she asks, "Where the fuck is Zack?"

A weaker man would crumble under her, but not me.

Without hesitation, I calmly reply, "He's gone. I fired him."

All three wide-eyed me. Jade's long arms lift to fall to her hips as her lips purse.

"You can't fire him! Get him back."

I take a step toward her and lock onto her sexy green eyes. "If I call him back, I'm leaving. If I leave and he remains in your charge, your stalker will surely have you in his/her clutches within a month. That man was slow, lazy, and unfit to guard you. So, you choose; him or me?"

If her eyes could set me on fire, I'd be ashes. "I don't even fucking know you."

I smirk and say, "The only reason you want him back is so you can take off on your own without anyone the wiser. He'd never notice you leaving and you like that. You'll never get away with that with me."

She turns to Alex and slams her hands on her hips as her weight rests on one deliciously firm hip. "Are you going to let this asshole fire Zack?"

Alex sighs and very sternly says, "If Arrow doesn't feel Zack is beneficial in keeping you safe, which is the priority, then yes, I support his decision."

My voice draws her angry glare my way. "Ma'am, you can go about your business, and I'll stay out of your way as long as you follow a few rules."

She acts as though I've slapped her with a horrible insult. "*Rules?* No. You will stay out of *my* way; that's rule number one. I'm paying *you* to do a job not the other way around. You do what *I* say. Are we going to have a problem?" She takes a quick, deep breath. "And don't ever call me ma'am."

This *Jade* has snap. My cock swells from the anticipation of the challenges ahead with this egotistical woman. An overdue spanking might knock that golden spoon right out of her ass. I know her type: she's spoiled and thinks she can do as she pleases without consequences. That doesn't fly with me no matter how much fame or money she has.

She's beautiful, I can't deny that. Her eyes; the colour of jade must be where her name comes from. They're heavy-lidded and surrounded in black make-up like she just woke up after getting fucked hard all night. She's tall. I'm 6'2" and she's not more than a few inches shorter than me with strong, long legs. How would they feel wrapped around my back while I'm balls deep inside her?

I step toward her and stop a mere feet away and keep my voice steady. "No. That's not how this works. *Alex* hired me to keep you safe and that's exactly what I plan to do. If you continue to defy me, you'll make my job damn near impossible. Do you want to die or worse: fall into the clutches of a psychopath who may carve you up slowly for his own entertainment? If the answer is no, you'd better listen to my rules and abide by them. Do *you* understand *me*?"

Her beautiful full lips part and close several times as she battles to think of something to say to put me in my place. Having come up with nothing, she growls from between her teeth as she storms down the hall to the last door on the right. She stands with her back to us with her weight rested on one leg.

With his hands in the pockets of his grey dress pants, Alex wears an apology in his eyes. "Sorry. She can be a bit… Anyway, give me a few minutes to calm her down and I'll come talk to you."

He doesn't rush as he makes his way down the hallway to meet up with the angry woman.

How much fun would it be to tame that wild bitch? No. That's not why I'm here.

The bodyguard stands by the elevator with his eyes on me as he awaits instruction.

"Brick, can we chat?"

The big man is in front of me in a second. He moves swifter than I thought possible for a mountain of muscle.

"Look, I'm not here to bust your balls, but I won't hesitate to let you go if I think you could hinder the job of keeping Jade safe."

Brick's hands barely fit in the front pockets of his oversized pants. "Hey, when it comes to keeping Miss Jade safe, I'll do whatever you say. Her safety is priority number one, always has been." His head drops and one palm rubs the back of his neck. "I've failed her by not keeping this stalker asshole at bay."

"How long have you worked for her?"

He straightens to his impressive 6'6" height and rubs his mitt over his thick chest. "I've been with Jade for five years."

"And this is the first time there's been an issue," I ask as more a question.

Brick's throaty voice carries a hint of concern when he looks at the closed door to the room the guy I fired has vacated. "No, no issues."

"That guy's gone. Which room is yours?"

Brick rocks foot-to-foot as if worried he may be next on the chopping block. "I'm not on this floor. My room is on the fourth floor. My job is to escort Miss Jade back and forth from her gigs. It's my size. People don't try to get too close."

A lot of men would be threatened by Brick's size. I stand at 6'2" and usually look down at people's eyes, not up.

"You're the size of a house, and that's beneficial for intimidation. But can you fight?"

"I wouldn't be at this job for as long as I have if I couldn't, sir. I'm trained in MMA, mostly Muay Thai and Judo, but I've studied the art of boxing as well." A proud smirk lifts his lips into a smile bearing perfect teeth. "I can hold my own."

He sees me looking at his perfect smile, so I say, "Don't smile when you're protecting her. Your smile makes you look kind and that won't be helpful. If we're not in public, smile like you've won the lottery if you choose to."

"Thanks, but, ah," Brick points a fat finger at his teeth, "these are fake. I lost them in the ring. The guy punched me, and my guard flew out. Before the ref could pause the fight, a powerful kick to my face broke my jaw in four places and took out five of my front teeth. That ended my dreams of having a professional MMA career."

My eyes narrow and my nose crinkles. "That's a bad break—pardon the pun."

Brick chuckles to laugh away the pain of a lost dream instead of wallowing. I like that.

I hand him the key card to the room across the hall.

"You're now the second in command. I like you. Don't fuck that up."

He accepts the room key. "I'm your guy."

"The room isn't clean, but you can call housekeeping to do their magic. Stay with them while they're on this floor. Anybody not on the list can't walk around on this floor unattended."

Brick pats his pockets on his pants and dress shirt as his head shakes. "What list? I haven't seen any lists. Shit! Did I lose it?"

A chuckle rumbles from my core. "No. Relax, man. I haven't given you one yet. I'll get something going as I get to meet people. The list can change at any time, but you'll be updated accordingly." A heavy sigh and a glance down the vacant hallway have me feeling the strain of the day's tension. My stomach growls to remind me I've skipped lunch. "All right. Nothing's happening here, so go get your stuff and call housekeeping. Tell them they aren't to walk too far past the elevator without an escort. Be here before they come up. Eat when you can because there may be times where you'll regret skipping a meal."

"Yes, sir."

My hand reaches toward him. "Give me your phone."

He pulls it from the back pocket of his oversized black pants, unlocks it, and hands it to me.

"I'm putting my number in your phone. My name will be 1, so it's the first one you'll see. If there's something important, I don't want to wait to hear about it while you scan through your contacts to find my name. Also, if my door is closed, yours is open. There will always be one of us on duty to watch that elevator and stairway at all times. Once I meet the other guards, I'll arrange a schedule."

Brick begins to fill me in. "No problem. The metal door near the end of the hall is a latched fire door and doesn't have a pull handle on the other side, so it's unlikely anyone will enter there, but not impossible. I checked it when she arrived three days ago. The lights flash in the hall when the door is opened. I suppose that's their idea of added security."

"Good. It's good to know you're not only here for the paycheck." I smile as best I can and walk back into my room while he quickly lifts the phone to his ear and opens the elevator using his card.

CHAPTER FIVE

"No way!" My heels smash into the carpeting as I rush into my suite and yank off my jacket, tossing it to the sofa. "There's no way some guy I don't know is going to follow me around. It's bad enough those damn security apes follow me to and from gigs, but that guy?" My finger points at the wall in the direction we left the bald man with a chip on his shoulder.

Alex closes the door even though it'll close on its own. His silent determination irritates me. He seldom raises his voice or moves quickly as if he were raised in a rich society. Alex is kind-hearted, but don't cross him. The man knows how to calm me down when I'm on the path to losing my temper. It's a short path, and I often sprint.

He slowly approaches me as I pace, stopping only long enough to take off my earrings and necklace and hold them in my hand which rests on my hip.

"You will and that's the end of it."

It's a losing battle but I can protest. "That's what you think. Why can't one of my regular guards be in charge. Why that fucking guy? He thinks he's king-shit and can tell me what to do? Fuck him!"

Why am I so enraged? Why? Because the man in the hallway isn't someone I can walk all over. The way he stared me down without flinching when I flashed my sexiest, do-what-I-say eyes had my pussy on fire. He can't stay because I need to run; I have to get away on my own and disappear among the crowds. He's going to lock me in this fucking room like a goddamn prisoner. I should be furious, and I am, but I can't stop imagining him slamming me against a wall, pulling my hair, and telling me he's going to fuck me into next week. Being owned in the bedroom is one thing, but not otherwise, and that's what he's threatening.

"Arrow is better. When it comes to your safety," Alex rests his hands on my shoulders, "I am not taking any chances. Someone is after you and they're getting too close."

My face drops to see my fingers fiddling with the finely gold trimmed diamond earrings. "I'm not afraid."

"Yes, you are." He pauses until I meet his eyes. "If Arrow doesn't work out, we'll find someone else. That's the best I can do, Phoebe."

Only a few people are privy to my real name—Phoebe Moore—and Alex is one of them, but I'm more Jade than Phoebe these days.

"Is he going to follow me everywhere? What if I have to use a public bathroom?"

Alex sighs as his blink runs long. "When do you ever use a public bathroom?"

My palms rise before me as my shoulders rise and fall. "It could happen?" Keeping my smile at bay proves more difficult than I'd hoped. "You talk to me like I'm a spoiled diva."

He steps away, but his gaze lingers on me with his brows raised higher than they probably should. "You *are* a spoiled diva."

My shoulder lifts as my head tips toward it. "Okay. You have me there."

"No more discussion about this. I need a nap, and you need to wash that make-up off your face before you plug your pores and we have to battle a pimple before your next concert."

My mumble sounds more like a pout. "Yes, Dad."

Alex frowns at the reference, as he always does. He's not my father, at least, I doubt he is. Alex is black, and I'm so damn pale you can see my veins clearly through my skin.

I unzip my boots and drop them to the floor. Moaning with each step toward the bedroom seems to ease the ache in my arches.

As the make-up remover solution eats away at the mascara and eyeliner, pale brown eyes haunt my thoughts.

That Arrow guy has the intimidation factor down solid. The way they locked onto my eyes and didn't even blink was his way of challenging me for dominance. Did I blink? Not right away but holding the gaze of a man who never folds was pointless.

What secrets does he hold dear to him?

Does he have a wife and kids?

Would he lie down his life to protect me, as I'd expect is in his job description?

Arrow seemed indifferent toward me, but would he strip down and make sweet, passionate love to me, or fuck me like the angry man he portrays? I'd bet he fucks like a demon, pulls hair, and bites as he calls his women nasty names. I could use a little of that but *not* with him. He's my bodyguard and if we get too close keeping his mind on his job will be more difficult. A distracted bodyguard makes room for psychopaths to get too close to me.

A shiver runs up my spine, so I point at my reflection with anger in my eyes. "Stop it. Nobody's going to get too close to you. You won't allow that Arrow guy anywhere near your body no matter how many screaming orgasms he might be able to give you. Arm's length, bitch. Keep him at arm's length." My clean-faced reflection nods as her back straightens with promise.

I slip out of my show clothes and into yoga pants and a sports bra with a delicate crisscross design on the back. With the proper footwear and a baseball cap with a wide brim allows my long ponytail to swing behind me as I walk, I pull open my door and make my way down the hall with my room key tucked in the tiny pocket at the waistband of my yoga pants.

Cautiously, I peek around the doorframe of Arrow's room to ensure he isn't watching the hallway from inside his room. I rush past and press the elevator button. It's ting is low and I cringe. Did he hear it?

A warmth at my back has me spinning around. I yelp and startle away from the man standing directly behind me. *Arrow!*

"You scared the hell out of me! What's wrong with you?" My hand presses to my chest. "You of all people should know sneaking up on someone is a bad idea. Fucking asshole!"

The bald man's head and face are smooth as if keeping himself hairless is his priority. Is the rest of his body hairless, too? A hint of leather and spice tickles my nostrils, and I crave more, so I breathe him in.

"Ma'am, where do you think you're going unescorted?" The tone of his voice was level and unemotional. Shouldn't he be angry with me for trying to sneak away?

"*Ma'am?*" My hands rest on my hips as my weight rests on one leg. "I told you not to call me ma'am. I'm not old enough to carry that title."

His eyes remain locked on me. No matter the tingles running down my spine, I will not look away. The elevator opens and neither of us moves, remaining locked in a power struggle.

My eyes drop to his fat tongue when it pokes free to moisten his lips. His lips lift at their edges in triumph as if getting my eyes to drop just set the pack order, and he's the top dog.

If I didn't think he'd laugh at me, I'd kick myself in the ass for losing our staring contest. Instead, I step into the elevator and immediately hit the close the door button and the button for the gym. As they begin to slide, Arrow reaches his muscular arm against the right door, and it opens for him. Still wearing that damn smirk, he steps in and allows the doors to close.

As we descend, he clears his throat.

I refuse to look at him. My arms cross beneath my breasts to boost them to where I'm sure his eyes will fall. If he wants to be the top dog, I'll make sure his desire for me makes it extremely hard not to want me. The only way teasing him won't work is if he's gay. Judging by how he looks at me, I doubt he's on that side of the fence.

"What?" Insolence carries in my tone.

There's a pause before his deep voice whispers. "If you think you can slip away from me and put your life at risk, you'll fail every time. I'm always watching. I'm one step ahead. I'll find you every time. Is that clear, little girl."

My mind spins as the memories I hope one day to suppress flash like a movie through my thoughts and it's a battle to hold back my vomit.

My words rush from between clenched teeth. "Don't ever call me *little girl! Never!*"

I will not cry! *I will not cry!*

With a tilt of his head, Arrow tries to read my reaction. "You didn't like ma'am. Tell me— why does *'little girl'* offend you so much?"

My attitude shifts from victim to vixen. "As you may have noticed, I'm not a little girl. Why can't you just call me Jade like any gentleman would?"

Arrow narrows the space between us. His voice is deep and breathy. "In case you haven't noticed, I'm no gentleman."

Fuck! Did my ovaries just kick out an egg?

His hands rest at his hips while his voice remains low and steady. "Lady, everyone calls you Jade, but I'm not everyone. I'll come up with something suitable? What's your real name?"

"Wouldn't you like to know?" This asshole will never call me Phoebe. He is not in my inner circle and never will be. Only people who know how I've suffered under that name can use it.

He squints as if I've said something stupid. "Well, yes. I did ask."

Unsure of what to say to get one up on this man, I thank the universe the door slides open, ending this battle for dominance.

Arrow follows close behind me without a word as I walk past a group of people in a lobby leading to either the pool or the gym. My head tips down to hide my recognizable face below the brim of the baseball hat. I lead the way to the gym using my key card for access.

There's only one man in the dim room despite the large windows overlooking a well-maintained garden of various flowers with a few boulders shimmering beneath the sunlight. The sounds of quick, heavy breaths from the middle-aged man on the pulleys blends with calming instrumental music similar to what plays in the elevator.

I pass the free weights and stair-climbers and step atop the first of three treadmills.

Damn! I forgot my water bottle.

As the machine beeps with each press of the speed and inclination buttons, it hums to life. Set at a brisk walk to begin, I notice Arrow guarding the door with his arms crossed over his chest and his feet shoulder-width apart. While he studies the room and the lone man minding his own business, I have a moment to examine his physique without the risk of him noticing.

The man's thighs and crotch are testing the strength of his dark blue jeans with wear marks not from purchase but from years of use. They fit him perfectly and the bulge he's sporting as he stands so steady has me curious to know what he's concealing. Black boots only add to his strength. To me they represent power and superiority—like a cop or navy seal.

But the way the black t-shirt fits snug to his biceps and a waist tight with muscle has my lip pinched between my teeth.

How long has it been since I've had sex with anyone other than my vibrator? Several months ago, Alex hired a high-priced male escort to entertain me for a night. The oral sex was amazing, and the man could kiss like it was his only job. His cock was big and always hard, but I don't just fuck anyone, so I wouldn't let him fuck me. Sucking his cock and him eating my pussy like a superstar was good enough for me. He was sweet, mid-twenties, and sexy as a magazine model, but he didn't thrill me. He only came to my room because he was being paid to, but when he saw it was me, he was so excited to meet me. That excitement quickly died when he realized I didn't want to talk, just sex and then get the fuck out.

Just once I'd like to find a man who doesn't know I'm famous or rich. I want a man to want me – the real me and not my persona.

Panting, I notice Arrow watching me. "Hey, can you get me a bottle of water?" His head shakes. "Why not?"

"I'm not here to serve you. I'm here to protect you. How can I do that if I'm running around getting things for you? So no, I'm not leaving your side to get you a bottle of water. If you want one, go get it yourself, and I'll follow."

"Are you fucking serious? You're an asshole."

He snickers as his head tips to the right. "Are you just figuring that out?"

The middle-aged man has stopped wiping his face with the towel draped around his neck to watch the tension between us. He stares at me as if trying to figure out who I am to know why I'd need protecting.

"Excuse me," he says from across the room.

Arrow's glare locks on the man.

"Yes," I say and continue walking.

The man seems uncomfortable with Arrow assessing him, so he doesn't approach. "You have a bodyguard. Are you famous or just rich? I—I can't seem to place you."

With a shrug, I slow the treadmill to a stop. "I'm no one important – just rich."

"Oh. Okay. I'll leave you to your workout. Stay safe." The man gives a lazy wave before he nears Arrow. "Good luck keeping her safe, sir."

Not showing any emotion, Arrow looks at the man. "She's trouble, but I can handle her."

The nameless man glances at me and nods before he departs.

The door clicks to lock as I mimic him in a sassy voice. "*I can handle her.* Like fuck you could handle me."

On the wide navy-blue mat suitable for eight bodies, I face away from Arrow to look out the window and begin stretching. First my arms followed by my legs. My legs part shoulder-width and I bend at the hips until my arms dangle to the mat giving Arrow a view sure to grow the bulge in his pants.

Who's going to handle whom? Fucker!

CHAPTER SIX

My phone buzzes in my pocket.

Brick: *I'm in the room. Is your door closed? Where are you and is Jade with you?*

Me: *She's with me in the gym.*

Brick: *Do you want me to come down?*

Me: *I've got this. Take down names of anyone entering the floor and take their photo. Follow them wherever they go but keep your ears tuned in to the elevator doors.*

Brick: *I got it. It's quiet at the moment.*

I slip my phone back into my back pocket and look up to see a firm, round ass bent over with her legs spread as if inviting my cock to slip into her. Yoga pants leave little to my imagination as the crease between her rounded ass cheeks is deep. She's doing it on purpose. Otherwise, she wouldn't be looking at me from between her legs with that *'I caught you'* expression seared on her beautiful face.

To stop myself from ogling her, I pick my phone from my pocket and send a text to Fixer.

Me: *The woman is a tyrant.*

In seconds, bubbles dance on the screen.

Fixer: *Good. You could use a challenge. Maybe she'll shake you out of your funk.*

Me: *Piss off. I like my funk.*

Me: *Do me a favour and get me all the information you can on this woman. I'd like to know what I'm dealing with. Maybe someone from her past is trying to make a reappearance.*

Fixer: *You got it.*

Me: *Thanks. Talk soon.*

Fixer: *Have fun!*

Me: *Fuck you, asshole.*

I glance up to see her well-shaped bicep strain under the tension of a pulley. Her lips are pursed, and I wonder if her asshole is as pretty as her lips. It's obvious she's annoyed that I turned away from her and didn't continue to check her out.

Maybe Fixer's onto something because this little power struggle between her and I is fun. There's more to this woman than what she shows people. The way she pushes people away has me sure someone hurt her. Maybe more than one person. Fixer is the best I know at researching people. He'll find out her secrets.

Damn, she's strong. The weight she uses isn't for the meek. Her body is fit, tight, and she's proven her flexibility. Most singers need to maintain their physique for their costumes and to perform on stage without dropping from exhaustion.

I'm curious to see her perform even though rock music sounds like screaming voices over squealing guitars and pounding drums. It doesn't interest me. I prefer softer music where the words are easily distinguishable.

She's lost in her thoughts as she moves from one apparatus to another. Her expression doesn't reveal what's rattling around in her mind. Where is she? What is she thinking about?

Sweat beads on her skin emphasizing the peaks and valleys of feminine muscle. Beneath the sheen, her cheeks are flushed, and her parted lips seem puffier than usual. This is how I imagine she'd look impaled on my cock during a hard fuck. Maybe a good pounding would loosen the stick she has wedged up her ass and she'll come down off her high horse and be kinder to us nobodies.

It's not easy to keep myself from ogling the beauty doing curl-ups with weights on her chest.

Her workout is grueling, but she never makes a sound louder than a heavy breath rushing free.

She slowly walks toward me. "I'm done. You know, you look like you work out. Next time, you should get a workout in, too."

How long was I lost in thought not to notice her approach? Her emerald eyes hold me captive.

"I might have if you'd given me notice rather than putting yourself at risk."

She blinks and allows her eyes to drop to my chest. "I'll do that next time."

"I appreciate that."

A quick glance through the glass door proves an empty room, so we exit while she walks ahead with her face tipped down. People carrying the weight of fame are well skilled in the art of hiding in plain sight. They know how to blend in. It's a talent learned from years of running from screaming people with intentions of touching her, taking a chunk of her hair, or something more sinister.

In the lobby, a tall man a few meters away tips his face to study her more closely. Before I can move up beside her to block his view, she's already noticed him and shrouds her face with a dab from her towel. The man loses interest and returns to his conversation with a short woman in a business suit.

The elevator doors close and I tap my card on the scanner which prevents the elevator from stopping anywhere other than her floor. Her sigh weighs heavy as it's set free with no discord for discretion. Safely locked in a metal box as it's gradual climb to her personal floor may be the only place she feels truly safe. She yawns with a gaping mouth. My stance shifts to ease the pressure of my semi-hard cock. How nice would my shaft feel pushed deep into that cavern?

Stop! Fuck! She's your ward, not your next play thing.

The doors open. A second later, Brick steps from his room with a dangerously stoic expression. His bright blue eyes catch mine before they glance at Phoebe, and light up with kind-heartedness. "Hello, Miss Jade. How was your workout?"

Her palms press to his chest as her genuine smile ignites. "Brick, how many times have I asked you to dump the *Miss*? From now on, every time you call me Miss Jade, I'll call you Mr. Brick."

The way Brick's cheeks flush vibrant red is a dead giveaway that he's taken by her. If she invited him to her room for a quick fling, his cock would tear through his pants in anticipation.

He swallows hard. "It's how I was raised; treat women with respect until they don't deserve it. You're kind to me, Miss Jade."

My loud throat clearing grabs their attention, and Brick takes a step back. "Maybe you should retire to your room, *Miss*." My emphasis on miss has her eyes roll met with a huff. "You asked me not to call you ma'am or little girl. Miss would be anywhere in between the two. Don't you think so?"

Her lips twitch as she searches for a comeback that never comes.

She storms down the hall with the towel swaying in her grasp. My eyes drift from her ass to notice Brick still drinking her in.

"Hey," my fingers snap to draw his attention "keep your mind on the job."

His shoulder pulls back as if to stretch out an old injury. "Yeah. No, I'd never— I mean, I wouldn't— Jade's great, but I respect her too much to take her to my bed. Besides, she wouldn't be interested in someone like me."

"Why not you?" What kind of man is she into?

"I'm the relationship type. She's not into that."

Not into relationships? I wonder why? Did some guy break her heart, and she's sworn off men? Again, I'll need to do my research.

"Has anyone come to the floor?"

"Just the maid. I took down her information and took a photo before I let her clean Zach's room—my room, I guess." His hand points to the door held open by his suitcase.

"You're still packed? I like that; prepared to leave on a moment's notice." My palm slaps his bicep as men often do for a job well done. "I'm going to Mr. DaVinette's room to copy her schedule for the week. When I return, I'll relieve you."

His deep voice seems to fade into the thick carpeting and doesn't follow me down the hall. "There's no rush."

I knock lightly on Alex's door. A few seconds pass and I knock a bit louder.

The door flings open.

"Arrow." Alex tries to focus on me between blinks. "I must have drifted off to sleep. Please, come in. Would you like a coffee or something a little stronger?"

"Water."

He nods and pulls at the waistband of his red sweatpants to straighten them before a tug at the shirt's hem ends his fussing.

"Please, have a seat."

Alex's room isn't nearly as glorious as Jade's, but it's equally impressive. Wall to floor windows allow for a full view of the city while the tint prevents the city from looking back. I sit on the white leather sofa facing the large gas fireplace situated below a monstrously large flat-screen television with a slight bow to the screen.

I'm handed a rectangular shaped bottle of water before Alex sits on the pillowy, black leather armchair across from me.

He sips from the large white mug with what I assume is coffee. "Did something happen? You look annoyed."

Where do I start? Oh, yeah. She's a fucking pain in my ass!

"Nothing I couldn't handle." I crack open the bottle and take a long swig before returning the cap. "She tried to sneak off to the gym without an escort. She failed, of course."

He sets the mug on the marble coffee table before he leans back. "Jade's going to test you. Don't expect her to be nice to you until she gets to know you. She can be stubborn, and she keeps her walls up. Just let her be her and she won't fight you as often."

Stubborn doesn't cover it. Little does she know she's met her match. Match? No, I fucking win! I *always* fucking win!

"She's welcome to do just about anything as long as we're informed ahead of time. Please explain that to her. Her safety is our only goal, but we can't do our jobs if she's determined to wander off on her own."

The man exudes intelligence. His elbow sinks into the arm of the chair as his thumb and forefinger stroke his well-trimmed beard. The silence in the room speaks volumes. He loves her and he's afraid for her, but he doesn't have much authority over her, and it frustrates him. Has he warned her many times before not to go anywhere alone only to have her do exactly that?

"But that's not why I'm here." I shift to sit more forward on the sofa and rest my elbows on my knees. "I'll need her schedule for the foreseeable future. Plans need to be made on my part, and I can't do this without knowing what's happening next."

"Yes! Oh, shit." As if startled, Alex rises to his feet and rushes to the desk in the far corner of the room situated next to one of the windows. "I meant to give that to you when you arrived, but I got distracted and—Well, here you go."

I'm handed a booklet with a blue cover void of images or words. Inside is an in-depth calendar. Each page marks a day and a list of tasks that would have anyone exhausted. How is she expected to meet with eight media outlets back-to-back and then go to hair and make-up to prepare for a photoshoot across the city? Wait! What city?

Alex leans over to pick at the pages to flip them one by one. "Here's today. She's free until 4am when we drive to the airport. We'll fly to Vancouver—I suggest you sleep while we fly. It'll only be about an hour, maybe a bit more, but it's what we all do."

Flipping the page to tomorrow has my brows rising and my gaze locking on his.

He shakes his head and nods. "Yes. I know. It's a lot, but it's her schedule. She likes to keep busy. The woman has superior get-up-and-go. Don't get too frustrated if you struggle to keep up to her moods. It's taken me years to figure her out, and she still catches me off-guard."

Alex is tall and keeps his greyed beard perfectly trimmed. Even in sweats and a t-shirt his look screams leader of a board meeting if he were to work in a multi-billion-dollar office setting. His style seems too sharp and classy to represent a rock and roll band.

Alex runs a tight ship. I had expected masses of fans clouding the hall and floating from room to room taking drugs and having wild orgies. Thankfully, I was way off on my assumption.

Closing the booklet, I stuff it under my arm and stand. I make my way to the door with the half-drank bottle of water gripped below the booklet.

"I'll go through it and take care of everything. Don't worry about anything. I'll hire extra people if need be, but she'll be kept safe."

"That's your job," Alex says with a confident nod of his head before he grips the door handle and twists but hesitates. She's been through a lot, so the more you push her, the more she'll push back. Do you understand what I'm trying to say?"

"Yes, sir. I do. But I won't stroke her like an injured puppy. She doesn't need that and it's not my style. There will be rules she's expected to follow, and if she doesn't, she'll be punished."

Alex straightens his spine and looks at me with concerned curiosity.

"Put it this way; if she follows my rules, I'll let the leash out a bit more. If she disobeys and pulls at the leash, she'll be put back in the cage."

"Oh." His brows furrow and relax as his eyes search the wall over my shoulder.

Is he picturing her in a cage? I am. How hot would it be to have her in a cage begging me to set her free?

No! Dammit!

My head shakes to rid the thought from my mind. "It's a poor reference, but the gist is there."

His finger waves between us. "I think we're going to get along well. You may be exactly the right person for her—" his mouth opens as his head jerks, "to protect her."

"I suppose we'll see." I shake his hand and leave his room.

The door clicks unexpectedly loudly as it closes. Jade whips open her door and she's standing before me with a white towel hugging her curves with another beehive atop her head.

Her eyes widen when it's me she sees and not the person I assume she had expected—Alex. When my gaze remains locked on hers, not scaling her body as she'd expected, her stance falls back onto her left hip as her slippered foot holds the door open.

My voice is smooth and fatherly, which should annoy her. "You've had your workout and taken a shower. Now, go to bed. We have an early rise."

Her hands land on her hips and her head tips back as she scoffs.

"Don't tell me what to do. You're just another mindless monkey under my reign, so don't think for one minute I'll take orders from you."

That's right, defy me. Fight me at every turn. I love challenges. I can't wait to break her down only to build her back up into an even stronger opponent. Play the game, little bird.

My eyes hold her tough gaze as my boots slowly carry me to her, stopping mere inches from her. We're so close I can smell her mango shampoo and flowery soap.

My cock strains against my jeans.

As I did before, my tongue pokes free to moisten my lips, but her line of sight doesn't shift toward it. Hmm, she learns quickly.

With a slow blink, my eyes slowly fall down to her cleavage before my head tips to scale her legs and back up to her cleavage.

"Little girl, my job is to keep you safe. This game you're playing will only get you punished. You can stop trying to taunt me into pursuing you. It won't happen." I lift my eyes to meet her wide green eyes. "The only contact we'll have is if you disregard my rules and try to sneak out. Keep it up and I'll spank your ass red hot to teach you a lesson."

Her jaw clenches before she swallows. Good. The seed has been planted and now she knows where I stand.

"You will never spank me!" She sounds so sure, and her shoulders pull back and her finger points at my face. "If you ever touch me, I'll have you put in jail. You'll be so sorry. Don't you ever fucking lay a hand on me. Got it, schlub?"

"*Schlub?* Really?" My chuckle is silent which purses her lips in frustration. "I could have a cage delivered to the next hotel and keep you in it. That's what we do to misbehaved pets. You'll look so pretty begging me for your freedom."

Her chest caves as a scoff rushes free. "*Never!* Don't you—You'll never—This is so—"

Disgusted, she storms into her room and fails to slam the heavy wooden self-closing door.

My whisper is low enough she won't hear. "That's right, pet. You'll learn your place."

CHAPTER SEVEN

"Jade, it's time to wake up."

I'm grateful when Elsa's soft voice wakes me from a dream.

I was staring into sexy brown eyes. Not just any eyes, but Arrow's. He had just slammed me against a wall, pinned me in place, and just about to kiss me. I'm torn whether I'd want to see how far my imagination would have taken it.

"Sorry, hon, but you have to get up now."

Through a not so lady-like yawn, I ask, "What time is it?"

"It's early; 3:45. The car will be here in fifteen minutes."

A full stretch along the cool silky sheet reminds me of the workout I did last night. I pulled extra weight hoping to impress my guardian. Impress isn't quite the word I was looking for; *tease* would be more suitable.

Her voice fades as she walks into the expansive closet. "What do you want to wear on the plane? Probably something comfortable." She's quiet for a moment while I slip my feet into slippers and stand with another stretch. "How about yoga pants and your oversized powder-blue hoodie?"

Elsa has been my personal assistant for three years. She's the only one of over a dozen that could keep up to my schedule without fucking up. One woman I hired was so distraught she lost my clothes to another flight at an airport in Kentucky that she couldn't stop crying. She was too panicked to track them down, so Alex had to do it. She was nice but I had to let her go.

Elsa is only about five-feet-tall and a bit chubby around the middle. With her birthday one week before mine, we share the same age of 32-years-old. Maybe we get along well because we're both Scorpios. I don't know.

I clear my throat to rid it of sleep and raise my voice. "Sure. That'll be okay. Crocs. I want to wear my Crocs, too."

She comes from the closet with the items and lays them on the bed. "There you go. Now get yourself dressed; there isn't much time."

"Is the band coming with me?"

Her head shakes as she folds a sweater before placing it in the suitcase and snapping it closed. "They're leaving later this afternoon."

"Hmm. Okay."

It's not unusual for the band to travel separately from me because the media seems to want my face up front and center. I'm the face of the band, but it's not my choice. Singers are often forced into that position.

If traveling by bus, I prefer to stick together. I like it better than flying, even though the downtime seems endless, and the boredom is quick to grow tedious. Being together like in the old days when we were just starting out was so much fun. As fame slid in, my heavy schedule kept us apart, leaving me feeling lonelier than ever. I miss them even though I see them all the time. They're so close, I often feel like an outsider.

My feet shuffle to the bathroom and I fear my eyes will bleed when I turn on the light.

A knock at my door will surely be met by Elsa, so I ignore it. It's probably Alex. If anyone else wants me, I'm too tired to deal with people, so they can fuck off.

The door opens as a deep voice calls out to me. "Let's go. Come on. We're going to be late if we don't hurry." Alex watches my feet shuffle me to the door while I fight the urge to pop my bottom lip out. "I know you're tired, but you can sleep on the plane."

I rushed down the hall toward Brick and the asshole, who were busy talking between them to bother to notice us. Brick looks tired but the ass looks freshly showered and wide awake. He's wearing the same jeans but has changed into a black dress shirt with the sleeves rolled up. Standing behind him in the elevator gives my tired eyes the opportunity to check out his wide shoulders, small waist, and firm ass.

Arrow looks over his shoulder at me with a knowing look as if he sensed me looking at him. When he turns front, I notice the mirror-like reflection above the elevator doors confirming he knew I was checking him out. My stomach sinks. He matches my eyes in the reflection, smirks, and winks.

Winks! What the fuck?

With my most convincing smirk, my head shakes. *Hell no, motherfucker!*

Arrow, Brick, and Elsa hear me clearly when I say to Alex, "He has to go. I don't want this asshole near me."

Alex is too tired to deal with me and it shows in his dismissive tone. "Well, he's all we have right now, so you'll have to deal with him."

Between clenched teeth, I grow more insistent. "Find. Someone. Else."

A deep breath fills Alex's lungs. "I'll work on it," he murmurs unconvincingly as the breath leaves him. He knows how much I hate to be dismissed.

The doors open before I can retort. The five of us climb into the back of a stretch limo but Arrow slides into the passenger's seat. Is she there for a better view of where we're headed in case trouble awaits us, so he can react quickly, or to get away from me?

The privacy window between us closes almost immediately. I don't want to look at him, especially if he looks at me with those sexy eyes and winks, again. What was with that wink?

The private jet is large enough to house us comfortably and has a bed in the back with Egyptian cotton sheets that feel like I'm sliding into butter. The rest of them stretch out in the comfortable leather loungers. Sleep takes me quickly, but not for very long, as I'm jolted awake covered in sweat. I was dreaming of those eyes looking down at me from above as his cock slid deep inside my pussy. It's not Jade he sees, but the broken soul I keep hidden from everyone. I wanted him to see it, to truly know me in ways I've never allowed anyone.

With a yawn and stretch, the lyrics to my newest song rehearse in my head, suppressing the dream from my memory. My lips move to shape the silent words as I make my way to the bathroom. It's not a huge space but much larger than any commercial airplane. The face glaring back at me carries the weight of too much on her plate and the exhaustion that accompanies it.

The suite we're brought to isn't the presidential floor, but the next floor down. It's not as lavish but the rooms are plenty elegant. Apparently, some billionaire with more sway than me bumped us out. If I see this guy, I'll ask him what the fuck his deal is.

It's no problem to be in the smaller suite, it's actually my preference. The less I have to walk around the better. My feet ache from the sky-high heels I'm expected to wear for interviews and during performances. Sure, they look great and form the muscles in my legs and ass to drool-worthy works of art, but they kill my toes.

The day already seems long even though it's only eight in the morning. Alex sits beside me on the sofa as he informs me of today's schedule. I'm supposed to sleep until 2pm and then be taken to the arena for pre-show testing. At 5pm I have make-up and wardrobe. At 6pm I have an interview with the local television news station to discuss tonight's concert. From there I'm driven back to the arena where I'm expected to rest for an hour, but the band will likely come hang out in my changing room. At 8pm make-up and hair will do their thing. At 8:30pm we'll meet backstage with the back-up dancers to go over any last-minute concerns while the previous band plays to warm up the crowd. We go on stage at 9pm and perform like trained monkeys until 11pm or so.

Directly from there we'll be taken back to the hotel where the band will party in Pony's room until they either pass out or take someone to their beds. Venus and Lacey always hide out in their room and have sex. Occasionally, they'll shower and go to Pony's room to join the band for a few drinks.

As for me, I'll go back to my room, take off my make-up, and cry.

Everyone has their ritual for coming down from the high energy of the performance. The adrenaline spike takes some time to die down, but when it does, insecurities and loneliness can eat away at the soul. I've curled into bed and begged the universe to not let me wake more times than I can count. It's not that I want to die, I just want… I don't know what I want. If I could trade it all in for a simple life where I work a regular job that doesn't pay enough and have to scrounge to pay the bills, would I want that? Probably not forever, but a month would help me to appreciate all that I have worked so hard for.

As Alex continues to dwell on my eating schedule where he insists I eat everything brought to me, I wonder when it was that I gave him the right to dictate my entire life.

My nude feet prop on the marble coffee table while my fingers weave together over my red t-shirt with the words "Go to hell. I'll see you there" written on the front.

He pauses, and I grumble. "As per usual everything is scheduled down to the minute. Um, I don't see any bathroom breaks on the agenda. Do I have to hold it all day?"

Alex lowers the portfolio and looks at me over his silver framed reading glasses. "Don't be a smartass. Of course, you don't have to hold it all day. You'll have a bucket whenever you need one."

His eyes laugh before annoyance wears heavily when his phone rings. He announces his name as he answers and rises, setting the agenda on the table beside his half-empty mug of coffee.

My arms cross over my chest and I slump down with my head resting on the fuzzy grey pillow and pull my feet up near my butt and my knees to my chest. If I can get myself small enough, maybe I'll be overlooked and can rest for a while.

A light slap to my thigh pulls me from the edge of slumber. If I were a dog I'd have lunged up and snapped. Instead, I swallow it down and sit up.

Alex's fatherly tone has me pulling the fuzzy pillow from beneath my head to cover my ears, but his muffle still radiates through.

"Eat this and then go to bed. You need the nourishment and sleep. It's going to be a busy day."

The pillow slides off my head and the dryness of my throat makes my voice husky. "Going to be?"

He pats my thigh a second time. "Come on, Phoebe. Eat, then sleep."

Against the resistant pleads from my body and mind, I sit up and stare at the cloth-draped table rolled in with silver hoods over the plates. My stomach growls, so I force myself to stand and cross the room to sample from the spread. Eggs, steak, salmon, toast, avocado spread, fruit, and a variety of juice bottles.

A motion to my right startles me. When did Pony and Lacey come to my room? How long was I asleep? It felt like seconds.

"Hey, guys." My voice is still coarse, so I crack open a grapefruit juice bottle and down half of it before I cringe at the bitter aftertaste.

Pony's long brown hair hasn't been brushed, so the slight wave to his locks have flattened in spots and extra curled in others. Heavy bags beneath his eyes prove he's been partying far too much. Has he slept or was he up all night fucking a groupie whose name he'll never be able to recall? My money is on fucking a groupie. He's such a male slut, and I love him.

Lacey's blonde and pink mohawk lies flat, not flowing like feathers as it does for photoshoots and performances. It hangs over the left side of her head with the bangs barely long enough to tuck behind her ear. Her face is squeaky clean of make-up. She doesn't look as tired as Pony, but her wife, Venus, likely insisted she sleep. Venus may come off as a badass, but she's gentle and affectionate when it comes to Lacey.

Pony doesn't lift his cheek from his palm supported by his elbow on the island, but his full lips quirk into an easy smile.

"Hey, girl." Lacey leans forward on her stool to rest her forearms on the island across from Pony, who remains seated on the tall wooden stool. "You look tired. Have you gotten any sleep? I mean, other than the twenty minutes you snored on the sofa?" Her quiet laugh has her exposed firm tummy tightening.

"I slept on the plane." With my juice in one hand, I carry the tray of freshly cut fruit to the island to share. "Alex wants me to sleep after I eat. If I could sleep while I eat, I'd be a happy woman."

Pony's smooth as silk voice cuts in. "You can. It's called an IV. We should look into getting some. I could use the boost. I wonder if they come with some hair-of-the-dog?"

I kiss the shoulder of his white t-shirt before wrapping my arms around his shoulders. "Pony, when are you going to learn? Hmm? Pussy will be there after you sleep just as much as if you stayed up all night petting one."

He scoffs. "One? Nah, two beauties rocked my bed last night. The brunette did this thing with her tongue that nearly—"

Lacey cuts him off, not wanting to hear about his sexual escapade. "Uh-uh, no! Gross!"

I laugh at the way her nose wrinkles at the thought of having sex with a penis. Even though she plays it up that she's all about the cock when she's performing, she's never even touched one and has no intention of changing that fact.

Pony has a body fit for fucking, which is what he loves to do when he isn't slamming on his Bass. He and I had a fling a few years back but we're too different for it to have worked out, so we decided to call it quits before things got ugly and split up the band, which happens far too often.

He was the best lover I ever had. That man knows his way around a woman's body so well he could draw a map and make a fortune selling it. He's had so many sexual partners since me I've lost count, not that I'd care to keep track. We remain close, but without the sex. I'll admit I do miss the way he made me scream through an orgasm. The thickness of his cock took some getting used to, but once my body complied, it was heavenly.

I pop a fat blueberry in my mouth while cupping several others. "So, what brings you two here? Shouldn't you both be sleeping?"

Pony groans his agreement, but Lacey flicks his forehead using her thumb and her middle finger. He sits up and frowns at her.

She picks up a strawberry and says, "Pony's here while Brick escorts the two chicks in his room to leave without filling their pockets with his stuff. I'm here to see how you're doing. We haven't had much time to catch up, so I thought I should check in on my second favourite girl."

Her wife is her first favourite girl, naturally. Venus is a tough, intimidating woman with a bite to back up her bark. A trained boxer, she can take care of herself and Lacey if anything threatening comes her way. She also has a huge heart not too many get to see. With more energy than a hummingbird, Venus's parents got her a drum set hoping it'd channel her focus and burn off some of the energy gymnastics and boxing lessons didn't.

"Where's Venus?" I ask just before a slice of peach has my taste buds screaming.

Her hand flops at the wrist making her bangles clink together. "She's taking advantage of the gym. Did you know there's a private one on the floor below us? It's only for the upper floors, so no dickheads or screaming fans will be there."

If I want to go, Arrow doesn't have to follow me like a lost puppy. He can stay here and let me work out in peace. Although, teasing him was fun.

My fingers shroud my lips as I push the peach into my cheek and say, "Maybe tomorrow if there's time."

I spend a lot of time working out because the pain in my body eases the pain in my thoughts. Besides, staying fit is essential if I'm going to dance and sing for two hours straight in front of 50,000 screaming fans on the regular.

Brick walks in through the open door and nods to Pony, letting him know the ladies have vacated his room. "Well, that's my cue. I'm out! My bed is calling my name."

Lacey shivers. "It's probably sticky with sweat and cum."

"Ew!" I laugh.

Pony stands and kisses my forehead before he turns to shoot her the middle finger making them both laugh. "I had housekeeping change them, so suck on that!"

"You couldn't pay me enough," she says and crinkles the shark features that make up her pretty face.

Pony leaves with Brick in tow while they chuckle about something said between them.

"So, how are you?" Lacey rounds the large white marble-topped island and sits on Pony's stool.

The stool to her right is silent as I glide it away from the island and take a seat. "I'm okay. Tired. That's nothing new. How about you?"

Her wrist flops again before she picks up a nectarine and begins to peel it. "Venus makes sure I'm okay, you know that. She insists on keeping our meals and sleep as regular as possible, so we don't burn out. But I like to push back just to keep things hot between us." She waves her brows as she pushes a slice of the orange fruit between her pouty lips.

"You're so bad."

"Yeah, but you wouldn't like me as much if I wasn't." She reaches out for my hand. "I'm here for you, okay. After the show, you don't have to be alone. Any one of us will stay with you, or you can hang out with Venus and me in our room. We can put on a sad romance movie and eat until we feel sick, or drink hoping for the same result. It's your choice. We're good either way."

"I love you, but I'm fine. Really, I am. It's my way of coming down." In case my words fail to convince her, the shrug of one shoulder accompanying a smile I force to reach my eyes should do the trick.

"Okay. The option is there." We hug and I watch her leave with her hips swaying beneath her shorter than short mini skirt.

After a few more bites, I leave Alex to his heated phone conversation. Why doesn't he loosen his collar or tie? There's nobody here to care if he gets comfortable. The man is almost always impeccably dressed.

The sheets are cool as my naked body slips between them like a caterpillar in a cocoon. Even my head hides beneath them to allow for even more darkness. I don't remember falling asleep.

CHAPTER EIGHT

Brick, Alex, and me have been standing at the elevator waiting for the princess to come out of her room. It's 1:45 pm and she's scheduled to be at the arena for the rehearsal for 2:00. Being late or unprepared for anything makes me twitchy. I literally twitch from the irritation, especially when someone else is the cause.

She's the stereotypical rock star; selfish and spoiled – a total diva. It's all about her. Fuck the other people waiting for her after working all day to get the arena set up. Fuck her band that left twenty-minutes ago. They'll be there on time.

This woman gets under my skin. Sure, she's hot as sin, and I'd love to throw her over my lap to teach her she isn't the fucking queen of England, but I should remain professional. I'm an employee and will clench my jaw and fists while I wait impatiently.

Her door finally opens, and she strolls out before Elsa. At least she's carrying one of the quilted duffel bags. Elsa has a bag slung over her shoulder and a purse under her arm. There's likely a ten-inch height difference between the women, which makes Elsa look like a child.

"Sorry I'm late," Jade says as she rummages in the side pouch of the bag. Her pinched brows relax as she lifts her phone halfway out before stuffing it back down. "Rachel called. She's getting on a plane now, so she should be here in a few hours."

Rachel who?

A soft ding precedes the elevator doors easing apart. My arm immediately extends to block Jade from entering. Two well-dressed men look out at us. One must be in his late forties and stands between us and a tall man in an expensive tailored suit that likely cost more than my truck.

The older man's eyes shift from me to Alex, Brick, and finally land on Jade. They remain focused on her. I can't blame him.

She's wearing very low-rise black jeans that fit her form like a glove, and a white off-the-shoulder t-shirt short enough to show her bra should she lift an arm. The thin fabric requires little imagination to know the black bra she's wearing has a lace design over her voluptuous breasts. Her hair is bundled in a messy bun and oversized sunglasses perch atop her head in anticipation of shrouding her eyes from possible fans.

Seconds pass before Jade shoves my arm out of the way. "For fuck sake."

She tries to push her way past me, but I remain at her side between her and the men.

"Hi. I'm Jade." Her arm extends to the man in the suit, and he accepts it. "You must be the guy upstairs. You stole the suite right out from under me."

The man is handsome, I'll give him that. His hair isn't grey like mine is when I let it grow some; it's jet black, short on the sides and sweeps to the side as if an entire can of spray keeps it in place. The dark hair emphasizes his pale blue eyes swimming with seduction like a sexy devil. He's a few inches shorter than me at about six-feet-tall. His hand is so clean he likely hasn't done an ounce of hard labour in his life. Born with a diamond spoon in his mouth, no doubt.

"Did I?" His voice isn't as deep as mine but it's smooth enough to convince a boardroom full of people his intentions are respectable, even if the proposal he's pushing is greasy. "Please don't hold that against me. My assistant makes all of my bookings. I'm Augustus Greyner."

Jade's fist presses to her waist as she shifts to face him with me still between them. "So, are you someone important?"

The man pauses before he turns to face her after nearly stepping around me. "I suppose if you haven't heard of me that would make me unimportant. And you are?"

Her chuckle fills the elevator. "If you haven't recognized me, I suppose I'm nobody important to you."

His laugh catches in his throat. "We could change that."

Jade's head dips to the left as her weight shifts to one hip. "And how do you propose we do that?"

"Have dinner with me tonight."

Oh, he's smooth like a viper in the night. Surely she's smart enough not to fall for this act.

Before she can respond, Alex doesn't shift his gaze from his phone as his voice is matter-of-fact. "Your schedule is booked solid tonight. I could pencil in tomorrow evening depending on how long the photoshoot takes."

The doors ease open, and we all step out with Elsa leading followed by Brick, Alex, me and the other bodyguard. Suit guy takes Jades fingers and brings them to his lips as he escorts her from the elevator.

While keeping an eye on him, my head is on a swivel. We need to keep moving. Standing in the lobby of a prominent hotel while numerous people linger could quickly become a problem. Brick has his back to us while he scans the patrons. Elsa and Alex have walked ahead in the hall toward the side entrance while they chat between them. Elsa's smile is slight, and Alex's gaze lingers a little too long. Are they lovers?

Jade stands far too close to the man as she slowly lowers her sunglasses over her eyes. "Well, I know where to find you."

Before he can say anything, she turns and struts away as her wedges clack the floor. His eyes locked onto her ass cradled perfectly in her snug jeans. The way his tongue grazes his bottom lip has me wanting to punch him in the face.

She's not an object for his pleasure. I suppose she could be if it's her choice. He can't buy her affection. Perhaps that's an attraction shared among the elite. As sure as the sun will rise, they've met countless people willing to give their dignity for a piece of the pie. With both parties having deep pockets that isn't an issue.

But he's a slimy wolf in a high-end business suit. Anyone can see that he's a mob boss.

Alex and Elsa have their phones in their hands while they compare notes. I'm not paying much attention to them. With my back facing Brick and the driver, I can hear their general conversation about the weather, but it's Jade who holds my attention.

Her elbow rests on the window as her thumbnail taps her front teeth. The far off look in her eyes proves her walls can lower. For the first time, I can see behind her rockstar façade. The sadness in her eyes screams loneliness.

Perhaps being someone who was cut deep makes it easier to pick out others with hidden wounds that never heal. Her eyes close as a breath fills her lungs. Is she on the verge of tears but too stubborn to let them fall? This isn't the time for tears, so when does she open the floodgates when she's almost always surrounded by people?

The car pulls into a parking lot and dips down the ramp, rounds a thick concrete wall, and stops in front of two metal doors with barred windows. A man's face appears through the window just as the door pushes open and locks in place. The young man steps out and immediately opens the car door. He's professional and doesn't speak but offers his hand to Jade before I can slide ahead of her.

Brick stands outside the dark tinted window beside me. I trust him to keep her safe until I can get out, which doesn't happen until after everyone has evacuated. That wasn't right and I'll have to speak to Alex about that. I need to be the last person in and the first person out.

I walk one pace behind Jade and Brick two in front. Both of us are on high alert as we're led through a maze of hallways until we finally come to a door with a white placard with Jade's name scribed in marker hung on the door. Brick walks through and, as if familiar with the routine, the rest of us wait until he's cleared the room.

With her tucked in that change room, six of us guards stand in the hall. Three men and one woman stand with us since the doors we're watching are near each other. They are here to keep the band safe. This is my first time meeting some of them. I've done research on each of them to be sure they're qualified.

The woman, Kina, although only 5'4" tall and weighing 135 lbs, is well trained in martial arts. She'd be a damn good opponent in a ring even for someone my size. I've worked with her twice before, so I know how professional she is. I trust her.

The three men are all large and have an intimidation factor that would likely have anyone reconsidering an approach to one of the band members. They're all trained in either boxing or martial arts. They've travelled with the band for several years. Eric is the newest to be hired last year.

While we wait, I use my phone to do a Google search on the slimy August Greynor. Sure enough, he's hooked up. He's the first son to Franco Greyner and is next in line. I knew there was something mob-like about him. Hopefully, Jade's not dumb enough to allow herself to fall victim to that life. Nothing good would come of it.

Half an hour later, Jade rushes from her changing room followed by Alex who looks like someone shit in his cereal. Nothing is said but there's tension in the air.

Jade's wearing black leather pants, a black bra, and a black mesh shirt. Why did she change just to do a trial run? Will she be doing the costume changes during the rehearsal? Odds are she's done this same routine at every venue she's performed at on this tour, and that's about two-dozen shows all across Canada and the US.

This will be my first time seeing her perform. During my research, I've heard her sing. One the song really stuck with me. The message of the song is about being down and out and riddled with pain. Although her voice was powerful in its gentleness, it's the way she sang it that proves every word was ripped from her soul.

Jade knocks on one of the doors and pokes her head inside. "Hey, dolls. Are you ready to do this?"

Female voices are muffled in the room. Jade crosses the hall and knocks on that door. Without waiting, she knocks on the next door meters down the hall. The first door opens, and Pony strolls out with a sleek looking bass guitar tucked under his arm. He's dressed in old jeans and a black t-shirt a size too small that clings to his ripped chest and abs.

The second door pulls open and Dex strolls out with a piece of wood pinched between his lips. It must be a reed since he plays some of the instruments requiring one. He's not dressed in anything special either; a pair of baggy blue jeans and an oversized salmon coloured t-shirt. The bright yellow high-tops on his feet grab my attention. Do they glow in the dark?

Three bodyguards lead the way while three of us follow as we make our way down two short halls before it opens up to a wider walkway. We round a wall of black curtains and the four of them hop up the stairs to the wide stage.

Blazing lights hurt my eyes, but the band doesn't seem to notice. Venus takes her seat behind her drums and touches each drum and symbol to ensure their proper placement, making adjustments where necessary.

Lacey picks up one of the three guitars to the right of the stage and flips the strap over her head. She turns in a circle and light glimmers off the diamond-like face behind the strings. She checks her pedals and turns to smile at her wife, Venus, who beams back at her.

Dex has squatted beside his trombone to affix the reed.

Jade slips the nearly invisible microphone over her ear while a man she called Dan lifts her hair to set it in place. She stuffs things in her ears and situates them.

Her voice thunders through the arena. "Can you hear me now?" There's a pause before a melody flows from her soul like an angel's kiss. "Here I am, lonely before you, if only you'd see me—"

The sound echoes after her words stop abruptly, and I desperately want her to finish her haiku. Seems a pity to hide her lovely voice behind such obnoxious rock and roll music.

Jade's voice returns to its regular pitch when she speaks to someone specific through her microphone. "How's the sound?" She raises her arm with her thumb in the air.

Lacey's guitar wails a high-pitched screeching melody, and I swear my eardrums just ruptured. Does it need a microphone? I think not.

A stagehand taps my shoulder. Before I can turn to look at him through watering eyes, he reaches in front of me with sound-blocking headphones dangling from his index finger. I slip them on my head as I nod to thank him. I may never hear properly again.

Jade faces Venus and nods a countdown. The music—*and I use that term lightly*—begins. They play through several songs while the lighting and sound techs do their thing.

An hour and a half later they've wrapped and leave the stage.

We lead the band back to the changerooms while they remain somewhat stoic in their silence as if they aren't preparing to play for a multitude of screaming worshipers. Shouldn't they be more excited than they are?

Ten minutes later, they dwindle from their rooms one at a time while their people follow them to the two cars in the underground loading dock. The band gets in one and Jade is led to the other.

This time, they get in first and I slip in last. I'll be the first person out after Brick, who sits in the front passenger seat beside the chatty driver. Brick handles the tedious conversation like a politician, and I'm thankful he sat with this driver and not me. I haven't much patience for small-talk when the idea of a wolf in a tailored suit pulling the wool over my little sheep's eyes has me chomping at the bit.

CHAPTER NINE

Jade

The band heads back to the hotel and I envy them. They can have a sit-down meal while I'm forced to eat fruit, cheese, and crackers from a tray in the limo on the way to the live TV interview for the local news station I've never even watched. I'll smile and make like those moments in front of the camera are the high-point of my day even if all I want to do is hang with my band back at the hotel and take a nap before the curtains draw back.

All too often the lead singer is the face of the band, whether that was the intention or not. Pony and Venus had an issue with being put in second place until they realized how exhausting the immense weight caused by the constant strain of the schedule can be. All too often they pity me but secretly thank me for taking the burden from them. That's not to say their burdens aren't extensive, but they have more time to enjoy the benefits than I do.

After make-up and hair have finished preparing me, I sit in the lounge where the live stream of the news plays. Fifteen minutes pass where I treasure the solitude. I'm the only one in this room and this will be the last time I'm alone until after the concert when the adrenaline drop will let the pain seep in nearly crush me.

Stop it! You're no longer a child, and *he* can't hurt you anymore.

Unable to sit still, I pace back and forth.

A woman's head pokes into the room. "Two minutes, Miss Jade."

Too many times I have to repeat the statement, "It's just Jade."

"I'll be back to collect you." She smiles and the door closes earning me a few seconds peace before Alex slides through the door as he slips his phone into the breast pocket of his light grey suit.

"Are you ready?" he asks as if I have a choice.

My shoulders lift and fall as my lips quirk to the left. "Yeah. Sure."

His head tilts back in that annoying way it does when he's about to scold me. "Phoebe, you only have to be pleasant for seven minutes and the cameras will be off. We'll be back in the car in fifteen minutes and on the way to the hotel. You can eat a decent meal," his brows rise when he looks at the half-eaten tray of fruit, "and then you can nap."

I groan as my lips push into a pout. "A nap. I'd love a nap—a long nap—like a week or two.

I'll get up to pee, drink, and eat, but then go back to bed." My eyes close and I sigh before they open. "That sounds heavenly."

His hands press to my shoulders. "After the tour, you have three weeks where you can disappear to Turks and Caicos if you wish."

"Three weeks." I pause to consider the possibilities of that time away. "It's not enough time."

"It never is, Phoebe. It never is."

There's a knock at the door before the same woman returns with a smile. "It's time. Follow me?" She asks as if I have the choice to lead or follow.

I'm rushed to a tall leather stool where a microphone is clipped to the upper pocket of my form-fitting red leather jacket. The crew is bustling around me as make-up and hair do some speedy touch-ups.

A tall, thin woman with impeccable stage make-up and long hair pulled into a swoop design reaches for my hand. "Jade. Hello. I'm Vicki Glasnier, the host."

She sits on the matching stool to my left and sets the paperwork in her hand on the narrow table between us and looks at it while talking to me and a woman picks at her hair with a sharp comb.

"Oh, you're doing a rock concert tonight. Singing." Is this the first time she's ever heard of me? "I'll be asking you about that and maybe we'll take a few calls if we have time. Is this all right with you?"

Do I have a choice?

My toothy smile radiates as would any seasoned performer. "Sounds like fun."

A man's voice calls out and everyone falls silent as they depart the stage. "Ten seconds."

My focus is on the interviewer as her primed smile doesn't crease her heavily Botox filled face despite her forty plus years on this earth.

"Welcome back everybody. I'm not sure if you know this, but here in our studio is Jade, the lead…"

Her voice fades from recognition as my concentration shifts to the camera pointed directly at the woman waving her hand to grab my attention. A light glows red proving that camera is live.

"Jade, tell us what it's like to be the center of attention with 50,000 people watching you."

That's a dumb question!

My amusement lifts my smile into something real. "Between the two of us you'd be the better person to answer that question. Don't you think? You're brought into hundreds of thousands of homes every single night. My standing is dull in comparison to yours."

Trained not to react until someone in her ear tells her what to say, she smiles as her holier-than-thou fluttering lashes bat at the camera lit up facing her. "My watchers see me, but I can't see them, unfortunately. You get to look at their happy faces as they sing along with you. There's more of an instant gratification."

Dance trained monkey, dance!

"I appreciate my fans. Looking at so many of their faces brings me so much pride in what I do. If it weren't for those wonderful people, I wouldn't be doing what I do."

"And you do it so well!" Her eyes flick from me to the camera as if she's ever heard my music. "In only a few hours, people will be pouring into the arena ready to rock with you and your band."

"They aren't just my band. We are the band collectively and share the spotlight." Dammit! I shouldn't have said that even if spoken without malice. I speak directly to the camera knowing the band will be watching. "Venus, Lacey, Dex, and Pony are my people. Without them we wouldn't exist. We've been together from the start, and each deserves equal praise for making our brand what it's grown into. If any one of them left the band, we'd shut it down. Without one we cease to exist."

Her face tips to the side and has yet to lose the smile. "Had we known that we would have asked them to join us today."

To smooth things over, I say, "They're so wonderful. They stayed back to get things prepared in my absence. Otherwise, they would have joined me here today."

If we weren't on the air live, she'd probably roll her eyes.

"Well, how selfish would we be to keep you any longer than we need to. How about we get some questions from our listeners?"

Like I have a choice?

Vicki sits a little taller as her shoulders turn ever so slightly toward the camera with the red light. "Caller number one, Michelle. What's your question?"

The caller's high-pitch excitement sings about the room as she studders through her praises. She asks a mundane question I've been asked a million times: "How old were you when you started singing?"

The camera locks on my face, so I confess how I began to sing in high school. "There was a talent contest my friend had talked me into entering. She was the only person to hear me sing. I was terrified. My anxiety eased away with each note, and I felt like I was where I needed to be. From that day on, I've been singing."

It's the truth, but there was so much more to it than that. I leave out my terror, the excessive fear-vomiting, and how Rachel had to drag me on stage—literally.

"Our second caller is John. What question do you have for Jade?"

A deep voice speaks slowly. "It's more of a proclamation than a question."

Curiosity rules Vicki's wide eyes. "Oh. Well, go ahead, John."

"I'll be attending the concert tonight and can't wait to see you. I can't wait until your gorgeous green eyes meet mine again."

My smile remains despite the cold shiver running down my spine and my fight or flight instinct holding my breath hostage.

"I've missed you. Have you missed me?"

Unaware of the threat, the host leans toward me sporting a wide grin and even wider eyes. "Awe, that's sweet. Do you two know each other?"

As my limbs grow heavy, I'm quick to say, "No."

John's tone grows more menacing. "Oh, but we will get to know each other very well. Soon."

Has all of my blood left my face?

Seeming to notice my fear, Vicki reaches for my hand and gives it a squeeze as she speaks to the camera in more of a scolding, motherly tone.

"It's not just you, John. Jade will see so many people tonight and each one will feel a special connection through her words."

My focus remains on the host's smiling lips while her voice sounds hollow as if coming to me through paper towel tubes like we used to do as children. My body stiffens but my smile continues to shine as if it's all my face can manage.

The glaring light pointed at us falls dark, jolting me from my daze. Did she ask me something, and I sat here like a silent fool?

She immediately leans toward me as everyone begins busying themselves by taking off microphones, rolling cameras away, and moving about to complete their tasks.

Vicki is absent of her smile. "Are you okay?"

"Um." A breath fills my lungs and it's the first in how long? "Somebody is— I've had a, um— There's been some threats. Sorry. I didn't mean to shut down."

People scatter when her perfectly manicured hand waves as her stiff brows fail to furrow. "Last year, I had a stalker show up *in* my house. Thankfully, my husband played hooky and we kept the kids out of school to enjoy an unscheduled mini vacation at the zoo. Had we not, I would've been home by myself that day since the maid and gardeners had the day off. I hate to imagine what could have happened if I were home alone. So, when I tell you that I understand your fear, I mean it."

How terrified was she and her husband knowing their kids could have come home from school to find their mother murdered? Worse yet, her husband could've come home to find them all dead. That puts fear at a whole new level. Thankfully, my concern revolves solely on me since my stalker shows no interest in the band, and I have no close-knit family to speak of.

"I'm sorry that happened to you. I had no idea."

She shrugs to lessen the memory of it. "Nobody knew because we kept it out of the media. How we managed that, I have no idea. That's why we pay big bucks to the right people." She stands and I take her lead. "Listen, if you ever need anyone to talk to about this, I have a great ear."

Without moving my head, my eyes skitter to the empty floor where the cameras stood moments ago.

She scoffs as her fingers quote. "Jade, I might be in the *'news'* business, but this could be a life and death issue, which isn't something I'd capitalize on by telling the world your troubles. I wouldn't want it for myself, so I won't do it to anyone else."

Before she can throw her arms up for a hug, I reach my hand between us.

"Not a hugger? Not a problem." She shakes my hand and leans in toward me. "You take care of yourself, okay? I hope they catch that son-of-a-bitch soon."

Alex steps toward me but it isn't him my eyes lock onto.

The pinched lips and flared nostrils of a deeply angry bald man grabs my attention and won't let it go. Arrow's eyes burn into mine before they jerk away as his phone presses to his ear. He's too far away for me to hear the words he's whispering to the person on the other end.

Beside me with his hand on my shoulder, Alex's sympathetic tone hopes to soothe me but it's more annoying than a hovering fly, so I wave my hand hoping he'll back away.

Arrow's fiery brown eyes lock onto mine when his phone slips into the inside pocket of his black suit coat. His white dress shirt has a few unfastened buttons, and his black jeans fit snug in all the right places. He's dashing in his casual dressiness.

The seriousness in his stare makes me feel like prey. But whose prey am I; the stalker or Arrow's? Which predator has me most fearful?

The stalker would do any number of things to me that could cause me physical or mental pain, but I've been there and would survive it better as an adult than I did as a child. But Arrow could crush my heart if I allowed it to him. I'd rather die at the hands of my stalker than risk that. What does that say about me?

Before I know it, I'm back in my hotel room lying on my bed in the fetal position. Men's voices rise and drop to a low hush as if not wanting to disturb me while they argue. I roll onto my back and stare at the tiered ceiling lined with sleeping lights. My fingers weave together over my forehead as deep, soothing breaths ease in and out of me.

Just relax. Soon I'll be on stage doing what I love.

I picture a set of eyes boring into mine from the audience as a gun barrel points directly at my face. My heart pounds and I gasp as I launch off the bed to the toilet and spill my guts. I flush and lie back on the black and turquoise marble tiles. The cold seeps through my t-shirt and the shivers are refreshing.

Get up, you big fucking baby! You're stronger than this.

My growl echoes through the bathroom as I rise to my feet and lock eyes with a face I barely recognize. Between the smeared tv-make-up and the absent eyes, she's a shell of sadness that weighs of disappointment.

Several wipes later and the make-up is gone, bringing back a woman I'm more familiar with. She's tired, but I can imagine her as a regular person set to do a mundane task, like go to the grocery store and push a cart up each aisle completely unnoticed by anyone. I'll never have that.

A knock outside the bedroom door pulls my attention from the reflection. With my toughness back in commission, I open the door with a straight spine and a relaxed expression.

Let the games begin!

My earphones hum with instrumental music to block out the hair and make-up crew as they decorate me with colour and flare. Dressed in yoga pants and a loose button-up black blouse, my Crocs are nearly silent as I make my way to the car. I've said nothing while being prepared.

I sit across from a man intent on staring me down and the limo revs to life.

What the hell is he thinking?

My brows pinch and my head tips to my shoulder. Arrow's smile is slight but for the first time I see him as a normal man and not someone incensed at life. I'm soothed by the calm way his chest rises and falls behind the suit jacket.

Neither of us dare avert our gaze first as the limo floats over train tracks and turns a corner, shifting us. So, we stare at each other.

Alex is texting while Elsa sits with her hands folded on her lap, eyes closed as she mediates. Soon we'll all be thrown into controlled chaos. None of that matters because when Arrow smiles and something inside of me shatters.

Tears spill down my cheeks much to Arrow's chagrin. Sympathetic eyes seer into me, and I hiccup, alerting Alex and Elsa.

I never cry in front of anyone. *Never!* What did Arrow do to me? *Fuck! Make it stop!*

Confusion swells in Arrow's eyes before they jerk away. At least he's willing to let me hang onto a shred of decency. Elsa reaches for me, but I lurch away from her as if she's electricity.

"No. I'm fine. I'll be fine." A deep breath fills my lungs as I lightly brush the tears from my cheeks, hoping not to smear my make-up any more than it already has.

Elsa's voice is somber as she pulls her phone from her satchel. "Don't worry, sweetie. We'll take care of this like it never happened. I'll call make-up and have them ready for you."

I skirt my gaze to Alex. His fatherly concern is overshadowed by the strength in the stiffness of his body language. He doesn't reach for me. Instead, his chin lifts, brows lower, lips tighten, and a slow nod of his head speaks volumes.

My tears instantly halt and my shoulders pull back. Chin held high; I take a deep breath. "I'm okay."

"Yes, you are," Alex says with an assuring nod and lengthy blink. He returns his attention to his phone.

If he had made a big deal about my little breakdown, I may not have stopped crying. He knows me well enough to know what I need from him and when I need it. He knows something in my past has shattered me and that locking away my emotions is how I hold myself together.

I was four-years-old when I was taken from my alcoholic mother and put into foster care. She always said my father used her when she was drunk and left before she sobered up, but I didn't know what that meant. I've considered doing one of those genealogy DNA kits to find him, but why would I want to find a rapist? If he took advantage of my mother when she was drunk, that's exactly what he is. I'm better off never knowing.

The first foster parents that took me in were the Gantry's. They were nice, at first. I had a full belly and soon my bones didn't stick out as much. I was clean with fresh clothing daily and brushed hair. The woman was so nice. She'd read to me while I sat on her lap in the rocking chair on the front porch in the suburbs. I wanted her to be my mom. But that image of the perfect family shattered when Mr. Gantry would sit me on his lap when Mrs. Gantry wasn't looking.

I remember the first time he touched me under my pink flowered underpants. My back was against his chest as my legs straddled his thin thighs. He smelled of stale cigarettes and whiskey. My yellow sundress was lifted to my waist. The muscles on his hairy arm would move as his fingers touched me *down ther*e. Sometimes it felt good, but sometimes it hurt and I'd cry. He'd rock me and tell me, "Good girls don't cry. Good girls get cookies."

Alex shakes my shoulders. "Jade! You're on."

I'm standing off stage while a roaring audience chants my name. I was just in the limo, wasn't I? When did I change into my black leather pants, and the long sleeved, black shirt that's mostly mesh but has leather bra cups with thin straps leading to the wide leather collar around the neck. I honestly can't remember. It's all a blur.

"Jade? What's wrong?" He shakes me again.

A smile spans my mouth as I step back and his arms fall away. Nothing matters but this moment. The only thing I need to think about is the song line-up and to let the words to the songs float from me as if I was born to sing them. It's what I do best.

"I'm okay. Let's do this!"

As concern has him hugging himself, I rush up the ten steps and past the heavy red drape and wave to the screaming fans as the sound of my black stiletto boots on the wooden stage drown in the noise.

In my earpiece, Venus's husky voice whispers a four-count. Lacey's guitar screams and my body vibrates from the disciples. The rest of the band roars to life as the first song in our set starts us off. Dex and Pony are to my left and plastered with the same fake smile I wear. Dex blows into his trumpet and my turn to join in comes in an eight count.

As I sing, dance, and do quick costume changes, my feet ache from the high-heels, but what hurts more is the concern that each set of eyes I look into may be my stalker. I want to be flirtatious, as is my persona, but the last thing I want is to lead them on even more. Somehow, I manage to push down my fear and do my job.

By the time we're taking our final bow, my body aches and my voice is hoarse.

Pony's long hair is slick with sweat. Dex has a sheen of sweat dripping to the waistband of his leather pants from behind the leather strapped harness crossed over his chest. They lead the way to the change rooms followed by me and a chatty Lacey who's still peppy with energy. Venus follows while complaining to one of the costume personnel about the way her leather shorts cut into her hips causing a rash.

Moments later we're whisked into the limos and rushed back to the hotel. I stare across the car to Brick, who is more interested in his phone than the silence filling the car. What a difference from a few moments ago when I couldn't hear myself think through the screams.

Arrow doesn't meet my eyes, even when we arrive back in my room. What is his problem? He's an asshole!

A thick bouquet of big, beautiful flowers is perched on a glass table just inside the foyer near the sofa. I'm drawn to it like a moth to a flame. The scent tickles me before I can pluck the card from the yellow envelope.

"Jade, Congratulations on a job well done. I'll be up late. Augustus."

The man is dashingly handsome, seductive, won't ask me for money, and has charisma coming out of his ass. He's the whole package. The way he stared into my eyes and kissed my hand awoke my pussy to her needs. It's been months since my body has had any attention other than masturbation.

I'm exhausted, need a shower, and want to murder a bottle or two of wine to forget the thousands of eyes that stared at me while I wondered if they wanted to harm me. So many eyes. Too many faces.

My heart thuds loudly in my ears when I re-read the card and consider the possibilities.

I tuck the card back in the envelope and set it beside the crystal vase.

Alex and Arrow seem upset as their voices remain hushed, but their body language is anything but calm. When Alex isn't tapping on his phone, his head shakes and his hand raises as if assuring Arrow everything is okay. The tension in Arrow's shoulders has him slightly hunched as his fists press to his hips and he paces before Alex.

Something's wrong.

"What's going on?" I ask as my boots drop to the floor one at a time.

Alex looks up from his phone. "Nothing's wrong, Phoebe. Go, take a shower and relax. It's been a long day; you must be exhausted."

Arrow turns to Alex as if that's the first time he's heard my real name. Did he really think Jade was my birth name? Famous people often change their names. If he gave it half a thought, he'd realize Pony and Venus aren't names often given at birth.

I remember the day Lacey crowned Pony with his nickname. She was behind me when I opened my bedroom door, so we could go in and change out of our swimsuits. He was changing, and we got a clear view of his monster penis. It's true. I've had him inside me on more than a few drunken nights. His cock is long and fat even when not erect.

Lacey fell in love with Venus almost immediately after being introduced. They were married in secret two years later and have been inseparable ever since.

Nobody can remember who crowned Venus with her nickname. She answered our ad online for a drummer and fit in like she had been with us from the beginning. Our original drummer moved away to start a career in real estate thinking it'd be more lucrative. Boy, was he wrong!

Dex is short for Dexter. He was crowned with that nickname in high school, long before I met him. He wore thick glasses and always had his face in a book. His grades were at the top of the chart. High school is challenging enough without keeping his sexual preference for girls and boys hidden. The only way he thought he could keep himself from being found out was to stick his nose in a book and not look up. While studying engineering in university, he met his first boyfriend, Rune. They dated for two years non-exclusively and were madly in love. However, Rune didn't agree with Dex having sex with a woman and couldn't move past it, so he broke up with him. Dex hasn't had a meaningful relationship since, but he's not opposed to a provocative night with a warm body. He and Pony have hooked up a few times that I know of, but Pony prefers women over men.

Lacey and I became friends in drama class during our second year of high school. That's when we started to dream about being in a band. We were so young at the time and had no idea how to get that going. She didn't go to college, instead she worked two jobs to help care for her ailing father. He passed away when she was barely twenty-two-years-old, leaving her on her own with only an aunt who lived in Florida. In order to make enough money to keep the house, she started dancing at the local strip club. She hated getting naked but loved the attention she got when she danced. As far back as I can remember, she's worn lace, hence the nickname Lacey.

As for me, I got my nickname because my eyes are the colour of jade. One magazine described my eyes as mesmerizing, soul seducing gems. My best friend, Rachel Hanover started calling me Jade when we met at six-years-old.

I moved next door to her with Mike and Leona Frewns; the good foster family. They raised me, yet I still don't consider them family. They were affectionate toward me, but because I was emotionally broken, I pulled away. I call them about once a month to check in, but don't go out of my way to spend holidays with them. Besides, I'm usually doing a concert or some kind of event during holidays.

Keeping people at arm's length is a defence mechanism and stepping out of that behaviour is too scary. No matter what I do, letting myself be vulnerable by allowing someone close to me is terrifying. The only person I'm really close to is Rachel, and it took years before I allowed myself to trust her.

Alex knows some of my story and hasn't allowed me to push him away. Do I love Alex? Sure, I suppose. He cares for me, and I care for him. He's just the right amount of pushy where he motivated me enough to build my career from near nothing to stardom. Would I miss him if he left me? Yes, I would miss his direction and support, and my chest aches at the thought of him dying or leaving me. Is that the definition of love?

CHAPTER TEN

Phoebe? So, that's her real name. How did I not know that? Fixer's dragging his feet on tracking down information about her; information that may be useful in unveiling her stalker.

Does *Phoebe* suit her personality? Absolutely not! Phoebe sounds delicate, soft-spoken, and driven by kindness. The only fitting part of that description is *driven,* but not by kindness.

I tried to find it when I researched her, but no name was associated with Jade. It's odd with the unlimited technology at our fingertips that someone can hide their past. All I know about her childhood is that she grew up in foster care and her neighbour became her best friend. I have yet to meet Rachel Hanover but know what she looks like from an online gossip magazine's snapshot of the two dining in public.

Rachel's pretty if you're into five-foot-tall blondes that might weigh 110 lbs soaking wet. Personally, I don't. I prefer women with meat on them; someone I can really toss around in the bedroom. I like to fuck like I'm bronco riding the meanest bull in the bunch and tiny women are too fragile.

My ward, on the other hand, she'd be one hell of a ride. But I can't allow that to happen, not that she'd even let me touch her arm. The woman has a chip on her shoulder. Before I said one damn word to her, she's already made her mind up to hate me.

Why the fuck am I even entertaining that thought? She's off limits. I may be a lot of things, but a rule breaker I am not.

Get it together, Arrow, there are more important things to think about than sliding my cock into something warm.

She received two deliveries of flowers to the lobby. The hotel's manager read the cards as he was instructed to. The bouquet sitting on the table she has her nose stuck in is from the asshole on the top floor. Although it irritates me to high-hell that he's sending her flowers, it's the photo in the second bouquet that has my hackles rising.

It's a picture of Jade on stage tonight as she leaned down toward the audience, smiling and looking directly into the camera lens. The stalker was that close to her, and she didn't know. They must not have looked familiar, or she would've recognized them, so the person is a stranger. Damn! That makes it harder to find them.

Jade stands between Alex and me, staring at him and giving him shit for not telling her what's going on.

"Something's up. Just fucking tell me what's wrong. Alex! Fucking look at me." Jade huffs and slams her hands to her hips, and he looks at her with squinted eyes from below perfectly trimmed salt and pepper eyebrows. "Thank you. Now tell me what's going on and don't deny there's a problem."

"Look at this picture." My voice grabs her attention, and she spins to face me with fire behind her eyes. "It's a long shot, but do you remember who took this?"

Her face softens for just a moment. Realizing she's showing weakness, she toughens her expression. She takes the clear plastic sleeve housing the small photo and examines it. Her eyes roam to her left before her head follows left but tilts to the right just as she is positioned in the photo. Her eyes close and her lips move soundlessly. It's as if she's singing to replay the moment.

She stands so close to me I can smell the sweetness of her shampoo and a hint of sweat. Is this how she'd smell after having multiple orgasms?

Her head shakes as her brows pinch together. Her sigh is heavy as her eyes open to meet mine.

They're glossy and extraordinarily green. I've never seen eyes that shade of emerald. She isn't wearing contacts because their depth is clear to her soul, and it surprises me that she has one.

"There were so many people taking my picture." Her face drops to hide under a tangle of wavy locks as she curses under her breath. Her head jolts up and angry eyes leer into mine. "We should've set up cameras to record the audience. I shouldn't have to think about setting that up. Isn't that in your fucking job description? Jesus, fuck!"

She storms toward the bar as more of her curses float about the room. She pulls the crystal plug from a bottle of red wine and fills an elegant glass nearly to the top before tipping the bottle back while her plump lips wrap around the opening, grabbing my attention. Her throat bobs three times before she sets the bottle on the bar top and walks away without recapping it.

My cock thickens from envying the wine. I shift my stance and wonder if she or Alex notice how snug my jeans are.

Alex and I share a look because she's right. I should have had cameras set up to capture the audience. Why didn't I think to do that? Where the hell is my head? What is it about this angry woman that has me out of sorts?

With his phone still cupped in his hand held at his waist, Alex runs his other hand around the back of his neck and grunts as his head pulls against it. "Phoebe, go take a shower and then go to bed, and for Christ sake, stop drinking."

She scoffs as her ass flops onto the sofa with her wine glass barely able to contain the red liquid. Her hand lifts as she gulps from the glass. It's half empty before she looks up at Alex and grins. "No."

"Get some sleep." He knows arguing with her is futile, so he nods at me before he leaves her suite.

With everyone out of the room, I kick the doorstop to release it and prepare to leave her alone with her wine.

She calls out. "Wait!"

With the door at my back, I look at her. "If you're going to yell at me or call me incompetent, don't waste your breath."

She scoffs and mumbles. "I didn't call you incompetent, but now that you brought it up."

I allow the door to close a little more to let her know I'm about to leave.

"Wait. No, I'm sorry. You aren't incompetent." Jade takes a breath, and I wonder if that statement was the best compliment she could give me without cringing. She stands and slowly walks toward me, stopping a few meters away. "Don't leave yet."

A flash of vulnerability is quickly erased when she straightens her spine. Weakness still seeps through her tough exterior by not meeting my eyes.

"You can stay. I want to shower but—" Her head swivels as she shifts a step away and stops. Her eyes don't rise from the nearly empty glass in her hand.

This is a side of her I never thought she'd let me see. She's afraid to be alone. This woman who an hour ago had thousands of people screaming her name is exposing a weakness.

I take a step toward her to allow the door to close. My voice is strong and smooth, which is what she needs. "Jaybird, look at me."

Her face contorts as she parrots me. "*Jaybird?* Is that my new nickname?"

"My nickname for you. Only mine."

Her lashes flutter and her mouth falls slack as if she's about to speak, but nothing comes.

More demanding, I say, "Look. At. Me. Jaybird."

A flash of resistance has her lips pinched in a line as her glare penetrates me.

My head tips back as my eyes glance down her throat to her chest and back to her eyes. "Come here."

She remains in place and her eyes skirt the floor proving the decision to walk or stay in place is a difficult one. With a loud clearing of her throat, she looks directly at me and walks toward me.

It's cute how she stares at me while complying to my demands. How much would she resist if I told her to take off her clothes? It's too soon for that.

She stops inches from me. Her eyelids are heavy as she lifts her chin to raise her eyes from my steady Adam's apple.

"I'm here. Now what? Are you going to tell me to jump around like a kangaroo?"

Imagining her hopping around the room has a smile twitching the edges of my lips that can't be suppressed. "No, but you will no longer talk to me like I'm a peasant. You will *ask* me to stay while you shower."

Her left eyebrow lifts. "A peasant. Really? I was thinking more along the lines of employee-employer." Her finger presses to my chest and then to hers.

I lean my face closer to hers as my eyes drink in her puffy lips, and whisper, "Never again will you talk to me like you do your other employees. I will no longer stand for your spoiled little brat routine. Do it again, and I'll throw you over my knee. Do you understand?"

Her tone is snarky as her face grows more animated. "I pay them very well, so I'll talk to them however I want. That includes you. You're paid handsomely, so I'll speak however I want and you'll take it, or you'll get the fuck out and not come back."

"As you wish, Jaybird." I smirk and leave the suite, allowing the door to swing closed behind me.

How far down the hall will I get before she comes out to either beg me to come back or give me another piece of her mind.

Five, four, three, two—

The door clicks and her voice purrs at my back. "Wait!"

A satisfied smile rides my lips as my feet plant firmly leaving my back to her.

"Come back," she asks in a sweet tone.

Fuck, this woman is like Jekyll and Hide.

My cocky smile fades as I turn to look over my shoulder, but not enough to look at her. I wait until she sighs heavily.

"Come back, *please*," she says as if the word was painful to say.

My body turns only halfway allowing me to look at her. Flushed cheeks shine through heavy make-up. She looks smaller somehow as she stands with her arms crossed over her chest with her foot planted to keep the door from closing and locking her out.

In no rush, I stroll back to her. She doesn't move to open the door further, instead her jaw is tense, and her nostrils flared. Swallowing her pride isn't easy for her. Perhaps nobody's put her in her place in a very long time, if ever.

My index finger lifts her chin to force her to look at me. Her breaths come heavily and there's a flicker of trepidation in her expression that suggests I move my finger away, so I do. She blinks rapidly before continuing to hold my gaze.

To ease her from whatever memory has her so stiff, I soften my voice. "I'm here, Jaybird. Tell me what you need?"

Jade swallows and sets free a ragged breath. "Can you stay while I shower? I'm not afraid to be alone, but I just don't want to—" She steps back before turning to push the door wider and going inside.

I follow and allow the door to close with a click of the automatic lock.

"It's okay to admit you're afraid. Anyone in your situation should be nervous to be alone."

"Yeah. Well, not me." She picks her empty wine glass from the table nearest the door and carries it to the bar where she refills it. "I've been alone for a long time, and I prefer it. Tonight, I'm just—"

My hands fold together over my crotch to hide the growing bulge. She's even more beautiful when she lets her guard down. If I thought for a moment she'd be accepting of a hug, I'd wrap my arms around her and tell her everything is going to be okay, but she'd likely punch me in the face and call me an asshole.

"Jaybird, I'll stay as long as you need me to."

Her eyes are glassier than usual, and I can't discern whether alcohol is the cause, or her emotions have broken through her sandpaper shell and she's welling up.

Leaning her hip against the bar, her finger circles the glass's edge creating a soft hum. "Why do you call me Jaybird?"

Should I tell her it's because I find her cackle annoying? "I know birds and Jaybird suits best."

She shrugs and sips her wine. "At least it's a pretty bird and not a vulture."

A smile tugs at my lips. "Vulture was a close second."

"I don't pick at someone else's scraps. I do the killing and let others pick at my scraps." She turns from me and swoops her messy locks over her shoulder. "Unzip me."

I step toward her back and imagine grabbing her leather collar and pulling her back to my front. I'd whisper how disappointed I am when she's being a bad girl while my fingers dipped below the waistband of her leather pants.

With my mouth inches from the ear bare of hair, I whisper. "Please."

Her beautiful lips part as her face turns over her shoulder. Her whisper precedes a breath heavy enough to swell her chest pushing out her breasts. "What?"

My tone is husky and unwavering. "Ask me nicely."

Her silver rings with skulls and daggers clack together as her fingers mesh before her chest. Mockingly, she retorts, "Please, sir. Will you be so kind as to undo a girl's top, so she may get naked and shower."

The crotch of my pants grows tight and my palm itches to spank the sassiness right out of this bitch. Instead, my jaw clenches as my hand slides around the leather collar. With a quick jerk, she yelps as I force her to take a step back until her ass presses against my crotch. She doesn't fight me off, which isn't surprising. Her breaths come heavily and ragged. The flushed skin on her cheek prickles beneath my hot breath.

"I like it when you call me sir. You should do it more often, just don't be such a sassy little bitch while you do it. I'm not opposed to punishing you. Keep that in mind."

My free hand unfastens the collar before I release her neck to glide the zipper down as my fingertips skim down her spine. It detaches and I take a step back, but she remains in place.

What will she do now? Is a battle going on inside her of whether to drop to her knees before me or walk away to take a shower, as was the plan?

"Thank you." Jade's hands clutch into fists at her sides. She takes a deep breath to collect herself and clears her throat. "I won't be long. Make yourself comfortable. Have a drink; you could use one to lighten you up."

With her back to me, she wiggles free of her top and tosses it to the floor. Her hair sways with each stride as it brushes the soft skin on her back. To let me know she won't be toyed with, she doesn't turn around. Little does she know hips are my thing, not breasts unless I have them squeezed in my hand, bound in rope, or the nipples are pinched between clamps.

Over her shoulder, in a clear voice, she adds, "Oh, by the way, I'll be hitting the gym tomorrow morning. You can babysit me while you get in a workout. We wouldn't want your muscles to shrink. Would we?"

My Jaybird's perfect ass sways beneath low-rise, snug, leather pants. She doesn't close the bedroom door, but I can't see in as the wall arcs to the left for added privacy.

She's probably pulling her pants down her muscular legs and stepping out of them. She'd be completely naked right about now. How would the dried sweat on her skin taste as I kiss down her spine to her lower back. Is her scent strong from being aroused during the concert and when my hand was around her neck?

Instead of rushing to that bathroom to stand outside the glass enclosed shower to admire her while she showers, my feet take me to the bar. A quick search proves there to be no whiskey. What bar doesn't have a bottle of whiskey? The bottle of tequila hasn't been opened, so I quickly uncap it and pour myself a double shot. There's a range of beer in the fridge, so I choose one and crack it open. I don't like the bloat I get from beer, but it'll be a good chaser.

Fuck! I hate tequila.

With my beer bottle in hand, I sit on the leather sofa and rest my feet on the coffee table.

Twenty minutes have passed, and the shower's still running. How dirty is she? Should I check on her? No. I can't go in there. If I see her hands brushing over her form through steamed, water dropped glass walls, my cock will tear free from its denim prison.

Another ten minutes pass and I've grown more concerned. I set the empty beer bottle on the coffee table and force myself to walk slowly while I listen. If she sounds like she's all right, I'll go sit back on the sofa and wait, but if I hear nothing, I'll have to investigate further.

There's no sound other than water, but before I can call out to her, a whimper weighs lightly on the mist. The scent of clean water tickles my nostrils before I reach the doorframe. Heat wafts from the open doorway, and I hear the sound again.

She's crying. Not a gentle cry, but a soul crushing sob. It takes more control than I desire not to rush to her and hold her while she clings onto me.

I stand beside the doorway and call out to her. "Jaybird, are you all right? I'm just checking in. You've been in there a long time."

"Close the door to the bedroom on your way out."

She's hurting, but too proud to let anyone see it. What happened to her to make her so heavily guarded? If someone harmed her, I'll fucking torture them in a manner that'll have them begging for a merciful death.

"I'll wait for you in the living room," I say loud enough to ride over the falling water.

Not ten minutes later she rushes from the bedroom wearing loose-fitting red silky shorts and a matching silky top that does nothing to hide her rigid nipples. White hotel slippers swoosh the tiled floor as she rushes to the bar. Damp hair hangs down her back leaving an unmistakable wet stain on her silky pajamas.

She doesn't look at me as she grabs two bottles of red wine and rushes to the main door.

What the fuck is she doing?

I'm quick to follow and grab the door before it clicks shut behind her.

As she rushes past the room with the open door, a shirtless Pony rushes out and calls to her. "Hey, doll. You look sexy as fuck. Where're you going?" It's obvious he's had his fill of alcohol.

Jade doesn't look at him when she turns around. Her eyes lock onto mine. "I'm going to get laid."

Pony whoops and whistles. "Alright! Go get yourself some, girl. Enjoy!"

A male voice calls his name, which directs his attention back to the party in his room. He laughs hard as he strides back into the room with his muscular arms swaying. The door shuts, containing a majority of the noise.

Jade's almost at the elevator when I catch up to her. Damn, she's quick when she wants to be.

"Where the fuck are you going?" My tone is harsher than intended.

Jade spins and holds up the two bottles of wine. "I'm going one floor up to have a drink with Augustus."

"It's one in the morning. Shouldn't you be going to bed – your own bed? Alex said—"

She snaps at me. "I don't give a fuck what Alex said! He's not my keeper and neither are you. Now leave me the fuck alone."

My nose twitches as she teeters on my last nerve. "Fine. If you insist on going, I'm coming with you."

"Like hell you are!" Jade's puffy eyes can't hide the emotions she's fighting to suppress.

She's going to get drunk and have sex with that mafia motherfucker. He's bad news, but she doesn't see it. Or does she? Is she self-destructive? If she were mine, she'd never get within one-hundred-feet of him.

"I know what it's like to have pain. I'd do anything to push down—way down into a dark pit where it can't hurt me."

She stares at me unblinking until the elevator's ding fills the hall. The doors ease apart and I want to throw her over my shoulder and carry her back to the room. Am I jealous or honestly worried for her safety? A little of both.

Standing at the back of the metal carriage is a tall, blue-eyed devil. He's handsome, I can admit that, but danger reeks from every pore. Is that what she's attracted to—a bad boy? If he fucking hurts her or gets her into any trouble… *I'm watching you, motherfucker!*

"Hello, Jade." His voice slithers as he steps forward and reaches out for her, taking one bottle from her, and admires it before his snake-like eyes drink her in. "You look lovely tonight. A little wet, but lovely."

My black boot prevents the elevator doors from closing while I hold his glare.

Augustus' perfectly white smile looks as fake as he is. "Don't worry about Miss Jade. I have plenty of security." His finger points at me before his hand slithers around her bicep. "Thank you for your service. You did serve overseas; is that right?" His grin proves he's done his research on me. "She'll be safer with me than anywhere."

That was a direct slap to my skills.

Jade leans into him and presses her chest to his. "I hope not to be too safe."

What the fuck?

The asshole leans in to kiss her but hesitates when the alarm sounds because I have yet to allow the doors to close.

He speaks slowly with a dangerous threat. "Step away. I'll bring her back in the morning."

Ignoring him, I speak directly to Jade. "Do you have your phone?"

Her eyes skim her body before meeting mine. "And where would I be hiding it?" Her attempt to stare me down fails where her blink drops her eyes to my tight lips before she looks away.

"And if you need me?" I ask as fire burns in my stomach. She's a danger to herself.

Augustus leans down to kiss her forehead, and her arms wrap loosely around his chest. "If I need anything, I'll call Alex."

They meet eyes as my foot retracts from the door. Their lips press together, and I can't watch. The doors shut, and I'm grateful, but more worried than ever. I shouldn't have let her go alone, but waiting in his foyer while sounds of their sex radiates through the suite doesn't sound like a fun night.

CHAPTER ELEVEN

Jade

It's 5am and I'm lying in a bed next to a man I know nothing about. Judging by the amount of security hovering around him, I assume he's important or lives a life of danger. Is he mafia? It would have been smarter of me to ask before I sucked his cock.

I don't want to know this man. He's a play thing to entertain me and satiate my body, which he did. While straddling his face, I had my first orgasm of the night. Later, I rode him like a fucking bull rider and got myself off while his gorgeous blue eyes burned into me.

Lying here with the moon hovering low in the sky outside the tinted glass wall, the rays are bright enough to create valleys where his relaxed abdomen muscles dip. His chest rises and sinks as low snores prove he's lost to the waking world.

His body is taught, but the muscles aren't as defined as Arrow's. Why did I run from him? Because he saw me through my bullshit. He fucking saw me, and he didn't run. What's hurt him? I can't imagine anyone doing anything to hurt that strong man. He's a pillar of strength and confidence. Was he always that way?

The air is too still; I have to get out of here. A balloon of emotional pain is about to erupt from deep inside me where I thought I'd hid it away.

Without rustling the covers, I ease out of bed and feel around with my feet for my slippers. My head spins from the effects of guzzling so much wine. I stumble but catch myself on the bedroom loveseat. I plant my ass on the satin cushion long enough for the room to stop spinning.

I sneak from the room and round the bar. I'm startled to find two well-armed men standing in the foyer. One of the men nods, but the younger of the two stands wide-eyed with his mouth ajar. Were they there when I was howling in pleasure? Oh, God! They'd better not have recorded it. They could sell it to the tabloids for tens of thousands of dollars if not more.

The younger of the two whispers, "You're Jade."

"I am." Like a trained monkey, my smile lifts into a sexy quirk. I stop one pace from the man and try to speak with confidence. "Have you two been here all night?"

His face flushes and his Adam's apple bobs, but he offers no verbal response.

Shit! He heard everything.

My feet remain planted when a deep voice behind me redirects my attention. "It's our job to ensure the safety of Mr. Greyner and his guests."

I spin slow enough not to lose my balance. The older man wears no expression, yet his premature wrinkles have etched deep on his forehead. He's obviously been working for Augustus for many years and the stress has chipped away at him.

"You needn't worry; we're locked in an NDA. Nobody working under Mr. Greyner would dare speak out about his personal life. You have nothing to worry about." He nods before he presses the silver elevator button to deliver me back to my floor.

The young man near me visibly shakes. Is he that much of a fan? The elevator doors open and the older man steps inside while holding the door for me. The young man stiffens as I lean in and press a soft kiss to his freshly shaven cheek. His breath hitches and I want more than anything to feel his crotch to see how hard he is, but I won't.

The older man clears his throat as a sign for me to take my hand away from the man's strong chest draped in a black dress shirt, as that seems to be their dress code.

After stepping inside, the black boot holding the door moves aside and his thick finger presses the button to my floor. He taps a card onto the black screen and the elevator begins its descent.

With a tilt of my head, I snicker. "You didn't have to come with me."

"Miss Jade, as I've explained it is my job to keep Mr. Greyner and his guests safe. When not under your own guard, you're under mine." The slight echo made his voice ring deeper than I had it earlier.

The elevator doors open and the man steps out before me as he quickly scans the hall before moving aside to allow me to pass. He follows me as I begin the walk toward my suite.

In my haste to leave, I forgot to grab a key-card.

Fuck!

"You're back." Arrow's familiar voice carries no emotion. He's the last person I want to see as I do the walk of shame. Unfortunately, I need him to unlock my door.

Why do I feel guilty as if I've done something terrible to offend Arrow? I had sex with someone—very good sex. It's been a while, and my body needed a release. It helped me push my pain down until I no longer cared to pay it a lick of attention. But a lingering sense of wrongdoing lingers in my gut. Will he threaten to throw me over his knee? My pussy clenches at the thought of him actually going through with it.

My arms lift and drop at my sides because I'm defeated. "Can you let me in my room?"

He's barefoot and shirtless, wearing grey sweatpants and looking sexy as fuck. His suit coat, jeans and dress shirt had him looking fit, but standing before me with the grey cotton material outlining his cock, my mouth is as dry as the Sahara Desert.

For fuck sake, look away!

My escort nods at me before shaking Arrow's hand. They say nothing as a silent nod of respect passes between them. The man rushes back to the elevator as Arrow stands a stride from me with his arms hanging at his sides and wears no expression.

Finally able to pull my attention from his abs and crotch, I motion toward the door. "Well?"

Arrow doesn't move. Is he trying to burn a hole in me with his glare?

Snarky, I cuss. "Fuck! What?"

Slowly and in a voice suitable for a couple in bed post sex, he says, "Have you forgotten to use your manners so quickly?"

My eyes close and the hallway spins from the abuse of alcohol, so I lean my shoulder against the wall for stability. "Will you open the door for me, *please*?"

His nostrils flare as his chest expands. I follow him to my door. He scans the card, and the door sounds the high-pitch alert before I push it open and walk through. The door closes with a click as I stagger toward the bedroom.

"Where are you going?"

I nearly jumped out of my skin. Before I can turn to yell at him to get out, the heat from his body radiates over my back through my silky clothing.

Slowly, I turn and we're merely inches apart. "I'm going to take a shower to get Augustus's sweat and cum off my body. Is that okay with you or do we have a problem?"

"You were rude to me before you left. We talked about that."

I scoff and twist my smile as my head shakes. "No. You talked and threatened me with a trip over your knee."

His chin lifts as his eyes bore into me. "That still stands."

"I'm too drunk and too tired for this." Before he can say another word, I'm in my bedroom with the door shut and my back pressed against it.

I skip the shower and flop face down on my perfectly made bed. The room spins quickly before the world fades away.

The weight of an elephant has found its way onto my body. I struggle to lift my face from the duvet. It's nine o'clock. With a loud groan, I sit on the edge of the bed and wipe the drool from the corner of my mouth. Nausea has me rushing to the bathroom sink, but the vomit doesn't come.

My head takes a few seconds to stop spinning. My reflection proves my head hasn't ballooned despite the sensation.

I brush away the fuzzy slippers coating my teeth while I shower with tepid water. The coolness helps with my equilibrium and clears my head.

Wrapped in the hotel's fluffy white robe and slippers and my hair turbaned in a towel, I make my way to the open concept room where the bar, small kitchen, and living room/dining room join. Neatly displayed on the dining table is a silver tray with two silver domes and a silver and black coffee urn.

I lift the larger dome and set it aside. There's oatmeal, eggs, turkey bacon, whole wheat toast, and a serving of Kraft peanut butter. Under the smaller dome is yogurt with raspberries and blueberries, and a large bowl of fresh mixed fruit. For now, I'll stick with coffee and toast until my tummy settles.

No sooner does my ass meet the sofa when there's a knock at my door. There's no point in quickly chewing and swallowing so I can invite them in with a yell or bothering to get up and open the door. History predicts it'll be Alex, and he has a key.

The door swings open and Alex enters followed by Arrow, Brick and Elsa.

We exchange greetings for a good morning, but the way Alex cringes when he looks at my face proves his disappointment.

"Rough night?"

"It was… stimulating." My eyes shift to the deepened groove between Arrow's eyebrows. I lift my toast to my mouth and before I bite into it, ask, "What's on the agenda for today?"

Alex pours himself a mug of coffee while Arrow and Brick remain standing in the foyer with a clear view of us.

Elsa sits on the sofa-chair without looking up from her tablet. "Okay. So, today—" her finger swipes over the screen several times as her face illuminates with a hint of blue light, "You're free until 5pm when the tour bus arrives."

My hand covers my mouth to hide the half-chewed toast. "How long is the drive?"

Her eyes plead for mercy as if she's about to confess something I won't approve of. "I figure it's about a six-hour drive. You could probably sleep most of the way. It'll help pass the time."

Alex sits across from me and sets his steaming mug on the coffee table before sitting back in the chair and crossing one leg over the other. One hand rests on his thigh while the other holds his phone up to see the lit up screen. "Pony and Lacey said they're going to work on what they claim to be the next gold record song."

"You already talked to them?" I savour the powerful scent of the strong black coffee before taking a sip. "So, you met with them first, and I'm the last to hear? Why didn't you come wake me up? I would've gotten up."

Elsa's soft voice follows her shrug. "I tried to wake you at seven-thirty, and you threatened to bite me. I thought it best to leave you to sleep it off."

My face scrunches and I scratch the back of my head through damp locks. "That sounds like something I'd say. My apologies for being a bitch to you. I honestly don't remember saying it."

She waves me off and tucks a stray lock of her natural red hair behind her ear. "Don't worry about it. It's not the first time and probably won't be the last."

Alex clears his throat and tips his face slightly as his brows rise in judgement. "Jade, you're free until then, but try to behave. I've assigned Arrow to be stuck to you like glue all day. It's not that I don't trust you not to go out shopping or do something just as stupid." He pauses as his eyes glance to the ceiling. "Actually, no. I don't trust you not to go out shopping or do something just as stupid. You're under lockdown. No leaving this hotel, and don't even think about trying to shake Arrow. Do you hear me?"

"Jesus, fuck! I'm not a child. Don't speak to me like I am, Alex."

He clears his throat and grows more sedate. "You've shaken off your security too many times after being asked not to, so I'll speak how I need to for you to listen to me. Do. Not. Leave. Arrow's. Side."

Great! I'm stuck with the one man I don't want to be around. Do I want to be around him? Yes, I do. But I don't want to want that. Not only am I stuck with him, I can't go anywhere.

I pull at the collar of the housecoat as if to hide myself away by ensuring the gap is properly closed. "Fine. I'll stay with him. I don't want to go anywhere today, anyway."

Arrow steps closer with his hands on his hips and it's now that I realize he's wearing gym shoes, loose navy shorts, and a fitted white t-shirt. This isn't his normal attire. I know him best in jeans, a dress shirt, and a suit jacket. But he looks damn fine.

While he looks at me, I prop my fists on my waist and purposely drift my eyes down his body. "Looks like someone doesn't skip leg day."

His smirk grows as he cracks his knuckles. "Today just so happens to be leg day. Last night, you said you wished to go to the gym for a workout. So, let's go. Get dressed and we'll get in a solid workout. It'll help you to sweat out the alcohol."

I mumble under my breath. "Or throw up."

He's quick to retort. "I'll bring a bucket. Let's go."

He's challenging me because he thinks I'll fail and show my weaknesses. This proves he doesn't know me at all. Functioning on a hangover is something I've had some practice at.

Let's go, motherfucker!

CHAPTER TWELVE

For two hours, Jade stretched, lifted weights, and walked the stair climber, and has yet to show an ounce of weakness. I'll give it to her; she's persistent. Her pores have spewed out so much alcohol it's a wonder she hasn't collapsed from dehydration.

Since nobody's in the gym I've let her go about her routine without needing to remain near her, which allows me to do my own workout. My legs feel like hot, wet noodles and my abs bear a gratifying burn.

I've been craving a solid gym visit for a few weeks. I've been using my home gym which doesn't offer a sufficient workout. Sprinting my property has kept up with my cardio. The silence has a way of making me feel peaceful. I can't wait to get home and away from this woman before I do something I'll regret.

Jade's raspy voice interrupts my thoughts. "Hey, are you about ready to go?"

"Ah, yeah." I quickly shut off the treadmill and see that I've run for a solid twenty minutes at a rapid pace. Sweat drips from my chin and my shirt's soaked.

A hotel hand-towel slaps against my face and she shrugs. I use it to wipe the sweat from my eyes.

"Thank you." With the towel pressed to the back of my neck, I take a deep breath and hold it to ease my pounding heart and cool my burning lungs.

How long has she been watching me?

Her pretty face is blotchy and her breathing is much calmer than mine. "I'd like to go back to the room and take a shower. Maybe we can go out to eat. I'm hungry and don't want to sit in my room to eat alone."

Teasingly, I ask, "Like a date? Are you asking me out on a date?"

Her defenses immediately have her stuttering. "What? No. I'm not—*no!* I just—I don't want to eat alone in my room. Alex said that you have to stay with me, right? And you have to eat at some point. So, you can sit with me, and we can eat."

"Together?" My fingers rub at my cheek as if confused whether or not this is a date. "I don't know. It sounds like a date to me."

She whips her towel hitting my leg, and I erupt into laughter while she storms off.

I follow her and chuckle. "If you admit it's a date, I'll say yes.

I nearly run into her when she spins to face me with her finger aimed at me. "Forget it! You can fuck off." She spins again and yanks open the glass door nearly hitting me with it.

"I was only teasing. Seriously though, you need to slow down."

Shifting into security mode, I notice a lot of people are in the lobby as she rushes along the wall toward the elevator. What I was hoping wouldn't happen is happening; people have noticed Jade and are leaving their luggage in place to approach her. Any one of them could be her stalker.

Fuck!

My legs feel rubbery from the workout, but I rush up beside her and wrap my arm around her shoulder to rush her. Her skin is damp with sweat as I pull her along quickly. The elevator opens just as we approach, and an elderly woman exits using a walker and stops to look around. I shove Jade to my other side hoping to get around the woman who's trying to figure out why a crowd of excitcd people are rushing in her direction. The doors are about to close when I wrap my arms around Jade and spin us past the woman and into the elevator. The doors close and I press my key card to the black screen.

With Jade pinned between the wall and me, the elevator begins its ascent. She's wide-eyed and her breaths are quick as we stare into each other's eyes. She doesn't push me away. Instead, she grips my biceps and pulls me in for a kiss. This isn't any ordinary kiss; she's aggressive.

My fingers grip her messy bun and jerk her head back. I kiss down her salty neck and press my growing erection against her pelvic bone. A soft moan rides her heavy exhale when I lightly bite her shoulder.

Our lips meet again, but I've taken control. I set the pace and it's a bit slower, less hostile. These are our first kisses, and I don't want to rush it. My hand frees her hair only to grab her throat to hold her back against the mirrors while I taste her mouth and let my fingers tease the waistband of her yoga shorts.

My right foot slightly kicks her right foot, and she spreads her feet, and her moan is sharp. My thighs surround her left leg while my hand ease under the waistband and into her panties.

Jade's kiss halts as a breath fills her body. As she exhales, she murmurs. "Oh, God. What am I doing?"

Before my lips press to hers, my middle finger slips over her mound and between her folds, while the others spread around her outer labia. She's so wet a tighter pinch is required to hold my fingers in place.

I whisper, "Nothing, Jaybird. You don't have to do a damn thing."

My hand jimmy's back and forth, pulling her labia as my middle finger presses against her clitoris firmly enough that my finger glides over the stiff bud while the hood pulls back and forth for extra stimulation.

She breaks our kiss by turning her head to the side. Her words aren't actual words as she mumbles between moans. Her fingernails dig at my shoulder while the other hand grips the bicep of the hand giving her pleasure. It's as if she will break it if I were to stop. Her hips try to buck but with one of her legs pinned by mine, her efforts are wasted.

A combination of sweat and excitement has her pussy slick. Her eyes are closed, and her face is flushed. Unintelligible mumbles carry her moans about the elevator as the metal box rises. She's so close. So close to giving me her orgasm.

My cheek rests on hers as my whisper warms her ear. "Cum for me, Jaybird. Give it to me. Let go."

The elevator slows, so I release her neck to press the button to hold the doors closed. She's so close to coming. If the doors open, she may snap out of her pleasure fog and push me away.

Her hand grips my bicep so tightly her fingernails have dug into my skin, but it's turning me on to know how excited she is.

"Don't stop. Oh, God! Yes. Oh, yeah! God. Yeah. Fuck. Oh!" A silence deafens my ears as she rides her high. Her clitoris swells stiffly beneath my fingers, but I don't alter my stroke even the slightest. She jerks and her legs quiver just before a wail so loud surely people on other floors could hear. I don't care. She begins to crumple, so I pull my hand from her pants, scoop her in my arms and carry her.

She wraps her arms around my neck as she catches her breath. "I can walk."

"I've got you."

We get to her bathroom, and I flip on the light before turning the dial to the dim setting. She releases my neck when I sit her ass on the cool countertop with beauty products lined up against the mirror behind her.

"Stay there," I say and glide my fingertips down her cheek. I spin the tap to the tub and plug the drain. It surprises me how quickly it's filling.

"Thank you for that—um, in the elevator—but you don't have to stick around. You must have shit to do."

Am I reading too much into her tone or is she about to fall over the edge of sorrow again? If I leave her, will she sob herself into a mess like she did last night? Will she go see *him* for comfort again?

With a bottle of Epsom salts in hand, I lift my finger to my lips. "You're welcome, but shh."

"*Shh?* You asked me to stay here but you said nothing about remaining quiet."

As the salts are pouring, I ask her, "Would you have obeyed if I had?

She leans back on her hands while her legs kick lazily. "No. Probably not, but 'A' for effort."

My abs tighten from a silent laugh as I stand between her knees with my hands planted on either side of her hips. "To make you stay quiet I'd have to gag you."

She fights back a smile. "Gag me, huh? With what would you gag me?"

"I can think of a few things: your panties, a washcloth, my hand over your mouth, a ball gag, or my cock. If you give yourself to me, I might let you choose."

Her pretty pink tongue juts out to moisten her lips. "And if I refuse to choose and prefer to give you an attitude?"

With no hint of humour, I reply, "Duct tape."

Jade's eyes narrow as her chin pulls back to her chest. "Duct tape? That would hurt like hell to remove"

"If my threat scares you, don't disobey me."

Sweetness in her tone feigns innocence as her wide eyes watch for my reaction. "Is the duct tape punishment for *all* insubordination?"

Her question is legitimate, but I wish she'd have asked without the forced innocence. It's demeaning for both of us.

I grip her chin in my thumb and forefinger and hover my mouth above hers, but don't kiss her. "How about you don't give me any shit and we'll get along just fine."

She snickers and wraps her long legs around my thighs. "I can't make any promises."

My fingers grip the hem of her sports bra and peel it off her sweaty body. Voluptuous breasts with light burgundy areolas pop free. It's not difficult to see that they've been enhanced, and I couldn't care less if they were real or bought; I'm a hip man.

"You aren't going to touch them? Most men can't keep their hands off them." Her lip pinches between her teeth as her head tips slightly forward. "Are you going to fuck me or what?" Luminous green eyes search from my left eye to the right and back.

More than anything, bending her over this counter and fucking her into next week is exactly what I want to do, but she's not ready for that.

My knuckles lightly brush over her butter-soft cheek. "Haven't you realized that I'm not like most men? I prefer to give women pleasure than take it from them. What I expect in return is to be able to have an adult conversation with mutual compassion and respect. I'm a dominant but that doesn't mean I'm an asshole. So, when I think you're ready for me, you can have me, but it'll be on my terms."

"Your terms?" Her lips pull into her mouth as if someone forgot to put in their dentures.

My hands grip around her ribs to lift her off the counter and set her on her feet. I squat and peel off her shorts and lacy thong.

Her vagina is inches from my face. The womanly scent mixed with the sweat from her heavy workout teases my nostrils. Her clitoris is still so swollen it's tip peaks from between her labia as if trying to seek the person who just abused her in such a delicious manner.

Off come her shoes and socks.

My cock is so unbearably rigid I have to press it with my palm to shift it to a position less restrictive. I ache to grip my shaft and stroke until I explode just to ease the pressure in my balls, but this moment isn't about me.

I stand and take her hand to help her into the large tub. She breathes through the heat as her exhausted body lowers into the heat. "Won't you join me?"

My head shakes as my arms cross over my chest. For a moment, I watch a calm satisfaction from the orgasm and the soothing hot bath take comfort in her features.

There's no doubt the bulge in my pants has piqued her interest the way she pauses and licks her lips. Now is not the time. I want her to want me—to want me to the point where she'll do as I say and be happy to please me.

"I have things to do." I quickly wash my hands and dry them while her questioning gaze drinks me in. "Relax and enjoy your bath. Like I said, when I think you're ready, you can have me. You aren't ready."

She swallows and shifts her eyes away. "You don't want me?"

"You have no idea how much I want you." We lock eyes for a long moment. "I'll see you in a little while, Jaybird. Don't leave this suite and let nobody in."

She calls out as I leave her bathroom. "Okay, I get it; you like birds, but you still haven't told me *why* you call me Jaybird."

CHAPTER THIRTEEN

We've been on the bus for two hours and Arrow has yet to move from the tan coloured leather lounger positioned behind the partition at the driver's back. Brick is in the passenger's seat reading a book. Elsa's been on her computer and made several phone calls, but her voice is so soft it didn't carry over the hum of the tires.

Dex is likely still hung over. He passed out on the sofa with his arms crossed over his chest and one foot on the floor.

Venus sits cross-legged on the floor by the sofa to be near Lacey and Pony. Pony has his guitar on his lap and Venus hums the beat while Lacey scribbles down some lyrics. It's their process. We all contribute to the music. If someone has a song idea, we help them bring it to life but give them all the credit on the album.

Alex is seated beside Elsa and bears a greenish hue. He's nauseous. He doesn't travel well on the tour bus and often gets motion sickness. We tease him, of course, but the vertigo sensation can follow him for hours afterward, and that's not laughable.

As for me, I'm lying on my back on the master bed with my fingers weaved together behind my head. I can't stop thinking about what Arrow did to me in the elevator. Nobody, including myself, has ever made me cum that quickly or powerfully. I saw stars. I've never cum that hard with another person.

Arrow is in clear view. His fingers are tucked into the front pockets of his faded blue jeans, his lounge chair is leaned back enough to allow him to stretch his legs. One big black boot is crossed over the other. Does he own any other footwear?

If he isn't sleeping, what is he thinking about? Does what happened in the elevator haunt him? I probably shouldn't have initiated that kiss. He's my employee and protector. I really fucked up. Then again, I want to know why didn't he come get me so we could go out for dinner as we'd discussed? Did he think I wasn't serious? It wouldn't have been a date, as he had teased about. Maybe he thought it would be? Either way, he should have called to say he wasn't joining me. I waited for him. When I was starving, I broke down and called room service. I want to be angry but more curious as to why he didn't join me.

He didn't show his face until we were loading ourselves into the tour bus. Brick and two of the hotel security ushered us out the back door into the bus. Screaming fans begged for autographs or photos. How the word spreads so quickly to our whereabouts has always baffled me. Hundreds of people were outside, and the noise was deafening.

I've had dreams where I'm walking through a shopping mall, going from store to store like any other patron. I'm unnoticed and it's peaceful. But that was then. I haven't gone to a mall in many years. I used to hate shopping, now I'd give anything to go to the grocery store unescorted.

My attention pulls back to Arrow when his leg jerks. He's dreaming. His head rocks side to side. He stills, and all seems calm until he suddenly sits up sporting the most bloodthirsty expression I've ever seen a man wear. His eyes dart around the bus as he takes in his surroundings before he closes his eyes and takes a purposeful deep breath, holds it, and eases it out. His shoulders slump slightly and his hand spans over his bald head flushed from his intense dream. As if sensing me, his eyes target mine.

I wave for him to come to me, but he hesitates as he looks to see what each person is doing. Again, I wave. This time I move up the bed and sit up with crossed legs like a kindergarten kid at story time.

His hand rubs down his face before he reluctantly stands, stretches his legs, and makes his way toward me. Nobody looks up from what they're doing as he passes them. He passes the bunk beds lining each side of the narrow hall and enters the room where I'm sitting.

My hand presses to the bed, and his chin rises, while his eyes squint to resemble Clint Eastwood. "I can't sit on the bed. It wouldn't be appropriate."

"Appropriate—shmappropriate. Sit." I pat the black silky quilt. "Nobody will care, and I'm not asking for another session like we had in the elevator. Although it'd be nice, it'd be inappropriate under the circumstances and could possibly draw attention."

"Do you think?" His hand rubs his cheek before he sits at the edge of the bed with one knee bent on the mattress to face me, and his other foot on the floor. "About earlier… I shouldn't have done—"

"If you're about to tell me you shouldn't have done that, or you regret it, or it shouldn't have happened, so let's pretend it didn't, I will kick you in the teeth."

"It'd be fun to see you try." His sexy smirk can't be concealed even beneath his hand still on his face.

My voice lowers to avoid being overheard. "Would that land me in the bad girl category?"

He's sure and serious when he replies, "It would be a punishable offense."

My high eyebrows boast defiance. "And what would that punishment entail? Just for shits and giggles, give me a scenario."

I lean back against the headboard and cross my arms over my chest to press my breasts together to deepen my cleavage peeking from the sweetheart neckline of my black t-shirt.

His voice is low and deep as his description lulls me into the fantasy. "I'd grab your ankle and use it to flip you onto your tummy and pin your thigh between my knees. You'd flail behind you trying to hit me, so I'd corral your hands and use my belt to bind your wrists behind your back. I'd unbutton your jeans and pull them down to your ankles, and kneel on the fabric, so you couldn't kick me." Pale brown eyes seduce my soul. How can anyone say what he just said and not have the tiniest of quivers in his voice?

My heart is pounding viciously. I can't speak, so I nod.

"Then, I'd use my belt to pull you up onto your knees while I shoved your shoulders to the bed. Your panty-clad ass would be mine for the taking." Arrow pauses for effect, and I want to scream at him to not stop. "Then—"

My eyes search for him for the rest of the scenario. When he doesn't continue, my voice cracks mid whisper. "Then what?"

His tongue graces his bottom lip as an enticing grin wrinkles the edges of his eyes. "Try to kick me, and I'll show you what comes next, but that'll require plenty of explaining to the people just outside the open bedroom door."

My leg itches to be flung in his direction. Although occupied, everyone's far too close to risk challenging Arrow. "Another time perhaps."

He nods with a lengthy blink. "Another time then."

"To change the subject—" My fingers pull at a loose string on the duvet. "What was your nightmare about?"

His eyes stare straight through me as he recalls the trauma he witnessed as if it's playing out before him. The colour fades from his face leaving him looking grey. His stare is hollow and unblinking. His teeth clench as his hands curl into fists.

When his head begins to shake, I wrap my hand around his bicep and shake him. "Hey. Are you okay?"

He startles, looks away from me and clears his throat to regain his composure. "Yeah. Yeah, I'm fine."

Concern weighs heavily in the air, and I'm sure he can feel it. "Was it the war?"

He's quick to snap. "I don't want to talk about it." His trembling hands brush over his bald head.

I might be better off not knowing what happened to put that level of fear into this hard as nails man. If only I could lift the heavy sadness that's aged his face in seconds, maybe the grey mood that surrounds him will become colourful again.

"Just know that I'm here if you want to talk. I know what it's like to be haunted by one's past."

He sniffs as his face twists and his large hands span around his thighs. Distraught eyes find mine. "And I keep secrets like a prime minister's campaign manager."

My back straightens quickly. "Wow! That'd be very tight to the chest. I'll consider it; if I ever want to talk… But I never do. I'm my own campaign manager." I fear my unconvincing chuckle didn't mask the pain I carry, but Arrow's considerate enough to delve deeper.

He pats my thigh and returns to his lounger while I memorize how his strong thighs lead up to a small, tight ass. What would it be like to wrap my legs around his hips and dig my nails into his flexed arms as he drills his cock into me?

I can't help but wonder if or when that will happen, and if I'll be prepared for what comes afterward. Sex is sex; we both get what we want and then go back to our lives. However, Arrow doesn't strike me as the fuck and run type.

CHAPTER FOURTEEN

Getting everyone off the tour bus and into the hotel safely went smoothly. We were driven to a back door and led by an older gentleman who smiled far too wide for it having been 11:30 at night. He brought all of us to a private elevator, which took us to the fourteenth floor.

A pretty brunette's smile is also not mirrored by any of us. We're too tired to be cheery. Her voice is soft but sure. "If the band would like to follow me, I'll lead you to your suites."

Jade steps toward the door to follow, but the gentleman raises his arm to stop her. "We have you situated on the upper floor, Miss Jade."

"It's just Jade," she says in an automated response. "I can't be on this floor with my mates?"

Concern he did something wrong crosses the man's face.

Alex doesn't glance up from his phone as he mumbles, "You're on the upper floor, Jade. Don't fight it. The entire floor is yours, so you'll be safer there."

My phone pings, so I pull it from my back pocket. It's Alex texting the code and instructions for how to lock the elevator from coming to her floor. It's an added security feature, and I'm grateful for it. The only people who can get through that code are Alex, Elsa, and now me. Even the hotel staff can't enter.

The band, Elsa, and Alex move slowly as they carry their overnight bags from the elevator.

Jade sounds defeated as she says, "Yeah, but—"

My voice is low and deep, so she'll understand my words as more of an order than a suggestion. "Say thank you to the man for ensuring your safety."

Dex's hand strokes down Jade's arm before he pecks a kiss to her cheek. "He's right. Don't worry, we'll see you tomorrow, love."

Jade looks up at me as the doors ease closed and the man taps a key card to the screen. She doesn't look away as it lifts the four of us up one floor before the doors reopen directly into the presidential suite.

I expect her to ask if I'll be staying with the others on that floor or upstairs with her, but she doesn't. Without another word, Jade heads straight to her bedroom and collapses atop the covers.

Before Brock and I can rest, we check each nook and cranny for anything worrisome like bugs and cameras. The suite is clean and secure.

The dark-haired beauty doesn't look so tough in the fetal position with a pillow tucked between her arms. Her mouth is agape as tiny snores ride on her lazy breaths.

Before I realize what I'm doing, my index finger is brushing a lock of hair from her forehead. My stomach hollows when an overwhelming urge to slide in beside her and hold her while she sleeps like I used to do with—

I jolt away from the bed and stumble as I back out of the room dreading she'll wake up. I turn out the lights and close her bedroom door. My head thuds against the solid wood and a deep breath held calms my pounding heart.

Don't cross that line.

That's something a romantic partner would do. I'm not that guy, and she needs to understand that.

Brick's eyes are closed as he leans against the wall beside the elevator door with his arms crossed over his chest. The sound of my boots on the marble floor must startle him because he pulls away from the wall and drops his arms. His lids struggle to remain parted above deep purple grooves.

My voice carries a hint of humour. "Brick, were you just asleep standing up?"

His fists rub his eyes so hard he'll surely see stars. "Yeah. I think so. Sorry, boss."

With a chuckle, I lift my phone to set an alarm. "Go to bed. I've got it from here."

His arms drop at his sides. "But you need to sleep too."

"Don't worry about me. I don't sleep much. Get some sleep because I'll need you sharp tomorrow."

Too weary to argue, Brick presses the elevator button. It opens and he saunters inside with his overnight bag dangling at his knee. He nods and the doors close.

With my phone in hand, I search for Alex's message and follow the instructions to punch in the code to lock the elevator doors.

It's just her and me in the suite. We could do anything we want up here and not worry about being intruded on. Unfortunately, I'm far too exhausted to even consider the possibilities.

I flop on the sofa and cover my body with the fuzzy grey blanket draped decoratively over the back. Sleep comes quickly.

A sense I'm being watched jolts me awake. I'm immediately on my feet with my fists raised. The large windows ensure the sunlight is like giant spotlights destined to scorch my retinas as they search the room for enemies.

A bewildered beauty stands beside me with her hands on her hips. Small silky shorts and a matching crop top are all that conceal her curves from my wandering eyes. If she turns around, I'll likely see the bottom of her ass cheeks from her too short shorts. I'm suddenly aware of how snug the crotch of my jeans are and I question whether it's morning wood or the simpleness of her beauty that has me so engorged.

She looks better without all that make-up obscuring her God-given perfection. The simple woman standing before me is a goddess and more real than the princess of sin she becomes when made-up.

Her weight shifts to one hip as her arms hug her chest. "If you're worried I'm going to make a break for it, you shouldn't sleep so heavily."

Jaybird's genuine smile is captivatingly beautiful. White teeth with a slight crookedness welcome anyone who is fortunate enough to see her in person. But does anyone other than me see the sadness behind her eyes she strains so hard to conceal?

My arms cross over my chest as my feet remain shoulder-width apart. "I'm not worried you'll try to escape, especially after the lobby incident yesterday. I worry more about someone entering without permission. An unchecked maid could conceal a weapon. You'd be defenseless in your sleep."

"So, what? Were you going to take them out with your snores? Was the objective to deafen the intruder?" Jade's stance shifts as she feigns innocence with a flutter of her lashes and her palms press to her chest. In her best southern belle accent, she swoons. "*My hero!*"

I can do without the sarcasm. If she agreed to be mine, a comment like that would earn her a stiff spanking that would have her ass cheeks hot all day.

"Keep it up, Jaybird."

She scoffs. "*Jaybird…* In case you haven't noticed, I'm a hot-blooded woman, not a bird."

"No, you're definitely not a bird." As I close the distance between us, her arms lower to her sides. "Hot-blooded, unquestionably. You're a whole lot of woman for any one man to tame, but goddamn I'd love to give it a try."

Jade's unmoving and wears no expression. What's she thinking? Have I pushed the boundaries too far?

More than the air I breathe, I want to kiss every inch of her body.

Is she the type of woman to take control and ride me until she shudders above me, or would she lie on her back like a limp starfish and expect me to pleasure her? If I were a betting man, I'd bet my wealth on option one.

Her eyes follow the sway of my fingers as they brush over the stubble on my chin. I hold my hand between us and turn it front to back while she pinches her lips together. Is she thinking about how I got her off in the elevator? The way she licks her lips and swallows is proof enough that she is. My tongue pokes free, and as I figured she would, she looks at it. Reading her is almost too easy.

Her dreamy eyes meet mine, but I make no advances. If she wants me, she'll have to make the first move, like she did in the elevator. The last thing I need is for her to say I pushed her into doing something she didn't want to do. So, I'll wait while she considers her next move, but the silence of the passing seconds is as torturous as nails on a chalkboard.

With her chin up, her words flow slowly and pointedly. "And if I were to invite you into my bedroom, what would be the first thing you'd do?"

My cock is so hard it's knocking at the inside of my zipper.

She doesn't retort when I step so close to her that our faces and bodies nearly touch. My hands press to my hips, and it's an open invitation for her to touch me, but she doesn't.

Her head tips to the right, so I lean in and hover my lips over her neck. As if the heat of my breath seduces her, she stretches her neck for more. Without touching her, my lips glide up her neck until the warmth of my words in her ear prickles her skin. "Invite me and find out."

Her quickened breath suddenly hitches in her throat. "I shouldn't. Everything about this is wrong. We'll be breaking Alex's number one rule—don't sleep with employees."

Still near her ear, I whisper, "Jaybird, I can assure you we won't be sleeping much."

She moans when my lips touch her throat. "If you want me, take me."

My fingers span up the back of her head and grip a healthy wad of her messy brown locks. My lips crash to hers as my tongue claims her. With my arm around her waist, I walk forward and make her walk backward. At the sofa's side, her thighs press to the puffy arm. She yelps in surprise when I push her back.

She lands with her shoulders on the seat part and her hips resting high on the sofa's arm. I squat and lift her dangling legs, placing her right thigh on my left shoulder. She watches me past her chin as two of my fingers slip beneath the thin fabric to brush over her outer labia. Her heat and scent of sex tempt my patience.

My eyetooth nips into the fabric of her shorts. One quick tug and the gusset tears in two, setting free her pretty pussy. No panties; I like that. One swipe of my fat tongue glides from her asshole to clit. Her back arches and her moan sounds as pretty as her singing. I engulf her clitoris and suck while my tongue tickles and teases the swelling nub.

Her calves are pressed to my back so tightly it's not easy to shift enough to stretch one arm around her thigh to hold onto her while my thumb and forefinger spread her puffy labia. With my tongue and lips savouring her clitoris, I push two fingers into her drenched pussy.

Jaybirds moans grow wild. This position forces her to remain still, but pleasure has her body desiring to move. She tries but fails to buck her hips when I press firmly on her tummy just above her mound.

My fingers glide slowly in and out of her as my lips encircle her swollen clitoris. I suck hard as my tongue whips back and forth beneath the hood. Her pussy clenches around my fingers; a sure sign she's close.

She wants to know what I'm all about, so I'm going to give her a taste. I pull my fingers free and yank her legs off my shoulders. She moans disappointment as she reaches down intending to stroke herself to ecstasy.

"Oh, no, Jaybird. Not yet."

With a tug of her hips, I have her face down with her ass in the air over the sofa's arm. She lifts herself with her arms and tries to stand but I grab a wad of her hair and slap her ass with my palm.

"Stay where I put you. Do you understand?"

She says nothing but stills.

"Arch your back," I instruct, and she sags her lower back, giving me better access to her pussy and asshole, should I choose to incorporate it in the festivities. "When I give you an order, comply and you'll be rewarded. Don't comply or outright disobey and I'll punish you. Tell me you understand."

"What if I don't want to play your little game?" Her question is a legitimate one.

I release her hair and help her to stand. The shorts hang awkwardly from her hips. The backs of my fingers brush over her flushed cheek and tuck a tangled lock of cool hair behind her ear before coming to rest at the back of her neck. Her heavily hooded jade-coloured eyes look more sleepy than sexy.

My voice is low and clear. "First, it's not a game. This is who I am. If you want me, this is the only way you can have me. I don't do romance, so if that's what you're after, you won't get that from me. I don't do dancing under the stars, walks on the beach, or candle-lit dinners.

I'm rough around the edges and sometimes a little cruel. But I'll never push you past your limit. Follow my orders and I'll make your body hum. I'll be here to keep you safe until such time as I'm no longer needed. After that, you'll go on with your life, and I'll go back to mind. So, knowing this, I need you to decide if you still want me?"

Her fingertips fondle the buttons on my black dress shirt but don't release them. "If I say yes and you ask me to do something that could damage my career or reputation, will I have the ability to decline that order?"

"One-hundred percent. First off, I'll never ask you to do something that won't make you better. I'm obligated, as your master, to keep you safe; physically and emotionally, and help you grow." My hands brush down her shoulders and gently wrap around her forearms, not moving her hands from my chest. "I will be here for you however you need me, but I won't do chocolate and roses. If that's what you need, I'm not the man for you. Call your mafia guy and have him touch you gently, but if you do, I'll never touch you again. If we're together in this, we're exclusive until the day I set you free."

Jade's jaw clenches and her chin lifts which is her tell that her walls are going up. She's not the commitment type, so why is she staring so intensely at me? What did I say that offends her?

More than anything, I want her in my arms, beneath me, clawing at my back as I bury my cock deep into her.

Don't shut down.

CHAPTER FIFTEEN

Until the day he sets me free.

I was a fool to think Arrow was different than most men because he doesn't put up with my attitude. But he only wants me for my body and the pleasure he can take from it, just like all the rest. Why did he have to say all of that? Why didn't he just tell me to follow his orders? He should've stopped there, but he didn't. His heart is off limits.

From the time I was young, men I thought loved me used me for their own needs. As the years ticked by, I learned how to turn it around and use men for my needs. It's worked so well for me, so why did I want Arrow to want me? Truly want me—all of me.

Suddenly feeling cold and exposed, I step back and slide my arms from his warm grasp before crossing them over my chest to protect myself.

Disappointment pinches his brows together, but he continues to study me. The tension in the air is like pea soup and I have to get away.

"Um, I have to get ready for the photoshoot, so—" My lips pull in between my teeth and I bite a little harder than I should. "Besides, Alex and Elsa will be here soon, and—"

"What was that?"

As if he slapped me, I stood frozen beside the sofa. "What was what?"

His head tilts as his hand brushes over the buttons on his shirt to smooth them. "You shut down. What are you afraid of? Why did you pull away?"

That's a question I'd need a shrink's help to answer.

Arrow's the first man to tell it like it is; to tell me exactly what he's going to take from me and what he's not willing to give. He's open and honest, and it's more frightening than if he'd professed his undying love for me, and then stolen from me, cheated on me, and dumped me in a humiliating way.

My body holds stiff as my head shakes far too much. "I can't do this with you."

He doesn't come toward me, which I appreciate. "Why not?"

"It's too—" Too, what?

"Too honest and you aren't familiar with that. It scares you. Am I right?"

He isn't wrong, but the next sentence has my hands fisted at my sides and panic welling up inside me.

"Someone hurt you when you were young, and it haunts you. Because of that, you don't trust anyone with your heart. You're worried we'll start this unique relationship and you'll begin to trust me only to have me leave you like everyone else has?"

Did all of the blood in my body sink to my feet? "H—how do you—"

He steps toward me, and I shake my head as a silent plea not to touch me. If he puts his hands on me, something terrible will happen. Maybe I'll pass out, die, scream like he's murdering me, or fall into his arms like the weak women in those romance novels I spend too much time reading.

There's softness in his eyes as he glides toward me seemingly in slow-motion. He stands before me with his arms wide, but he doesn't touch me. Instead, his voice softens to say four little words that could absolutely ruin me if he doesn't mean it. "I'm not going anywhere."

Why is he doing this?

"Stop, please. I don't—I can't."

Pain wells in my throat before an eruption of tears and heavy sobs has me falling against his firm chest. I'm scooped up and carried. He drops onto the sofa keeping me on his lap and holds me tight in his arms.

It hurts: my throat, my eyes, my chest, and I can't breathe even though I'm gasping. Arrow simply holds me. He says nothing because there are no words to soothe me.

Why did I let him break me down?

How long he's held me on his lap is anyone's guess, but I don't ever want to leave this spot.

The door unlocks with a click before the sweet alarm sings it's warning of visitors. I've never moved so quickly in my life. In a flash, I'm in my bedroom with the door shut, leaving Arrow's lap still indented with my butt print.

Alex and Elsa can't see me like this. They'll know I've been crying and there will be so much pity in their questions as they try to placate me. Letting Arrow see me like that is bad enough, but I can't deal with pity at the moment.

I shut the bathroom door and turn on the shower. After stripping, I shove my pajamas in the trash and cover them with balled up tissues, so nobody will notice the torn crotch and ask questions. That would be difficult to explain especially since it doesn't feel like it even happened.

I step under the hot water and let it pink my skin. Maybe my brain was foggy from the endorphins from the oral sex and that enabled him to break me down. But did he break me down or did I do it to myself? I let myself imagine a future with him. How foolish of me.

There's a knock on the bathroom door before Elsa's tender voice calls from the partially opened door. "Jade, we need you to be ready to leave in twenty-minutes. Can you manage it?"

My voice cracks from the swell of emotions I haven't yet suppressed. "Yeah. I just need a few minutes. A coffee would be helpful."

"You got it." Elsa closes the door.

The water washes over my face and I wish it would drown me. Facing Arrow after that disgusting show of weakness is at the top of a list of things I don't want to do, just above shoving a fork in my eye. He's here until we find my stalker. I have to suck it up and get the fuck out of the shower.

The fan blows so ferociously it's damn near impossible to hold my eyes open. The photographer continues to plead with me to look at him as the click-slide sounds of his camera prove hundreds of photos are being taken.

"This is bullshit. That fucking fan is drying my damn eyes," I say and step off the platform while the train on the nearly sheer red gown trails behind me.

The photographer doesn't sugar-coat his frustration as he calls out, "We'll take a break. Shut off the fan."

The fan shuts down and the bright lights turn off one by one.

I storm over to Alex as each blink feels like my lids are scraping over sandpaper. "It's too much. My eyes are so fucking dry."

Alex shrugs and flashes a pitiful expression that tells me I have to put up with it. Why does the magazine need me to look like I'm falling from an airplane?"

"From where I'm sitting, you look amazing. It'll make for a great cover." He pats my shoulder and smiles. "Just a little longer and they can cut you out of that dress. You'll be back in your yoga pants in no time."

"If I could cry to make the shoot stop, I would, but it's the Sahara fucking desert in here." My finger aims at my eyes.

Before I can continue my argument, the green-haired make-up artist comes at me waving a bottle of eyedrops and a tissue. "We can't have that; you'll ruin your make-up and we'll have to start all over again." She leads me back to the platform and the woman who sewed me into this dress lifts the train before I sit.

Earlier, the hairdresser hardly said more than two sentences to me while she styled my hair, leaving me to assume the purple arcs under her eyes and paleness of her skin are from a wild night of partying. She stands patiently in front of me holding a brush in one hand and a can of hairspray in the other, staring off into space as if her brain has temporarily shut down.

My head tips back and the make-up artist plops some drops in my eyes and cautiously dabs away the runoff before it can ruin the masterpiece she painted on my face.

I look flawless, unlike a natural woman. Nobody's skin is this smooth. Why do they bother with so much make-up when the artist is sure to photoshop the shit out of the photos until I'm barely recognizable?

I'm helped back onto the small stage and asked to sit with my legs tucked at my side. My gown is spread out around me.

The photographer nods his hand to his assistant as he gives me instruction. "Look straight at me and wear no expression."

The lights go out and I do as he says. The sooner he gets the shot, the sooner I'm out of here.

A strobe of light to my left accompanies the click-slide of the camera lens. I do my thing;

197

turning my head this way and that, changing my expression ever so slightly, and lifting a shoulder while dropping the other. The silent lights flash all around me and only the camera sings.

I stare into the darkness just to the right of one of the flashing lights. Each flash proves Arrow's still standing there, watching me. My deep breath nearly bursts a breast from the barely-there cups struggling to contain them.

Why is he staring with such an intense expression? Is he angry or concerned, or is he done with me? Have I pushed him away? It's what I do, and I have reason to. I'd never admit it to anyone, but my heart is paper thin. A moment of vulnerability with the wrong person could tear it into a million pieces.

The photographer's gravelly voice breaks me from my thoughts. "Okay. Great job, Jade. I'm going to take a look at these. Can we get a costume change?"

The lights are turned back on, and I'm led to the room aside the platforms where the costume designer snips the stitching so she can remove the dress. Stripped down to my beige thong, I dress in professionally torn pantyhose, black cut-off denim shorts, a simple black bra, and a white t-shirt with the neckline cut off to allow the fabric to hang off my shoulder. It's so thin the black bra shadows from behind the bleeding rose image on the chest. My feet are slipped into army-style black boots with a four-inch heel. I like how unique they are. Maybe they'll let me keep them.

A thicker coat of eyeshadow and liner are added for a more intense look, along with a touch-up to the bright red lipstick. As my hair is being fucked with while I observe the photographer and a balding man in an inexpensive suit huddle and coo over the images on a laptop. But it isn't them I care to see.

For a distance, Arrow's also studying the screen. There's a moment when the jaws of the two men fall slack. Arrow strides three steps closer and stares at the laptop wearing the same expression of awe as the men.

I want to see what they're looking at.

The bald man's right arm crosses his chest to hold his left elbow while his finger taps his chin. "That's the shot."

"It's perfect." The photographer steps back to tilt his head left and right, then leans closer to the screen as he zooms the photo, I assume, since I can't see the screen.

The way Arrow looks at me holds me prisoner and threatens to break down the walls containing the pain that is my life. I can't look away.

What is it about this pushy bald man with the 5 o'clock shadow? I've known him for four days, and he sees deeper into me than anyone has. Worse yet, I think I want him to.

The very real possibility I'll never recover if he hurts me terrifies me. If I survive it, broken and tattered, who will I become? I may no longer be the same Jade; a tough woman who takes no shit from anyone and always suppresses her emotions behind an angry facade.

Why did he have to come into my life?

CHAPTER SIXTEEN

That photo haunts me. Each time I close my eyes, her green eyes captured in the image steal a little piece of my soul. The way the light shadowed and illuminated her face had the green looking like they're ocean deep and her ruby lips were kissable and pouty. But the sadness within her beauty is what makes the photo so incredible.

Jade isn't one to show weakness, but the vulnerability captured at that moment burrowed into me. I'll never lose that image. I never want to even if it haunts all of my dreams. I'd prefer that over the nightmares I'm currently laden with.

At a posh restaurant, myself and Eric, wait for our dinners at a small table just inside the room where Jade's team are dining. Brick and Kina sit at a table just outside the room. If there's a threat, we'll be on it long before they can get to Jade.

Jade's best friend, Rachel, surprised her by showing up at the shoot just as we were getting set to leave. Had she been five minutes longer she'd have missed her. They sit with their backs to me and haven't stopped chattering like fourteen-year-old girls after a weekend apart.

Why do women not outgrow the need to tell each other everything? Should I worry she'll tell her about what happened between us this morning? Should I care if she does?

Full from eating one of the best tasting chicken breasts and mixed vegetables I've ever had, I could use a nap. In fact, I could use a week of sleep. Ever since I got here, I haven't spent a full night in bed. My back aches from sleeping on the too-soft sofa, and when I stand too long, the ache in my knee is a constant reminder I can do without.

I hadn't noticed Jade pass me with her clutch in hand. She says something to Brick I can't hear, and he sits back down. She walks away and he looks to me to question whether he should follow her. I set my napkin on the table and hurry to catch up to her.

She's quick, but I easily catch up. "You can't walk away like that."

"I have to use the ladies room. Do I need supervision while I pee? The door is right over there. One way in. One way out." Her black painted fingernail points to the hall by the washrooms a short distance away.

My hand aims toward the small of her back, but I pull it away before I make that mistake. Surely, someone in her party will see and ask questions or a random shot of it will be splashed all over the fake news rags. They may claim we're getting married because she's pregnant with my baby.

"Yes, Jaybird. I'm coming with you."

She speaks to me low over her shoulder. "I really want to know why you call me that."

A smug grin lifts the edges of my lips. "Because it suits you."

We arrive at the closed door to the ladies room and she turns to shoot me an eye roll. I crack the door open and yell inside. "Is anyone here? Say so now because a man's coming in."

Nobody replies, so I look at Jade and say, "Follow me in."

"Wait! What? You're going in with me?" She stands with shocked eyes and a gaped mouth. "You're not going to listen to me pee."

My eyes lock onto a waitress when she passes behind Jade to pass through a door marked for the staff.

"I'm not staying inside, but I'm not leaving you out here when I go in to ensure someone isn't waiting inside to stab you. So, if you have to pee, follow me in." I hold the door open and step halfway in.

Again, she rolls her eyes and uncrosses her arms.

As she passes me, I whisper, "Rolling your eyes is very rude."

Just inside, I ask her to wait before I check each stall. I grip the door handle, but she grabs my arm before I tug it open to leave her to do her business.

"Okay," she says and clears her throat.

Confused, I ask, "Okay? Okay, what?"

"This morning." Her shoulder lifts as her head tips toward it before she looks anywhere but at me. "We can try it your way. At least you're honest about what you want from me. I have one condition; I need a guarantee you won't make promises you have no intention to keep."

Did I hear her right? She's agreeing to submit to me. My cock springs to life, and I'm thankful my suit coat shrouds it. My index finger lifts her chin until her glassy eyes reluctantly meet mine. A hint of a plea lifts her brows.

The weight of the situation steadies my tone. "I keep my promises. I also have a condition. If for any reason you need it to stop, you'll say the word 'red.' Everything will stop, and we'll discuss the situation. Agreed?"

Her nod is slight, but it's enough to lift a smile that deepens the lines at the edges of my eyes.

She whispers, "We need to keep this a secret. Promise me."

"I promise I'll never tell anyone about anything private that happens between us. Your secrets are safe with me."

"Like a prime minister's campaign manager," she reminds me and chortles.

My index and middle finger rise side-by-side. "Do you need me to swear on my Scout's honour because I will."

She laughs at me and slaps my fingers down before shewing me out the door.

Everyone is safely back at the hotel before nine o'clock. My shoulders roll to ease the tension before I use a washcloth to wipe the steam from the mirror. I'm wearing a fluffy white hotel towel around my waist when I answer a knock at the door.

Eric, the dark-haired man I ate dinner with holds two dozen long stem roses in a crystal vase. "Sorry to bother you, but these came for Jade. You said you wanted us to alert you to any suspicious gifts."

"Yeah. Come in. Set them here."

He carefully rests the expensive vase on the desk and leans in for a sniff from one of the plump roses. Why he felt the need to lean in baffles me because my whole room has been poisoned by their scent.

I'm not a fan of roses. They remind me of funerals, and the one I missed because I was recovering from surgery in Kandahar. I arrived back in Canada a day late, and I'll never not be angry about that.

My knee aches at the memory of how painful it was to nearly lose my leg. The constant ache is miniscule compared to the pain of regret I'll forever carry, but I deserve nothing less.

I tighten my towel on my waist and notice Eric's subtle scan down my body. He apologizes before turning to look at the emergency exit sign permanently fixed to the back of the door. Is he gay? I don't care if he is, and I don't care if he looks at me; it's no sweat off my back.

The white envelope holds a small card with a rose on it. How fitting.

It reads: "Hello Jade. I'd love for you to join me for dinner at Louisiana's tonight for dinner. Augustus Greyner."

Well, fuck!

It's bad enough that mafia billionaire asshole fucked my girl—well, she wasn't my girl at the time—but now he wants to have dinner with her. Do I allow Eric to deliver them to her or should I turn them away? If I don't, and he calls her to ask about the bouquet, she'll be pissed at me. So, I have no choice.

Surely she'll call him to say she's not interested. She will... Right? She'd better. Would I be able to make him disappear? He's very well guarded, so it would take planning. I could break out the long-distance rifle and do what my nickname predicts; I can shoot straight as an arrow, and I rarely miss. *What the fuck am I thinking?* I can't kill the man no matter how much I want to. She'll turn him away, and we'll never hear from him again.

Reluctantly, I slip the card back into its envelope and into the bouquet. "You can give them to her."

Eric turns back and lifts the bouquet with the utmost care. To help him, I hold the door open.

As he walks out, I lower my voice and say, "Eric," he looks at me from over his shoulder, "It's okay that you looked at me. It's not up to me to tell anyone about your preferences. It doesn't change who you are."

The stocky man forges a smile and keeps his voice low. "I'm not hiding in the closet, but this profession calls for strong men and women, and a gay man doesn't fit that stereotype."

I smile and nod. "Well, nobody said we're a logical group." His laugh is deep and hearty. "Alright, go ahead and give the flowers to Jade. I'll be up there shortly to relieve Kina."

"Kina won't mind if you take some time to catch some shut-eye."

The last thing I want to do is close my eyes and relive my nightmare. I'd rather stay awake. "I function well on very little sleep."

Eric shrugs and holds my gaze before offering me a nod. That nod means more than a simple greeting. It shows in his eyes that he believes I won't tell anyone about his sexuality. I won't. I have no right to. Besides, who gives a fuck? Really? If anyone gave him a hard time about it, I'd fire them in an instant.

Before I leave my room, I examine myself in the mirror. My black dress shirt is pressed and is button correctly aside from the top two which I've left unfastened for my comfort. My black jeans are clean and not wrinkled, and my boots have been shined. My head and face are freshly shaven and my aftershave has been applied sparingly. I'm set to go, so why the hesitation?

To my reflection, I whisper, "She's just a woman like any other. She'll wise up and send you on your way. Until then—" My palm drags down my face before I sigh. "Just keep your shit together, motherfucker."

Tiny Kina's standing several feet from the elevator when the doors open to Jade's suite.

"It's nice to see you again. Thank you for coming on such short notice."

"It's my pleasure." Her voice is huskier than her size presents.

"Kina, is there anything I need to know?"

She sees me notice the leather office chair seated nearby still bearing her ass print. "Sorry, Arrow."

My head tips as a smile rides my tone. "No worries. I'd rather you sit than fall over. It's okay with me."

Her stance eases as her hands slide into the pockets of her black dress pants.

Black liner emphasizes the almond shape of her soft brown eyes, and her chocolate skin is as smooth and unwrinkled as I remember it to be.

I worked with Kina on another case where a hitman was trying to take out a millionaire. It took some investigating, but it was soon apparent his son was the person behind it. Apparently, money doesn't buy loving kids.

Kina's resume is impressive. With her parents deceased shortly after her birth, her twenty-four years on this planet were spent under the watchful thumb of her grandfather. She had a tight schedule of home-schooling along with martial arts training from the time she was old enough to walk. The woman is nearly unbeatable in hand-to-hand combat.

She keeps her personal business personal, and she's all about the job. I hadn't taken the time to ask about her hopes and dreams the last time we worked together, and we probably won't be here long enough to worry about creating a lifelong friendship.

We won't be here long enough… Will I leave one day?

Kina smiles and brushes the red tips of her long black braids back and forth over her open palm. Nervous habit perhaps. "Miss Hanover's inside with Miss Jade. She arrived at 9:37pm. She was carrying a bottle of champagne and two small tubs of ice cream."

"Ice cream and champagne? Interesting." My effort to force my smile to not reflect my disappointment seems effective.

Jade agreed to be mine and follow my rules. I understand her friend showed up today and they need time to catch up, but I thought—no, I'd hoped—she'd agree to be mine tonight.

"Did she say how long she'd be staying?"

The blank stare Kina wears has me wanting to kick myself for asking. Why the hell would Rachel offer Kina a timeline for her visit?

"Um, no, sir," she says as she pushes her pony-tailed braids over her shoulder to hang down her back to her bum.

If I didn't know how dangerous she can be, I'd believe her to be a typical college student with an innocence not yet shattered by reality. But I see past the gentleness of her face and can't imagine the lessons she's endured to become the warrior she is.

She shoots me a side-eye. "Was I supposed to ask?"

My hand rubs over my dome to stall while I consider a reason. "If they had plans to go to the pool or the hotel bar, they may have said something."

She nods but her lips pull tight and her back straightens. "I can stay all night if you want to get some sleep. Brock told me you've had night duty and most of the day watch since you got here. Humans need ample sleep to regenerate the mind and body. I can call you if anything should arise."

A blast of laughter radiates from the main living area which is hidden from our view.

I lean a shoulder against the wall as my arms cross over my chest. "Champagne and ice cream? They're probably in for the night."

Kina rocks back and forth from heel to toe and grins. "Sounds like they're well on their way to eating and drinking themselves into a coma."

We share a laugh, but I fucking hope not! I had plans.

"In that case, it'll be an easy night. You sleep and be back around 6am. At seven the band will be joining us for a recorded interview with a television show I can't remember the name of. At eleven o'clock, everyone will be boarding the private plane to fly to Toronto—their hometown. When we arrive, the band will head off to their homes. I'll stay in her guest room, and you and Brick can get settled in the hotel. It's only a few blocks away. If anything seems suspicious, you two will be at the ready."

Without hesitation, she asks, "How far from the mark's residence is the hotel? We will need a few routes marked on a map and cars for travel."

"That'll all be taken care of. Brick's handling it. I'll work out a schedule. You, Brick, Eric and I will be on call even when we aren't on shift. Hopefully, the stalker won't show up at her home. So far, he's been quick to know where she is at all times, so it's likely he'll make himself known. We'll have to stay sharp."

With eyes that understand how horrible things can turn in a hurry, Kina says, "It's easy to protect a mark in a hotel with only one entrance door. Her home will have plenty of entry points: windows and doors. We'll have to ensure they remain locked at all times." She looks to me before resting her hands on her hips and rocking from foot to foot. "My suggestion would be to have one guarding outside while the other remains in the residence within earshot of the mark."

My hands rest on my hips as I look at her from below my brows. "You make for a great personal bodyguard. Seriously, you're right on the mark of what needs to happen."

Her arms rest at her sides and her chin lifts to prove she's powerful, yet her tone is whimsical. "I'm not only a pretty face, I'm also a trained killer."

I like her sense of humour and snicker. "Well, *trained killer with a pretty face*, get out of here. Go get some sleep. I'll see you in the morning."

"I wish you an uneventful night." Her head jerks a quick nod before she strides off quicker than someone with such short, thin legs should be capable.

Muffled laughs flow from behind the thick door, drawing my attention. I've never heard Jade laugh so heartily. It's easy to differentiate between Jade and Rachel's voices. Jade speaks in a raspier manner than her much higher-pitched friend.

More laughs make my stomach tighten. I want to be the one to make her laugh that hard. It should be me.

I'm jealous? What the hell?

CHAPTER SEVENTEEN

Jade

Rachel snorts through a laugh which has me laughing so hard the melting ice cream in my mouth dribbles from the corner of my mouth. Tears pour down our cheeks and my stomach muscles ache.

There's just something comforting about being with my bestie. There are only two people in my circle who know about my past: Rachel and Alex, but he doesn't know as much as Rachel. Still, there are awful things that happened to me I will never tell her about. The details of what the monster did to me would horrify her, and there's no need to put those images into her head.

Having her here is a double-edged sword: I find comfort in her humour and the familiarity she brings. With her around, no matter where we are, I feel like I'm at home. On the other hand, her presence is a constant reminder of the mental struggle I went through to grow past what happened to me. She helped me by just being there and not forcing me to talk about it like the psychologist tried to do.

We were only six-years-old when I moved next door to her, so she wasn't told of the sexual abuse he put me through because it was beyond her comprehension. Hell, I experienced it first-hand and didn't understand why he was doing what he was doing. It felt wrong, but he told me it was expected of me, so I went along with it. It was easier than and less painful than when I fought back. He'd hold me down, tie me into embarrassing positions, and cover my mouth and nose with his hand to stop me from screaming. I blacked out so many times, but it was better than being awake.

"Hey! Where'd you go?" Rachel's hand is patting my forearm. "There you are. I lost you for a minute. Are you okay?"

My ability to suppress everything and crack a convincing smile has been perfected over the years. "Yeah. I'm fine. I just—"

A deep breath fills my lungs. She knows about my steamy night with Augustus. But I have yet to tell her about Arrow's proposition. I tell her almost everything, as besties do, so why does this confession make me hesitant?

She sets the cardboard ice cream tub on the living room table beside her champagne class and turns to face me as her legs curl beneath her. Her head and shoulder leans onto the back of the sofa.

"What's going on?" And don't tell me that you're fine. There's something you aren't telling me."

Here goes nothing!

With a voice low so whomever is standing at the elevators won't hear, I say, "Arrow." My face contorts as my shoulders lift almost to my ears before dropping.

She leans in with a hanging jaw and wide eyes. "The bald guard? What about him?" Her eyes light up as if she's seen something unexpected. "You and him?" No! Come on. Are you serious?"

"Yeah. I mean, we haven't fucked." Why am I so twitchy and nervous? This is Rachel! She never judges me. "He's fingered me and ate me out once. Bastard didn't let me cum on his mouth, and then—"

Captivated, her eyes shifted from my left to my right. "And—and then what?"

Unable to hold her gaze, I watch my spoon poke at the lump of brownie stuck in the vanilla ice cream. "I don't know. He asked me to be his submissive, and I questioned it. I wanted to know what that entailed, and it ruined the mood."

"Oh. Submissive? Really? Okay. Continue." She studies me with narrowed eyes, reaches for the pale-blue throw pillow behind her, and hugs it to her chest. "Start at the beginning and don't leave anything out."

It's easy to tell her about how dominant he is and detail the incident in the elevator because it was all about the physical act, but when it comes to what happened on this sofa, I'm more reluctant, and she can sense it.

"Stop holding back." She lightly slaps the thigh of the one leg I have bent on the sofa. "So, why did he stop?"

Hold it together!

The spoon slides into my mouth, and I let the ice cream melt on my tongue. "I'm not nearly drunk enough for this."

She's quick to take the ice cream and spoon from me, set them on the table and hand me the half-empty glass of champagne. "Drink and then spill it, bitch."

After taking a bigger sip than champagne calls for, it bubbles in my throat forcing me to cough. "I asked him what would happen if I didn't want to play his little game."

"And what did he say?" Rachel is way too invested in this!

My thumb glides up the flute to erase the dribble from my lip. "He suggested I give it a shot, and then he basically said he'll be leaving as soon as we catch my stalker, so this isn't a heartfelt thing—it's just sex." My sigh is exhaustive. "But I don't know if I can do that."

"Why not? You aren't into the whole hearts and flowers, *love me until the day I die* relationship, anyway." Her head tilts as her eyes assess my reaction. "Are you?"

I say nothing as I search the wall behind her for the answer. The air seems too heavy to breathe. "Maybe I am. I—I mean, I don't have time for a relationship with my schedule being so tight, but having someone to hold me at night doesn't sound so awful."

Rachel leans back with squinted eyes and a scrunched nose. "Are you serious? Since when?"

After a shrug, I take a smaller sip of champagne and swipe up the glass with my thumb. "I'm getting older, and my career is at an all-time high. Where else am I going to go from here? I have three platinum records, I'm in the hall of fame, and I've sang in stadiums all over the world. I'm not saying I'm done, just that there has to be… more. I want *more*."

Her tone has a hint of jealousy. "You want more. Fuck you… You have everything." Her hand rises between us as her head sways. "Don't take that the wrong way; it's not a slap at your success. I'm very proud of you."

I mumble, "Sure sounded like a slap."

"Sorry. I just… I'm worried about you. I mean, this guy—*Arrow*? Nice name, by the way—he told you he wasn't staying."

With a groan, I stand and stride a few steps away before walking back as my arms flail for emphasis. "I know. He's leaving. There's no chance of a relationship. It'd never work out. He's too— And I'm too— We're so fucking different, but—"

I turn to face Rachel and my face tightens as my lips pinch between my teeth proving my inner turmoil.

She walks to me and takes my hands in hers like she used to do to calm me down when we were children. I despised hugging—not much has changed. Holding my hands was her way of letting me know I wasn't alone. She didn't really understand what I went through, and it didn't matter because she was present and it was all I needed. It's what I need now.

She takes a deep breath as her chin rises, signalling me to copy her. Like we did back then, we'd tip our heads back and exhale to let all the pain go up to the heavens. I couldn't understand her belief in a god that would allow someone to do such horrible things to me, but I accepted that she did.

"Okay. Why do you feel so close to him?"

"There's pain inside him. I can feel it. It sounds weird but his pain comforts me. It's like we're silent sufferers and knowing that makes me feel like it's okay to—" My shoulders lift and drop making our hands swing between us. "I think he'll understand me better if he knew. Do you know what I mean?"

My face begs for her to understand, but I'm not sure she can. How can someone who's never experienced trauma understand the true meaning of the word?

Instead of smiling to ease my mind like she always has, she releases my hands and strolls to her glass, picks it up, but doesn't sip. Not turning back to face me, she says, "You can talk to me about what happened. I'm your best friend and I'll never judge you."

As she turns back, tears have pooled in her eyes. I didn't know how much my secrecy had affected her. Holding back on the details was meant to save her from the disgusting imagery she'll never be able to shake from her mind. Would I even be able to tell her what I remember without shattering into a million unrepairable pieces? I've repressed so much that I fear awakening those memories could bring back some of the more horrific things I don't want to remember.

"That's not it. I know you won't, but it hurts too much to even think about it. He did things to me that should never be done to a grown woman, let alone a little girl. I didn't understand. He always said I made him want to do those things to me. Of course, I know now he was a child rapist and deserved what he got." Mind-fog blurs my vision as a flood of hot, sticky, red liquid drowns me. "Someone hit him and he rolled off me. There was so much blood."

The simple act of her hands tightly gripping mine pulls me back from the memory.

She whispers, "Just breathe. Breathe in. Breathe out."

After a few deep breaths, I force a smile and thank her with a nod.

"I'm tired. Is it okay if we talk tomorrow?"

Rachel tucks her blonde hair behind her ears. "I can stay with you while you sleep, like we used to do."

I remember how safe I felt when she'd hold my hand, and I'd close my eyes. He would never touch me if someone was in the house. Even though I knew he could never hurt me again, I'd have the best sleep when she spent the night sleeping beside me.

This time my smile is genuine. "I love you for offering, but no. I'm okay. Really, I'm okay."

Rachel picks up her half-eaten ice cream container of Rocky Road, walks past the bar and kitchen, and takes a step back when she nears the foyer. Her laugh is so silent her face flushes partially hidden behind her palm.

My voice is barely audible. "What?"

She waves me over and points for me to take a look. I lean slightly forward and see a bald man sitting on a leather office chair with his elbows on his knees. His back is to us and his focus is on his phone as his fingers move lightning fast over the screen.

I pull my short friend back to the kitchen and fan myself as I feign a swooning southern belle. "And there he is, my protector."

Her mouth twists as her hips sway side to side. "He's hot in that dangerous, mysterious, *I'm-going-to-hurt-you* way."

My voice hovers below a whisper. "I suppose he is."

"So, are you going to invite him to join you for a drink?" Her eyes study me for a beat before I shrug.

Should I?

"I don't know. Probably not. I'm tired."

She leans forward as I lean down to peck air-kisses by each other's cheeks.

Rachel struts to the foyer with her hips swaying as if trying to be sexy, but too much alcohol has her trying too hard. She's doing it as a joke because she'd never go behind my back to sleep with someone I'm interested in.

Arrow is on his feet and doesn't look impressed by Rachel, but he smiles politely as she runs her hand down his bare forearm. With the sleeve of his dress shirt rolled up past his elbow, she strokes his skin. She gazes over her shoulder and mouths, "Hot!"

Arrow presses the button to call the elevator which takes her away from him. He looks at me with a minuscule smile while she dances to the music in her head.

With a wave over her shoulder, she dances with a slight drunken sway into the elevator.

When I'm home tomorrow, Rachel can sleep in the guest bedrooms she's proclaimed as hers. It'll be nice to be home. It's been too long.

The elevator doors close and my breath catches. I'll be at home tomorrow. Security will be in my home, meaning Arrow will be in my house, too. Why does this scare me and excite me simultaneously?

Arrow's deep voice saves me from the anxiety I was edging close to. "How much did you drink?"

My back rests against the wall, and I suck air between my teeth. "Three glasses in two and a half hours. I had intended to drink more, but the ice cream was far more entertaining."

He wears a funny smirk as his eyes drop to my throat. "Did Miss Hanover skip the ice cream?"

I chuckle and nod. "Yeah. She's never been good at holding her alcohol. Four glasses and she's tanked."

"She looked like she was having a good time."

"Until tomorrow morning when the tiny miners with pick-axes are in her head." My lips fold in between my teeth before they pop as I set them free to gloat. "I'm a rockstar. Rockstars can hold their alcohol. It's a requirement according to the stereotype rules and regulations."

Arrow slowly draws nearer to me with his gaze affixed to mine. The tension is high, and my pussy is reacting favourably. I want him inside me, but first I want him to eat my pussy like he did before and let me cum this time.

Should I invite him in for a drink as Rachel suggested?

CHAPTER EIGHTEEN

Jade looks so fucking delicious in her oversized t-shirt hanging past her hips. What do her panties look like? I might die from arousal if she isn't wearing any. Her hair is tossed into a messy bun and she has no make-up on, which is how I like her best.

A hint of mango shampoo teases my nostrils. What would it be like to bury my face in her hair while I fill her full of my cock?

I stand so close her rapid breaths brush her nipples against my dress shirt. My body aches to feel her buttery soft skin, the warmth of her breasts in my palms, and taste her stiff nipples.

Being only a few inches shorter than me, her chocolate scented breath brushes over my neck. Beautiful green eyes stare at me. She says nothing even though her lips part and close several times. She has questions, doubts, and hesitations. As do I.

Jade swallows when I lean in and brush my cheek against hers, and shudders when the heat of my breath on her neck precedes a gentle kiss below her ear. "Invite me in, Jaybird."

"Are you a vampire now? I have to invite you in."

I'd love to eat her but not in a bloodsucking manner. Perhaps my eyes reveal my shameless thoughts because her whisper becomes powerful despite its gentle tone.

"Only if you continue what you started before I fucked it up." Her laugh rides a nervous exhale.

My fingertip delicately brushes a lock of hair from her forehead after it escapes her messy bun.

She did nothing wrong. Something traumatic happened to her. Was it before she was fostered by Mike and Leona Frewn or later as an adult? My jaw clenches to stop myself from wanting to kill whoever hurt my Jaybird. I swear to God I'll fucking make them suffer. But I have to remain calm and in control, so she trusts me not to make her pain about me. As soon as I take it on through anger, she'll clam up. She needs to set all that pain free. So, for her, I'll set my promise for vengeance aside and be here for her.

"You didn't fuck anything up. Everything happens as it should. Invite me politely."

With painful patience, my lips brush up her neck, over her jaw, and onto her puffy lips. Fucking hell, they're soft. They're like pillows I want to nestle into and stay forever. I catch my moan too late, but it seems to spark something within her. Her arms wrap around me to pull me into her, and our bodies thud against the wall but neither of us cares.

Her breathy words quiver. "Arrow, please come in."

With our arms wrapped around each other, I walk her backward further into the suite. Neither of us breaks our gaze as I hold her to me and guide her all the way to her bedroom.

The bed is draped in a white and black duvet with six pillows propped against the tall, cushioned, leather-bound headboard. The bedroom has a dim glow bleeding in from the light surrounding the bathroom mirror. It's illuminated just enough where one won't trip on anything in the night as they walk about but not enough to keep one awake.

As soon as we near the bed, Jade grips the hem of her shirt and attempts to lift it, but I stop her.

"No. I will unwrap you when I'm ready to see you." She tries to kiss me again, but I press my palm above her cleavage. "Patience, Jaybird."

I take a few steps back as my eyes drink her in from head to toe. "Take your hair down."

There's no hesitation before she reaches up and pulls the clip from her hair. Long tresses of deep-brown locks flow down over her chest and frame her beautiful face. Her hands fist and relax at her sides as if she's unsure of where to put them.

My cock strains in my jeans and more than anything, I'd love to rip off my clothes and bury myself deep into her. But this isn't about me. I'll take mine when it's time. It isn't time.

The light is behind me, so she probably can only see my outline as my arms slowly lower with each button unfastened. Watching how she squeezes her legs together ensures she's enjoying the show. She wants me as much as I want her, and the torturous wait has her growing more needy. Good.

My shirt slips off my shoulders. Knowing I'll need to put it back on and look like the professional that I am, I'm careful to fold it before putting it to rest over the white leather sofa chair a few feet from me.

I step closer to her where she could reach out and touch me, then stop. Her eyes follow my hand as it glides down my strong stomach, unfastens my belt, and pops the button on my jeans. The ting of my belt buckle is the only sound to break the silence, and it may as well be a church bell.

She whispers, "Please."

My thumb brushes over her jaw as I cup her chin with my fingers. "Patience, Jaybird."

Her stance shifts and her heavy breath reveals annoyance. "We have to hurry. What if someone comes?"

"Like who?" My eyes follow as the back of my knuckles ease down her throat and stop at the cleft.

"My security team. What if Brick comes to relieve you and you aren't standing there. He'll alert the others, and they'll come bursting in here thinking something's wrong."

I lean in but don't kiss her. "Nobody's coming. I have the night shift. I'm all yours."

"I think you have that backwards. You meant to say that *I'm yours*."

My voice rumbles low. "*Are* you mine?"

Despite the low light Jade's eyes glow a brilliant green. "I haven't fully decided."

My head tips and she must sense my hesitation.

She adds, "Convince me."

Fuck, yes!

My fingers grip the hem of her shirt and pull it over her head and toss it on the bed. Her hair floats down over her full breasts, igniting my jealousy for each strand. She stands before me in a pair of black boy-shorts and nothing else. A tinge of blue radiating from the bathroom light accentuates her curves. As much as I'm dying to grab those breasts to suck and nip her perfect light burgundy nipples, I must resist. This isn't about me. I want to please her; to prove I'm worthy of her—of all of her.

My fingertips tenderly brush her hair off her shoulders to drape down her back. My eyes capture her wide-eyed gaze. My palms skim down her shoulders and arms before gathering her wrists to lift her hands and place them on my chest.

Her lips part and her chest rises and falls quickly.

My voice is low, words unhurried. "Do you feel me?" My hands remain over hers to hold them to my chest, and she nods. "Do you feel my heart pounding for you?"

Her brows pinch together when she looks at her hands. "Yeah. Why are you— Can't we just… do this? Like, why are you hesitating?"

She tries to pull her hands away, but I hold them to me.

"Stop overthinking. Look at me." I'm quiet until she reluctantly looks at me with a tilt of her head.

How will I feel if she pushes me away again? Will I try again or leave her be? Has nobody ever taken their time with her? That would be a pity if no man has ever savoured her body and mind. It's not making love if the emotion isn't there. Right?

Worried she'll run like a scared gazelle if my voice is too demanding, I remain composed. "At this very moment, what should you be thinking about?"

"Okay. This is stupid." Frustration has her face contorting. "Don't you want to fuck me?"

My brows couldn't lift any higher. I lead her left hand to the solid bulge in my jeans and her eyes drop to watch. "Jaybird, what do you think?"

Trepidation has her whisper unsteady. "Then, why aren't you inside me?"

Before she can torture my cock by rubbing it outside my jeans, I put her hand back on my chest and cup her jaw to force her to look at me. "Because this isn't about me. I'm here for you. I won't fuck you until I think you're ready."

She laughs too heartily for the situation. "Trust me, I'm fucking ready."

"Hasn't anyone ever made it about you?"

"Sex is sex." She shakes her head with a heavy sigh. "Are we doing this or not?"

My grin and glare grow wicked. In one quick movement, I grip her waist and toss her back on the bed. Before she bounces back up, I'm between her thighs with my weight rested on one elbow while the other hand pushes below the thin waistband of her boy-cut panties.

She didn't lie; she's ready for me and dripping wet. My index finger slides between her folds to collect some of her juice before pulling back until my fingertip rests against her clitoris.

Her breath catches and her hips struggle to rise beneath my weight.

My index and ring finger rest outside her outer labia and press lightly as my middle fingertip brushes up and down over the protective hood of her clitoris. Each time it pulls back the light brush over the sensitive bundle of nerves has her tiny moan easing free.

"Now, if I had rushed, like you had insisted, I wouldn't take the time to play with your clit. I'd simply rip these fucking panties off and ram my cock deep into you in one thrust. I set the pace, Jaybird. I know what I'm doing. So, stop trying to top from the bottom and enjoy the moment. Do it again, and you'll regret it."

She frees her lip from between her teeth and moans as her lower back settles against the bedspread. "How will I regret it? Will you make me cum a million times until I beg you to stop?"

"Done some reading, have you?" My finger's pace increases as my other fingers move alongside it. She whimpers and wraps her ankles over my calves hoping to pull me into her more. "Quite the opposite. I'll hold off your orgasm until you're screaming my name and begging for permission to cum."

Her eyes lock onto mine as a mixture of fear, confusion, and intrigue flash through them. "Please don't do that."

"Tell me you'll behave." When she fails to respond, my fingers lift away from her pussy.

Frustration has her struggling beneath me, but when she fails to break free, she grips that wrist and tries to make me touch her. To prevent her from taking control of the situation, I pull my hand out of her panties, much to her chagrin.

"*Why?* Don't stop!" Her body contorts as she struggles to lift her pelvis high enough to rub her vagina against my hip for some relief, but she fails. She speaks through clenched teeth. "*Fine!* I'll be good."

As tenderly as I can, my lips press to hers instantly easing her frustration. Her lips spread as if to welcome my tongue, but she won't direct me, so I kiss the corner of her lips, over to her cheek, and down her throat.

This is fun. Not only am I in bed with a sexy-as fuck woman who knows how to ride my last nerve but teasing her to the point of desperation puts a gleaming red cherry on top.

I roll and pinch one nipple while sucking and nipping the other, and then I switch breasts.

The coolness of her palm on the back of my neck to hold me to her makes me wonder if any woman has ever gotten frostbite on their fingertips while sitting in her living room on a hot summer day. I'll allow her to put this little bit of pressure on my head because she isn't directing me. Knowing her, that'll change soon enough.

By the time I've kissed down to her mound, Jade's moaning softly through rushed breaths. She grips the back of my head with both hands as if hoping that'll force my mouth to her pussy. Instead of getting her wish, I rush up her body and glare down into wide eyes laced with confusion.

My tone is deep and powerful. "What did I say about topping from the bottom?"

Jade swallows before a jovial smile crinkles the edges of her eyes. "Not to do it. Are you going to forbid me to orgasm because I'm a bad girl, or will you spank my ass raw?"

Fuck, yes! Taunt me, Jaybird.

I try to memorize how beautiful she looks with her hair spanned out across the bed.

"I'll let you choose." There's no way in hell she'll choose orgasm denial. My palm has itched to spank her from the first time she sneered at me.

Her face scrunches before a questioning grin reaches her eyes. "Seriously?"

My brows rise as I nod. "Mhm."

"Maybe I'd prefer the latter because I'll be damned if I'm going without an orgasm tonight." She bites her bottom lip.

Even in the low light, I can see her cheeks flush pink. If my cock had hands, it'd be stroking itself for some relief.

"You'd rather I spank you than deny you an orgasm?" She nods, and my voice deepens. "Woman, welcome to my world."

Before she can do anything but squeal, I roll onto my back, while I flip her over and shove her torso until she's face down with her hip over my legs.

Jade laughs and wiggles her ass as if this is a fun game. I'm glad she's finding this amusing. In some ways I am, too, but my palm is itching to redden her cheeks for all the bullshit she's put me through.

Still smiling, she lifts onto her elbows as she looks over her shoulder. "Are you going to hurt me now?"

My finger traces the waistband of her panties and slowly pulls them down to reveal the crack of her luscious ass. "Do you want me to hurt you?"

With sarcasm dripping from every word, she says, "I thought I wasn't supposed to top from the bottom." She rests herself on her elbows and makes a point to buck her ass up and down several times before she relaxes her hips on my lap.

How I remain so in control to keep my voice smooth and unrushed has me wanting to pat myself on the back. "If I ask a question, I expect you to answer. Until I know your limits, I need to ask. I don't want to push you too far by doing something you don't approve of."

She looks over her shoulder again as her fingertip rests on her bottom lip. "You can make it hurt."

My cock may never recover from the pain it's in.

"What word will you say if you want me to stop?" I ask as all four of my fingers slip beneath her panties to caress her smooth as silk ass cheeks.

"Um, how about *shih tzu*?"

"Shih tzu?"

"It's the first word to come to mind. Besides, I've always wanted one." She doesn't hide how the word choice amuses her.

"*Shih tzu* it is. Are you ready?"

Without a sound, she nods before turning her face to look at her fingers nervously fiddling with the bedspread.

I ease my hand from her panties before lifting it and coming down on her right ass cheek. Jade jolts and takes several quick breaths before nodding for me to continue. Again, my palm comes down on her right buttock, and I leave my hand in place so she'll feel the warmth of my palm on the reddening handprint. This time, she holds her breath before releasing with a cross between a moan and a groan. She nods just as my hand lifts and cracks down on her left buttock. As her cheek sinks to the bed, her back arches to lift her ass for more.

My whisper sounds quiet after the sharpness of the spanks. "What is your safe word?"

"Shih tzu," she replies with a quiver in her voice.

In rapid succession, my palm smacks her ass ten times; five on each ass cheek. I immediately lift her and flop her onto her back, yank off her panties, and dive my mouth over her clitoris. She cries out and grips my bald head. To stop her from directing me, I grip her wrists from around her thighs and pin them to the bed alongside her hips. She pulls hard to get away from the restriction, so much so I let her go. I expect her hands to return to my head, but they rest in place where I had them imprisoned.

She doesn't like to be held down. *Damn.* Maybe we can work on the trust to build up to that.

My mouth gapes as my lips take as much of her vagina in my mouth as possible. I suck and release her labia as my tongue laps at her stiff clitoris. My lips close in around the bud and suck with varying pressure as the roughness of my tongue glides beneath the hood.

Jade's lower back arches as her head rocks side to side. Her low moans grow louder with each breath. She whimpers when I glide my fat tongue from her asshole almost to her clit, but suck her right labia instead, and let it pop from my mouth before repeating.

She's so distracted she doesn't realize I'm pulling my pants off, and if she does, she isn't saying so. But when I fist my erection, my moan can't be helped.

She tastes sweet and tangy like a woman should, and it's arousing me even more than I already am. Her scent coats my face, and I can't get enough. Needing to be inside her, I glide two fingers through her wetness before plunging them inside her vagina.

Jade unabashedly cries out as her face tilts left to right.

My lips encircle her clitoris and suck as my tongue rapidly glides up and down and side to side. My fingers push toward the front as they glide into her with a steady pace, not too fast but not too gingerly.

Her hands grip her breasts as she pinches her nipples between her thumbs and forefingers. She pulls and pinches as she twists them in a way that looks like it's causing her pain along with pleasure.

She pants and moans as the tight muscles in her abdomen flex and relax. "Oh, fuck, yes! Don't stop. Please, don't stop." Jade falls silent and her chest rises as she inhales deeply and holds it for several seconds. Her wail accompanies bucking hips. "I'm coming. Yes! Oh, God!"

Her rapid short breaths grow into increasingly loud cries until her head pushes into the mattress and her muscles from head to toe grow taut. She stills everywhere except the pressure and pulsing around my fingers. Her pussy squeezes as it throbs making it impossible to fuck her. Her clitoris swells and stiffens between my lips.

Everything stills; her body, me, the air, and everything the world has to offer. Nothing exists to her except my tongue and the euphoria she's lost in. I'm envious because I crave for my own release but watching her let go of whatever haunts her is better than any orgasm I could imagine.

Jade collapses as her body jerks each time my tongue dares press to her super-sensitive clitoris. "Holy fuck. I need you inside me. Please."

I climb up her beautiful body and kiss her belly shimmering with a light brush of sweat. My lips press to hers more aggressively than before. She isn't hesitant to taste herself on my tongue and moans into my mouth. I hug her to me and carry her with me as I roll onto my back.

She straddles me with her pussy hovering above my cock that rests along my belly like a steel pipe.

As we kiss, I whisper, "I don't have a condom."

"Good thing I do," she replies and leans away to reach into the nightstand drawer. In seconds, she's straddling my thighs and ripping a condom package from the roll before discarding the other nine with disregard to where they land. She tears the package with her teeth and smiles down at me.

My hands rest behind my head, so she understands that she has full control. I don't know what happened to her in her past, so to ensure she takes what she needs from me without it coming back to haunt her, I'll give her this control.

"Impressive," she comments and fumbles a bit as she rolls the condom over my length.

Painfully slowly, she eases her pussy down over my shaft and I swear to God I see stars flickering around my eyes. More than anything, I want to buck up to bury myself into her, flip her onto her back, and fuck her until every muscle in my body aches, and she begs me to stop.

So tight. So wet. So hot! Like the perfect fitting glove, her vagina swallows my aching cock, soothing it like warm honey on a sore throat. To stop myself from erupting like mayonnaise from one of those ridiculous squirt bottles, I mentally slap myself in the face and repeat, *This isn't about you.*

The light from the bathroom glimmers over her parted lips, down her slim neck, over her luscious mounds, and down her torso. Shadow hides her mound when she's sitting her weight on me with me sheathed inside her velvety soft walls.

Her hips begin to buck; slowly at first. In less than a minute, she's bucking wildly and moaning like she hasn't been filled in a very long time. I'm not hung like a porn star, but I'm hard as fuck and long and fat enough to pleasure a woman.

If she continues to fuck me this insatiably hard and fast while looking like a wet dream, I won't be able to hold off much longer.

My fingers bite into her thighs but it seems to ignite her fervor that much more. "Slow down, Jaybird. Slow down or I'll cum."

Her hands press to my chest as she pinches my nipples, sending shockwaves of pleasure straight to my cock. The wickedly sexy smirk on her parted lips pushes me over the edge.

"I'm coming. Jaybird—" My fingers dig into her ass to rock her hips faster. My breath rushes from me in wailed pants as the intense tickle of my orgasm grows increasingly more painfully delicious.

Jade sits up and her head tips back. I buck her like she's my own personal fuck toy and she cries out in pleasure. "I'm coming! *Fuck!*"

Her body stiffens, so I have to work harder to keep her hips rocking to ensure my orgasm is euphoric instead of dimming equivalent to a release I give myself in the shower.

I want more. I want it all. And I want it with *her*.

My hips lift as my ass muscles clench hoping to burrow deeper inside her, as if that's even possible! It's all I can do to not scream like a woman when my orgasm finally crests. The bed spins as the room darkens. I no longer feel the warmth of her skin or have the ability to use my arms to make her rock her hips. She's fucking me under her own power as her pussy walls spasm around my explosive erection.

I feel the burn of semen rush through my shaft and it's hot like lava. I'm a balloon floating above the spinning bed in the whirling room of darkness with a gorgeous brunette above me. If only I could open my eyes to see her beauty, but I'm bound by orgasmic bliss. I never want it to end, but in seconds, I'm back to reality. My lungs burn as I gasp for breaths. Every muscle in my body aches from the joy of a spastic climax.

My eyes finally ease open. Jade remains on me with my shrivelling shaft inside her.

But her flat expression gives me pause.

Fuck! What is she thinking?

CHAPTER NINETEEN

Jade

My thighs burn from the exertion, and a delicious exhaustion has swept into my entire body. My nose and lips are numb because I held my breath for too long but was finally able to fill my lungs when the first spasm bolted through me like electrocution. More than anything I'd like to collapse on top of Arrow and hold him while I let my emotions take over, but I can't give into them.

Arrow's warm palms brush up my thighs waking me into the reality of too many thoughts and emotions. Why does my brain have to take over after an orgasm? Why can't I enjoy the serene calmness so well described in the romance books I've read? I want that, but with Arrow? He's temporary, so no.

The slow glide of his tongue over his bottom lip draws me from where my thoughts were about to travel—where they always travel; into the darkness.

He gazes up at me from below heavy eyelids, and he's never looked more handsome. "Where did you just go?"

His wilting cock slithers from my vagina making us both shiver through a brush of hyper sensation, thus rescuing me from answering his question. My refusal would likely end in an argument, but I can't tell him the truth. I'd be crushed if he were to look at me the way the cops and my foster parents did after they learned the gory details of what that monster did to me. It's my personal hell, and Arrow can stay the fuck out of it.

A warm hand cups my cheek. "Hey, come back to me."

When did he sit up beneath me? The erotic moment has passed. It's done. We're done.

I shuffle away from his hand and off the bed, leaving him sitting up with his shrunken cock still sheathed inside a cum-filled condom. A look of confusion and sadness christens his expression, and I've seen enough.

"I need a shower," I say with a smile that my career has taught me how to pass off as real. Before he can say anything, I've shut the bathroom door. The lighted mirror shines over my hands as they press to the back of the door. When I'm sure he hasn't followed me, I back up and turn to pull the knob to start the water. My fingers wave beneath the stream as it quickly warms to near scalding.

Three quick steps have me gasping and fighting back a scream as the blistering hot stream slaps against my flesh. My eyes squeeze tight and my fists clench at my sides. From my neck down, the front of my body feels like it's being boiled. It's the only way to get clean from the memories that make me feel dirty.

I need this to set me free.

Strong hands grip my biceps and yank me backward as the water ceases to rain down on my reddened skin. Off balance, I topple against a hard body and we both sink to the shower floor. His arms wrap around my waist and pull me against him. He hugs me and refuses to release me despite my screams and struggle to get away. His legs spread wide when I give in and pull my knees up to my chest, tucking my feet beneath his thigh, and I rest my head on his firm chest.

Soothing words stroke my conscience. "I've got you. You're safe. It wasn't your fault."

It wasn't my fault?

He's right—it wasn't. I was a little girl and afraid. I knew struggling would only hurt more. At four-years-old, he was so big compared to me. It was nothing for him to hold my tiny hands in one of his and pin them over my head. He didn't like me looking at him, so he'd cover my face with my bed sheet. For me, it was better because I didn't have to see the way his face contorted when he forced himself to fit inside my body. It used to hurt a lot, but over time, it got better. I learned not to scream or cry too loudly because he'd press his hand over my mouth, and it was hard to breathe. It scared me more than anything.

"Phoebe, it wasn't your fault."

He used my name.

A flood of tears carries my pain as I scream through the agony of setting it free. I tremble so painfully I need to wrap my arms around his chest for stability.

Oh, God. It hurts so much. I can't make it stop.

His relaxed whisper nearly breaks me when he repeats the phrase that so many have said before him, but it meant nothing. When he says, "It wasn't your fault," for a third time, something inside me cracks open and bleeds.

Will I die? It's okay if I do because I'm so tired of carrying this disgusting secret.

I'm so cold as my weight shifts. Curled in the arms of someone warm, I'm being carried but exhaustion has me unable to refuse.

"It's okay, Jaybird. I've got you." Warm lips press to my forehead.

An achy shoulder wakes me enough where I roll onto my back to escape the dull throb. The last thing I remember, I was on the floor of the shower in the arms of a tender man, shivering and blubbering like a fool. My forearms cross over my face and a lazy groan expresses my humiliation.

Half expecting him to be in my bed snoring beside me, I slowly turn my head to check. Thankfully, the bed is empty.

"Why the fuck did I do that?"

My embarrassment slips to the back of my mind when I remember the events of last night. So hard I orgasmed with him. Arrow made me cum like I never have with anyone. Sure, I've had orgasms with men, but nothing like that. It wasn't just my vagina that felt it. My entire being was rocked. He rocked me so hard I broke.

A breath fills my lungs as my hands cover my face with the hope I'll smother beneath them and not have to face him. I cried in his arms and screamed. He saw the worst of me. He held me while I tortured myself with guilt and anger. I always do that alone. I swore nobody would ever see me break.

I won't survive if Arrow wears the pitiful expression the social workers, foster parents, and police wore in my presence. Why did I let it out in front of him? Fucking why?

I don't remember coming to bed, but I vaguely remember him carrying me. I was so tired. How long did we sit on the floor of the shower while I spilled my emotional guts?

Another groan has me sitting up and arching my back to release some stress. Failing to accomplish that goal, my shoulders slump forward as my hands drop into my lap. How will I face him today?

A knock at the bedroom door has me rolling my eyes because I know it's Elsa. It's time to start the day by picking away at the schedule. At least it'll be a distraction from my penetrating thoughts.

Elsa enters and startles when she sees I'm awake and sitting at the edge of the bed. I'm naked. Having seen me nude on so many occasions, Elsa isn't fazed.

Even in the dimness her vibrant smile can't go unnoticed. "Good morning, Jade. How are you this morning?"

The light flicks on, momentarily blinding me and making me cranky. Why don't most hotel bedrooms have a dimming feature to their light switches?

"That's too fucking bright." My face scrunches. Fearing wrinkles, I force myself to relax my expression. Reluctantly, I ask, "What time is it?"

"It's six o'clock."

Frustration mixed with self-pity rings heavily in my words. "In the morning?"

Her laugh is slight. "Yes."

Elsa heads directly to the walk-in closet and hangs a grey clothing bag before setting a large navy duffel on the floor and reaching inside to pull out a shoebox. She lifts the lid and sets the strappy three-inch-high black shoes with red soles on the floor.

She steps out and closes the door before standing with her hands on her hips and still wearing that smile too annoyingly cheery for me, while I secretly wallow in regret.

"You look tired. Were you up late?"

My palms press into my eye sockets and rub until white stars flicker behind my lids. "Yeah. Something like that."

"A shower will help wake you up. Get a move on. We have to get you ready for the early morning show. "Fair warning; they're going to ask you about your relationship with Augustus Greyner."

"What?" Shock has my eyes widening too much for having just woken. "How did that get out? I mean, what the fuck? How? Who squealed? Nobody knew about it except for our personal staff. Nobody at the hotel knew anything. Do we have a rat in the mix?"

Elsa giggles and shrugs. "Maybe, but I don't think it came from our end. Nobody on our staff would sell that story." She glances at the bedroom door before her brows furrow.

"What?" I stand and cross the room toward her; still nude.

She bites her lip before meeting my eyes. Her arms cross over her chest and she clears her throat. "Well, your regular staff have proven they wouldn't say anything."

It's my turn to bite my cheek and glance at the door. "Are you saying Arrow might have something to do with this?"

Her shoulders lift near to her ears before dropping harshly. "I don't know. Maybe. I mean, unless it was someone under Augustus's employ, but I'm pretty sure he would have vetted whomever is around him. He's not in the *forgiving* business, so it's unlikely anyone would cross him."

She's right. He's been described in the news media as an untouchable mobster with a cruel history, but nothing sticks to him in the court system. Somehow, he's never served a moment in prison despite the horrors whispered about him.

Augustus was nothing but a gentleman toward me. He was kind and smooth with his words, but when it came to fucking, he wasn't as rough as I like a man to be. Perhaps he held back because he didn't want to scare me off. That's proof right there he doesn't know me. I don't know him either; not really.

"So, are you suggesting Arrow had something to do with it?"

She shrugs again as her head tips to follow the slant of her lips. "No matter who spilled it, it's out there, so you need to nip it into felonious gossip. Deny, deny, deny."

"Who cares who I fuck? Honestly!" I storm to the bathroom and pull the shower knob. When it's warm enough, I step inside and shiver until it grows hot enough for my liking but not scalding.

A toothbrush scrubbing and a coffee awakens my brain, and I'm soon ready to face the day, but not necessarily Arrow.

Elsa hands me a towel to dry off with before she helps me into the fluffy white robe provided by the hotel.

"Make-up and hair will be here in…" she glances at her watch, "about five minutes. So, let's get some more caffeine flooding your system and food in your belly."

My feet slide into the hotel slippers, and I shuffle behind Elsa to the kitchen area.

I pick at the tray of fruit and eat the strawberry yogurt but grimace at the eggs now cooled into rubber. The yolks stare at me and I'd swear they're judging me.

A knock at the door has Elsa rushing to open it. In comes Gail with her trolly of make-up and hair products. The slightly overweight woman is smiling wide like a happy-go-lucky morning person. Don't these people realize it's too early to be so damn happy?

Before she has me turn on my stool to face her, I gulp the last of the brutally strong black coffee from my mug and hold it up to Elsa and nod. "Bar keep, fix me up."

She scoffs her laugh and takes my mug.

"Good morning, Jade. Are you ready to get started?" Gail holds a large white hair clip and waits for me to give in to the tribulations of the make-up and hair ritual.

"Why not?" I say and flash the best smile I can manage.

Elsa sets the mug on the marble countertop behind me and rounds the island before she flops onto the cushiony sofa with her mug and tablet. She immerses herself into her work, paying no attention to Gail and me.

"So, anything new and exciting?" The forty-something woman whirls my hair into an easy bun and clips it out of the way.

"New and exciting? Every day is a new day. Every day offers something I have to do whether it be exciting or simply interesting depends on the tasks. As for today, I'll be on a television program denying my relationship with Augustus Greyner. It's so ridiculous that I even have to say anything. People have nothing better to do than gossip about my personal life."

Gail opens a drawer on her cart and shakes the bottle of moisturizer before squirting some onto a foam puff. She dabs it around my eyes first and works out from there. "No, people have nothing better to gossip about. You're the *'it'* singer and people are curious about what you do in your spare time." She stands straight and lowers her brows while her lips quirk into a grin. "What do you do in your spare time?"

My eyes roll as I drole my words. "Not you too!"

We both chuckled because she was only playing with me. She may be curious, but I doubt it. She's been around so many celebrities she knows more about them than they probably realize, but she keeps to herself and shows no real interest in the conversations I've had with Elsa, Alex, or anyone, for that matter. She simply paints my face and styles my hair to match my persona and moves on. I like that about her.

Half an hour later, I'm prettied up, dressed, and have used the bathroom for the last time before we meet up with the band and head off to the interview.

Elsa carries the large navy duffel, as she always does. What she has in there seems endless. Basically, anything I may need or ask for, she has in that bag: water, mints, gum, lipstick, make-up for touch-ups, a tablet to play games on in case I have to wait anywhere for too long. She doesn't allow me to get bored. When I do, I get cranky. Call me spoiled, but if I get to a gig and have to wait to perform, it frustrates me. Tell me what time I'm to be on and I'll be there for that time. I'm a busy woman. Well, not always busy, but they don't have to know that!

In the kitchen, the beautiful Kina sets a mug on the counter and stands with her hands clasped together behind her back. "Good morning, Miss Jade."

"Good morning, Kina. At ease, soldier." I smile as I reach for a strawberry, but Elsa slaps my hand away. "What the fuck?"

She busies herself with the zipper on the bag. "You don't need any seeds in your teeth."

"Kina, call me Jade. How are you today?"

She nods but doesn't smile. "Alert and ready to keep you safe, ma'am."

"Please, no *ma'am*. Just call me Jade. I appreciate the respect you're presenting, but I'm not uppity and would prefer not to be called ma'am. Ma'am makes me sound so old. I'm only thirty-two, not sixty." I smile, but her eyes jerk away quickly.

She'll continue to call me Miss Jade or something else respectful because it's her nature. She's lovely and nobody would ever suspect such a tiny woman to be so damn good at martial arts. Along with her eye make-up applied impeccably and her long braids tipped in red, her silky brown skin would be stunning on a magazine cover. But protecting me is the career choice she's made for herself. Sure, I pay very well, but wouldn't something less time consuming be a more interesting choice for a young woman?

I ask Elsa, "Where's Alex?"

While shuffling through the bag, she replies, "He said he had something to do but he'll meet us there." She curses and stops walking, so I pause and watch frustration wash over her features. "Do you have your phone?"

"No."

"Dammit! I'll be right back." She rushes back to the bedroom.

Kina follows as I continue to the elevator. Just before I reach the reflective silver doors, Arrow comes into view. He stands only a few feet from me. Our eyes meet but I look away. I can't see the pity expression he most likely will cast my way.

Arrow's perfectly pressed black dress pants, white dress shirt with two buttons unfastened, and the black dress coat make him look mouthwatering. Now that I know how delicious he looks when naked, I may prefer him nude.

Dammit! Stop thinking about the sex.

It was fun but it's over. He saw the worst in me. Nobody sees that. Nobody. But he didn't run away. He stayed. He stayed and held me through the worst of it.

Why? Because after the sex we had, he felt obligated. He didn't stay for my benefit; he stayed because he'd look like a fucking asshole if he'd just left. But he did leave. He put me to bed and left me in the suite alone to get away from me. If he'd slept with me, held me through the night, I'd know he didn't just use me. But he left.

I wish last night never happened. It'll never happen again.

CHAPTER TWENTY

Waiting for Elsa to return with Jade's phone may only take a few seconds, but how Jade looks everywhere but at me has my jaw clenched. What the fuck is wrong with her? We were so close last night. It wasn't only sexual, although that was admittedly primo sex. She let her guard down and we need to discuss it. Does she have a breakdown after every sexual encounter? The better question is *why* did she break down?

Look at me, Jaybird!

As I slide my phone into my inside jacket pocket, I clear my throat to get Jade's attention. Her eyes jerk to mine but flick to Elsa as she enters the foyer.

"Good morning, Jade." My voice seems loud amid the silence.

Her arms hug her chest over a black leather halter top with a deep V to expose the cleavage my lips were buried in not twelve hours ago. I'd give anything to grab the back of her neck and pull her face to mine. I'd kiss her hard and wanting, because I desire her to be sheathed over my cock as her curves sway like an ocean above me.

My stance shifts to better conceal my growing erection.

Dead puppies. Septic tanks. Old pudding with a rubbery crust. That worked; my cock has softened.

"Good morning, Arrow. Did you sleep well?" My beautiful Jaybird's eyes lock onto mine with a challenging tilt of her head.

As I'd hoped, her eyes drop to the tip of my tongue as it coats my bottom lip with saliva. Her stance shifts to pull her thighs together. She wants me as much as I want her. Still, she remains glaring at me, and it seems like a challenge.

"I slept better than I have in months."

Nothing too graphic should be said in front of Kina because she's perceptive. In my peripheral vision, I see her glance from Jade to me and back before she turns away from us and slips her hands in her pants pockets.

I woke at five o'clock on Jade's sofa and left her suite only to find Kina in the hallway doing a cross between martial art moves and gymnastics. As I passed her to walk toward my room, she breathed in. Our eyes met and her brows scrunched disapprovingly.

Somehow, she knew damn well what I was doing in Jade's room last night. Although she said nothing, her silent tongue-lashing was plenty loud.

I told her that after Rachel left, Jade couldn't sleep because she was too nervous about the stalker and wanted to talk. She didn't buy it, but I didn't confirm her conviction either. Plausible deniability.

Kina immediately went up to Jade's suite to allow me some time to shower and get some food in me before we were to set off to the interview.

The tortured soul inside Jade matches mine in that we both suffer deeply. Her trauma wasn't earned in a war like mine was, but a war she did battle. What happened to her?

I ask, "And you, Jade… How did you sleep?"

Jade's hands drop to her hips as her chin jerks up and her painted lips twitch. "I slept just fine."

Her throat clears before she addresses the woman doing her best to stay out of it. "Kina, how's your grandfather doing?"

At 5'4" tall, she's much shorter than Jade. Anyone would think she's the mark being guarded by Jade and not the opposite way around. Kina looks up at Jade and flashes a rare smile. It's fleeting, but I saw it.

When did the two women have time to discuss Kina's grandfather? In such a short time, Jade was able to get Kina to open up to her. Call me impressed.

Her voice is unsuitably gruff. "He's doing much better. Thank you for asking."

"Is he out of the hospital?"

Kina and Jade continue to chat through the entire elevator descent. Kina's head is on a swivel to keep aware of her surroundings. She leads Jade and Elsa to the expensive black car with the blacked-out windows. She opens the door and glances at me as Elsa slides in first and Jade sits beside her. I slide in beside Jade and our shoulders meet. For the first time since I carried her naked body to her bed, we're touching. The heat from her bare arm seeps through my suit jacket, reminding me of how hot her smooth skin felt against mine.

In the front seat, Kina brushes her gathered braids over her shoulder. The intricate weave of each braid has me wanting to praise the talent of their weaver. That takes skill.

From the edge of my eye, I see Jade turn her face to look at me. Without moving my eyes, my mental attention shifts to her. Patiently, I wait for her to say something, but she disappoints me and turns her face down to her phone's screen as it lights up.

Should I say something? It would have to be cryptic because Elsa is so close beside her. Sure, her attention is on her tablet, but she can hear us clearly.

How long will she and I sit in awkward silence before one of us breaks the tension?

Say something!

My cheek turns toward her, but my sights remain focused out the windshield. "So, ah… Are you looking forward to the interview?"

Jade scoffs a chuckle before she lowers her phone to her lap. "No, I'm not. It's going to be hell; I have to lie and deny my relationship with Augustus."

My face turns slightly more as a fire in the pit of my stomach erupts. "You *aren't* in a relationship with him. It was one regretful night and it's over. Denying you're in a relationship isn't a lie, is it?"

Her head tips so she can better see my face. "Mhm. Should my bodyguard be voicing his opinion on whether I regret having sex with someone?"

Fire. Burning. Hotter.

It takes a conscious effort to unhinge my jaw. "I suppose as your bodyguard, I shouldn't."

Sarcasm weighs heavily from her lips. "Well, you *are* my bodyguard, and that night isn't the one I regret. So, why don't you just do your job and keep your opinions to yourself."

Deep breaths in through my nose and out my mouth help simmer the explosion threatening to tear me apart. My shaking palms press to my thighs as I silently seethe.

She said she'd submit to me, but a submissive would never talk to her Dom in such a way. Fine. If this is how she wants it, this is how it will be.

We're done.

Kina stands slightly behind the curtain just off set while I position myself between the two cameras focussed on the well-lit Jade and the interviewer. The two women are posed with legs crossed as they face each other on the orange sofa chairs separated by a decorative wooden coffee table.

A man counts down as his arm drops to match the numbers and continues even when the last two numbers cut out.

The blonde host whose name escapes me, breaks from looking miserable to unfathomably happy. "Happy late morning, viewers. I hope your day is starting off well. We have a special surprise for you, today. Here with me is the brilliantly talented, stunningly beautiful Jade." She pauses and leans in toward Jade while she smiles to show too many gleamingly white teeth. "Welcome! I'm so excited to speak with you. This is the first time you've been on our show. Am I right?"

As practiced, Jade smiles, and her eyes shimmer beneath the lights. "It's so great to be here, Kathy. This is my first time here. I watch your show as often as I can and really wanted to join you. So, thank you for making my wish come true."

Oh, she's good!

Kathy sits straighter as her hand presses to her chest. "That just makes my little heart thud. You can come to the show anytime you're in town. We'd love to have you." She turns to the camera and asks. "Wouldn't we?"

The woman is so fake. How can anyone watching this show believe her to be genuine? The smile is fake, her behaviour is over-acted, and she's so obviously full of shit. Maybe I'm too good at reading people, but I'd never watch this woman even if nothing else was on.

"There have been some rumours floating around."

Jade nods as her lips pinch together in a smile. "There are always rumours. In general, they're spread by people who love to flap their gums whether the rumour is true or not. Those types have nothing interesting happening in their own lives, so they feel a need to butt into other people's private lives."

The interviewer's shoulders jerk back as if she were slapped in the face. I suppose her words were aimed at the interviewer and all gossipy talk shows. The woman's job is to do just that; spread more bullshit gossip. It's how she makes her living.

Her fingers fold together on her lap as she nods in agreement even though she wants to be snarky back to Jade. It'd be unfitting to the persona this woman has worked so hard to falsify.

After a beat, the woman nods. "And this is why you're here with us, today. Would you like to set us all straight?"

A deep breath fills Jade's lungs. She shifts herself to better face the camera without turning away from the blonde and brushes an imaginary hair from the thigh resting atop the other.

"Why not?"

The woman's glee is over-the-top as she turns herself to face Jade, not the cameras. "All right. I'll ask the question we'd all love to know the answer to." There's a pause while Jade stares unblinking at the woman while she wears an expression that screams *fuck off, you nosy bitch.* "Augustus Greyner; are the rumours true? Are you in a relationship with one of the richest, most powerful people in the world?"

Jade smirks as her eyes sparkle below the hot, blindingly bright lights. "A relationship? Sure, we're in a relationship."

The woman gasps with her hand on her chest as she glances at the producer standing just off set.

Jade continues. "You and I have a relationship; a working relationship. There are many types of relationships. We could develop a friendly or romantic relationship. As you can see, there's a difference."

The blonde's over hair-sprayed hair doesn't swing when she quickly shakes her head in denial. "Oh, we could never have a romantic relationship, Jade. I'm a married woman—to a man."

Jade's full attention returns to the interviewer. "I was only giving a reference for the definition of relationship. I'm absolutely uninterested in becoming romantic with you."

For a moment, the woman looks offended, which is exactly what Jade intended. She's quick to recover. "I see, but you didn't answer the question: Are you in a *romantic* relationship with Augustus Greyner?" Her head tilts as her Barbie smile and wide eyes could set Jade ablaze if it were possible.

Jade takes a moment to sip from the giant mug set out for her and sets it down before her forearm rests on the tall armrest. "I am not in a *romantic r*elationship with August Greyner. We met in an elevator when we were in Vancouver. Someone must have seen him kiss my hand before he went his way and I went mine which, as you know, is a common practice for a gentleman. Rumours begin from a grain of rice and quickly explode into an entire paddy field.

The woman nods toward the camera. "That's true. Tabloids are the worst for building a mountain from an ant hill."

"Not only tabloids. However, coming on shows like yours to confirm or deny these ridiculous rumours is helpful in stopping them from blowing up."

"Since we're on the topic," the blonde leans in with both hands perched on the same armrest, "is there anyone special in your life—a romantic partner, perhaps?"

Emerald eyes scan the people behind the cameras until she sees me standing with my breath held while my hands fist at my sides.

What will she say? Do I want her to announce our undefined relationship? Would that be a good thing for her career or dent it? And yet, if she denies I exist, will it crush me?

A throat clearing beside me draws my attention. Alex scowls at me. Has he picked up on what her glare means?

I'm so fucked if he has!

Jade doesn't speak until we lock eyes again. "There's no one. I'm not a romantic relationship type person. Who has the time? I certainly don't.

Besides, being held down by one person for the rest of my life doesn't sound pleasant. I can barely stand being alone with myself for too long let alone having someone stuck to me every day. So, no. I'm not *with* anyone."

The interviewer's silence proves her disappointment that she didn't break the hottest scoop wide open.

I couldn't care less about that woman. The green eyes that look down before glancing away have me questioning whether their owner believes the validity of her own words. People who are truthful don't turn their eyes down before looking away unless there's cleavage involved, of course. But that could just be me.

Nothing either woman says after that penetrates the fog of questions and doubts bouncing around in my head. I hear nothing, even when Alex speaks to me in a whisper. What pulls me back from overthinking the way Jade looked away from me, is the way Alex steps directly in front of me to block my view of the women who've stood and are shaking each other's hands over the small table.

Jade rushes over to another platform lit with red lights and Venus taps her drumsticks to count them down. The obnoxious music roars to life with screaming guitars and heavy bass. Fuck, I hate rock 'n roll. The only thing enjoyable is the way Jade's voice shifts from either end of the scale without wavering. She's good. She's damn good. It's just such a shitty music genre.

The song ends and the blonde rushes to shake all of their hands as she calls out their name and tells the cameras they'll be right back.

A man calls cut and the stage lights shut off as noise erupts throughout the studio and people bustle about doing their jobs.

"Alex," I say in more of a question when I turn only to be met with his flared nostrils.

He looks at me as if he were my father about to question my behaviour. "What was that look about?"

Play dumb!

My expression doesn't shift from neutral but my arms cross over my chest. "What look?"

He steps closer until we're too close for men to stand unless they're intimate or plotting something scandalous. "I'm not stupid. If you're pursuing her, you had better put yourself in check. Let me just say that if you touch her in an intimate manner, you won't be here very long. You signed a contract about conduct, and you are to adhere to it. So, no matter how tempting, leave her be. She's far too busy and above your paygrade. Do I make myself clear?"

Calmly, I say, "I've read the contract thoroughly, and in no clause does it state what type of relationship I'm permitted to have with Miss Jade. Nowhere does it promise my dismissal upon an intimate relationship with her or any other staff behind closed doors." I lean my face even closer to him and lower my voice. "So, don't threaten me. I was hired to protect Jade even at the extent of my own life, and that's exactly what I'll do if need be. She's a grown woman and can make her own choices. It would be nice to keep yours and my working relationship a pleasant one. Try to pull this shit again, and I'll see you in court."

Alex storms away and presses his phone to his ear. I have no doubt he's calling the lawyer who drew up the contract to question what I've said. If I were a betting man, I'd put money on that lawyer being fired for not adding it in a clause.

CHAPTER TWENTY-ONE

Jade

Before we sit in the car, I ask Kina to sit in the back with me. Would Arrow dare say anything when they're within earshot? Probably not. He'd give me the cold shoulder and stew beside me. Of course, he wouldn't let it show on his calm and cool exterior, but his jaw tightens when he's internally annoyed, pissed off, or holding his tongue, and that's what he's been doing since the interview ended. I just can't deal with him right now.

This plane is smaller than the one we time-share. There's no bedroom for me to shut myself into. I'm forced to sit in the same area as Arrow, so I choose the only solo seat near the back of the plane. No one can sit beside me and that suits me well.

Since asking Kina to join me in the back of the car, I've said nothing to anyone. They can deduce my mood as being rather grouchy. That suits me just fine even though I'm not.

On the left side of the plane, Elsa and Alex sit near the cockpit in the seats facing each other with a table big enough for two separating them.

They immediately open their computers and begin tapping away before the plane's engines rev to life. Behind them, Brick and Gail share two dark-grey leather loungers. Lacey, Venus, and Pony take a seat with a table between them. Pony brings out a deck of cards and starts to deal.

Dex, always the sweetest of the bunch, leans in and asks, "Are you okay?"

My leg crosses the other as I unfold a blanket the stewardess offered me. This halter doesn't offer much protection against the cool air.

"I'm fine, Dex. I promise."

His brows rise as if in disbelief. "You don't seem fine."

My sigh weighs heavily as my brows rise in their center. "I can't wait to get home. This break will do me a world of good." I set the blanket on my lap and brush my hand over his. "Honestly, I'm okay. I'd tell you if something was wrong."

Satisfied with my answers, he pecks a kiss to my head and slides into the seat beside Pony. They begin flipping cards as they study their hands. Euchre; it's their favourite game to play to pass the time. Personally, I hate playing cards.

My attention shifts to my phone when Arrow steps onboard. There are three seats to choose from, including one across the aisle from me. He pauses his steps to look at me, but I don't raise my eyes from my phone. Pretending not to notice him, I swipe mindlessly hoping to look legitimately preoccupied.

Arrow sits in the seat by the window in front of me. The only visible part of him is the top of his bald head. A loud grumbled sigh and the click of his seat belt fastening is a promise that he won't be bothering me any time soon. Good.

The flight was only two hours—two hours of me trying desperately to sleep, but failing, which is sure to make anyone miserable. If I could've shut down for a few hours, I'd have been happier.

Song lyrics have been dancing through my thoughts like a freight train. I'll write them down when I get home. Maybe I can make a hit song out of whatever emotions I'm feeling. What the fuck am I feeling? I'm embarrassed of my behaviour after having sex with Arrow, ashamed of how I've been taking it out on him and torn-up by how fucking stupidly I'm fucking up something that could be a lot of fun. Why do I have to be so fucked up three years with a shrink couldn't cure?

Kina taps my arm, and I jolt upright. We're on the tarmac with the engines now at rest. Maybe I *was* asleep.

My phone dropped onto the dark grey carpet at some point, so I picked it up and stood with a stretch to ease the crick in my back from the weird position I had relaxed into.

I don't see Arrow until we're on the tarmac. Him and three drivers are loading luggage into the trunks of the three black cars not twenty steps away. The sleeves of his dress shirt are rolled up, showcasing the muscles in his thick forearms.

"Jade, you'll be in this car." Kina points to the middle car with the back door wide open to welcome passengers.

My shoulders roll and my head tilts side to side hoping for a neck crack to ease away the sharp pain in the back of my head. Soon I'll have a migraine if I can't ease this tension. It's my own fault. I brought it on by behaving like an asshole. Arrow did nothing wrong. Could this have been avoided had I woken with him beside me? There's no point in asking myself what-ifs. Above everything, we have to keep us a secret.

Wait… *us*? Are we an *us*?

Lacey is first to wrap her arms around me and peck a kiss to my cheek. Did she leave hot pink lips on my face? "Call us if you want to get together."

Standing at her side is Venus. She understands my distaste for hugs, so she pats my shoulder instead. "Anytime, Jade."

The ladies walk arm in arm to a black Cadillac and slide in the backseat before Venus closes the door.

Pony's been standing beside the stairs with his guitar slung over his shoulder. He's texting. I'd bet my career that he's setting up a hook-up for tonight. The man is a real slut, but the people he sleeps with know so and always come back. If he ever settled down, hell would freeze over. He looks up, so I blow him a kiss and he catches it before pressing it to his heart. "Love you, girl. Have a good one."

Dex hugs my shoulders from behind, not wrapping his arms fully around me, which I appreciate. I turn to face his scruffy face, and he grips my shoulders. "Don't be shy to call me. I mean it. We can have a girl's night and eat heaps of junk food, drink lots of wine, and watch chick-flicks under a warm blanket."

"Girl's night? Dude, you may be gay, but you aren't femme." I snicker as I look down at the leather vest and snug leather pants. "You have the butchy-bitch thing down pat, but femme you are not."

His head bobs to the left as his eyes drift with the motion. "No, but I do love my ass stuffed by a burly beast of a man while he calls me a pussy. Does that count?"

We both laugh as I lightly slap my palm to his face. "I fucking love you, Dex. I'll see you soon. I doubt I'll even get out of bed long enough to get dressed." His one eyebrow rises as his lips pucker with a twist. "I'll give you a call. I promise."

He blows me a kiss which I return, then strides to his waiting limo.

I sit in the car, and Kina closes the door. Pony slowly walks to his waiting car, but his focus is on his phone. It's a good thing there isn't an open manhole in his path.

The windows are so dark my phone's screen immediately dims. The car bounces several times as the suitcases are loaded into the trunk. I'm alone in the car and it's quiet. Soon I'll be in my home where I'll control the noisiness or quiet. I'll be alone as I prefer it… I still prefer that, right?

My door flings open. It's so bright Alex is met with my squinted eyes.

"If you need anything, call me or Elsa. You won't be alone because Kina and—" *Please say Brick!* "—Arrow will be watching over the house. Just stay indoors with the doors and windows locked. If you have to go anywhere… Well, don't. Stay home. I mean it, Phoebe."

"Yes, Dad," I reply with heavy sarcasm. "You realize I'm a grown woman, right? If I want to go out, I'll go out. Their job is to protect me.

So, they can do what we pay them handsomely for."

"Dammit, Phoebe! You're the most stubborn woman I've ever met. Just do what they tell you to do. After we catch the son-of-a-bitch, you can do whatever the hell you want." His face softens, and he sighs. "Take care of yourself. Enjoy the next three days."

"I will." My quirky smile as I scrunch my face nod does nothing to reassure him.

His frustration flares his face red. "Stay away from Arrow. You know what I mean. He can't do his job if he's too busy getting it on with you."

All the humour in my tone is gone. If a glare could punch him in the face, it's the one I'm sporting. "Alex, you're overstepping. Back the fuck off. Remember that I pay you, not the other way around. Don't tell who I can or can't fuck. You may run my career, but you don't have a say in who uses my body. You may want to keep that in mind."

Alex stares at me with flared nostrils. He knows I'm right and says nothing. Instead, he slams the car door and storms to the car in front of mine. He slips into the back seat but leaves the door ajar.

Elsa has her purse slung over her shoulder and her phone in her hand when she taps on my window and motions for me to lower it. I do, and her smile lightens my mood. "What was that all about?"

"Nothing important. You know Alex; he thinks he rules my life and can tell me what I can and can't do."

Her face turns back from looking at the car he's in and smiles again. "You have everything you'll need. Your bags are in the back, your maid knows you're coming, so she has shopped to fill your kitchen with what you like. She's made some meals to just heat and eat and left them in the fridge. So, you have three days to relax and catch up on your sleep. Call me if you need me."

The sun adds vibrance to Elsa's lazy curls. Her lazy curls radiate a hint of orange to brighten the natural red hue.

She rushes to the car, leans in and smiles as she says something I can't hear. She slides in with Alex and closes the door. They can't be seen through the limo-dark window tint. They're in the car together? They don't live anywhere near each other, so why would they share a car?

Oh, shit! Are they fucking? No way! He gives me shit for my interest in an employee, meanwhile, he's fucking my PA? Asshole!

Alex is much older than her. Then again, they have been awfully friendly of late. They've always been friendly but there's been a closeness unsuited of their characters. Wow! They have no choice but to work together, so if their relationship fails badly, life with them will be hell on earth.

The driver's door opens, and I pay no attention, until the passenger's door opens, and Kina sits. I'd welcome her to sit with me in the back if she'd asked. My skin prickles when the door opposite me opens. Before I even look to see who's coming in, I know it's Arrow. The breeze carried his woodsy cologne into the car to tease my senses and flash my memory back to when my face was nuzzled in his neck while he held me during my most vulnerable state of mind.

The quiet hum of the engine vibrates the car, and we begin to roll.

Great! The next twenty plus minutes will be spent in uncomfortable silence. Why didn't he sit in the front seat and let Kina sit with me? Does torturing me with tension give him a thrill?

"No. I don't want you back here with me? Let Kina—"

Arrow raises his index finger to silence me as he presses the button to raise the window to separate us from the driver and Kina.

My stomach drops out like I've been pushed off a rocky cliff. My nerves are on edge as I anticipate the inevitable splat.

The instant the blackout window seals, Arrow turns himself to better face me but says nothing.

"What?" I ask because nothing else comes to mind other than apologizing, which I'm too proud and stubborn to do.

Arrow's voice deepens through a whisper. "You tell me."

His hands are at rest on his knees in a non-threatening way.

I feel ashamed at how I've treated him. What am I angry about? That he wasn't in my bed in the morning and left me unguarded when he took off to get away from me?

But did he leave? How would I know if I was asleep? Doesn't he realize that I'm just too fucked up to figure out?

My fingernails pick at nothing on my black pant leg to hold my gaze from his. "I can't… I just… I don't know."

"Take a moment to figure it out and then talk to me."

Why is he being so gentle with me? I've been a fucking bitch to him all day. A thick finger lifts my chin and turns my face to meet his bewildered eyes.

Calmer than I deserve, he says, "Since I wasn't with you when you woke, and you were already angry with me the moment you saw me, why the hostility?"

The magnetic tug of his unblinking stare is too intense, and I have to jerk my head to the left and stare out the window. Should I leap from the car and take my chances with being maimed or killed instead of trying to explain the mass of fucked up thoughts that make up who the crazy bitch that I am?

My cheek pinches between my teeth as I struggle to find the words. Unable to, I turn back to and silently beg him for compassion.

Arrow's pale brown eyes carry an understanding that is laced with support not pity. But he won't understand, and if I confess my history to him, he'll never look at me the way he is now. Sympathy will replace the strength his stare offers, and he'll never look the same. He won't see me in the same light as he does now. How could he?

My words don't come, so he speaks in a warm tone. "You don't have to say anything if you don't want to, but this is what I took from last night."

No. Please. I don't want to know.

"We had sex; the best sex of my life." His slight smile and the creases beside his eyes prove he speaks the truth.

My unsure whisper is barely audible as my fingers brush an imaginary lock of hair from my cheek. "Yeah. It was really good."

"Better than good, Jaybird." His warm fingers brush down my chilled arm until they meet my hand and surround my digits.

"But after—" I swallow but fail to keep hold of my personal pain and it leaks down my cheeks. "That was so inappropriate. You were never meant to see me in that way. It doesn't have anything to do with you or what we did. It was nice; what we did. Great, actually."

Arrow brushes his thumb over my tears but says nothing. Instead, his hand reaches for mine to give it a light squeeze to urge me to continue.

My eyes close for two reasons; to ebb the flow of tears and prevent me from witnessing the shift in his eyes that will break my heart.

"I was four-years-old when I was taken from my alcoholic mother and put into foster care. Shortly after, my foster father—" I hiccup and snuff the snot threatening to drip from my nose. "He did things to me no man should do to a child. He *hurt* me. He said he loved me, and then he hurt me. I was four-years-old and so tiny, and he was so big and strong."

Arrow remains quiet, so I glance into his eyes fearing the worst, but the strength in his face remains. It doesn't carry the poor, pitiful expression I'm so used to seeing.

"I don't remember how anyone found out, but I was immediately taken from the house by a woman police officer. A swarm of blue uniforms invaded the living room. The monster was shackled and handcuffed as well as his wife. The two other fosters—boys—sat on the sofa with wide eyes. The one had a red truck in his hand. Why I remember that so vividly seems odd, but it was clutched in his tiny hand while the other boy held his free hand. I don't know if the monster touched them like he touched me. We didn't talk about that stuff. I barely remember them at all."

Maybe one day I'll try to find them to see if they suffered at the monster's hand, too.

"Anyway, the next thing I remember is the white and pink hospital gown I was in. It was too big and as I walked down the hall, I kicked it with my feet covered in those blue booties they give patients." The memory brings a smile to my face. "I was so happy at that moment. The nurse holding my hand was so kind. She was pretty and smiled a lot. She gave me a funny tasting fruit drink and popsicles, pink ones because I liked them best. I felt funny and fell asleep. When I woke in a different room, that nurse wore a different expression; pity. She told me I never had to see those people again because some really nice people wanted to take me home with them. She said there was a little girl next door that I could play with, and I'd be starting school with her. She turned out to be Rachel. I liked that nurse so much and begged her to take me home instead."

My tears have dried, and I feel oddly relieved, especially when I study Arrow's face and see the lack of sorrow in his eyes. His eyes are relaxed and his lips not gaping, but lightly pressed together and tipped at their edges with a hint of something else; pride, maybe.

Instead of asking what the man did or what happened to him, Arrow speaks with understanding. "Things happen to us that we can't control. It's unfortunate, but a fact of life. We've all suffered from something that nearly broke us. Often, we gain strength from overcoming it. Look at you now; you're a strong woman with a powerful career, and you take shit from no one." The back of Arrow's knuckle glides down my cheek to erase a stubborn tear and then cups my cheek. "It wasn't your fault, and this pain you've fought so hard to keep to yourself for so many years, you don't have to hide it from me."

My cheeks flush hot from the shock of the acceptance in his response. My face rarely reddens even under situations more expectant of a rosy face, but here I am feeling like an internal fire will surely melt my skin. "Nobody needs to see my little tantrums. *I* don't even want to be there for them."

"You can be weak around me. You never have to go through that alone again. I will be here for you. Cry, scream, and hit me if it'll help set it free." Arrow draws nearer to my face. "Tell me you understand what I'm saying."

I grip his wrist and his hand lowers to my shoulder, but I don't let go. "I want to, but you're not going to be here forever. As soon as you get my stalker, you're out of here. That's what you said, and it is how it is. Let's call the elephant and elephant and not try to side-step around it."

"When did I say it?" He asks with confidence as if he knows the answer.

"I—I don't remember exactly, but you said it. It's the truth; you're leaving."

Arrow's lips press to my forehead and linger. "I said it before we were intimate. I'm not so confident in that statement now."

Is he suggesting he plans to stick around? Do I want him to stick around?

"You can't promise you'll stay with me. My life is far too hectic for a relationship. My schedule is so complicated I barely find time to hang out with Rachel, and an intimate partner would require even more time, of which I don't have much to spare."

Stop me before I go off the rails!

He snickers. "We don't have to figure it all out right now."

My voice sharpens as my shoulders lift and drop. "If not now, when?"

"You're such a Jaybird." His smile grows wide as his private joke humors him. "Take a breath."

"Okay. What the fuck is with the whole *Jaybird* fascination with you?" My arms cross over my chest as I lean away from him and purse my lips.

Arrow's laugh is nearly silent as his hand glides down his cheeks and pauses at his stubbled chin. "A Jaybird is a beautiful bird despite being in the crow family. In my opinion, they're the prettiest birds I've ever seen. The only problem with them is their cackle. To protect themselves or their young, they scream the most annoying sound that sends shivers up my spine."

The look of insult weighing on my face has him laughing heartily.

"You have to admit, you have a very sharp tongue and use your words to lash at people to keep them at a distance! And damn, woman, your voice wails piercingly sharp through certain verses." His hand rises when my jaw falls slack. "It's not an insult, at least, I don't mean it to be.

Your music is not a genre I listen to, but you can't deny my reasoning for choosing that bird."

"Couldn't you have chosen a better bird? Was I that obnoxious?" My shoulders slouch because the humour isn't lost on me. "I suppose you're right; that bird suits me. Just don't let anyone hear you use it. We don't need the media to pounce all over that. The nickname will haunt my career."

"Never. It's yours and mine only." Arrow unfastens his seatbelt and leans toward me. His fingers grip the back of my neck and pull my lips to his. His kiss is tender, warm, and filled with promise. His lips leave mine and he whispers through a wicked grin. "Besides, from the moment I met you, I wanted you naked as a Jaybird."

CHAPTER TWENTY-TWO

By one-thirty, Jade's at home and already looks more relaxed than I've ever seen her. She was wearing a thin pair of shorts and a lazy tee. Her socks were fluffy and somehow stayed white no matter where she walked in this huge house. We've laughed and joked, talked about everything people can talk about, yet the conversation of where this thing between her and I is going was avoided. There are issues hanging between us that neither wants to bring up.

After we ate some of the delicious meals her maid prepared, Jade needed time on her own, so she set off to her room to soak in her huge tub. She didn't invite me to join her, which has me wanting to pout, but she's been through a lot these past twenty-four hours, so I'll let her be.

With the phone pressed to my ear, I move my duffel from the blue quilt spread over the king-sized bed onto a white loveseat in the corner. I chose this guest room because it's the closest one to the main living area which is between here and Jade's bedroom.

This room was designed with simplicity in mind. Small white nightstands positioned on either side at the head of the bed each contain a lamp and a coaster to set a cup on. The hardwood floor is draped in a lengthy fuzzy blue rug that'll be the last thing my feet touch before I slide onto the thick mattress.

After two rings, Fixer answers. "Hey, Arrow. How're things playing out over there?"

Should I tell him all about my infatuation with Jade? Probably not. He offered me this job. If he knew I fucked the mark, he'd be less likely to assign me to guard anyone else in the future. My stomach sinks when I'm reminded that one day I'll have to leave Jade.

"We haven't found the stalker yet. We're still working on it."

"Any threats recently?" His voice echoes as if he's in a large room. What sounds like a pan or plate coming to rest on something hard confirms he's in his kitchen. I've been there many times and hate the way it feels so much colder than the comfort of my log cabin.

My hand slides up the wall in the bathroom in search of a light switch. The room wakes with warm lighting, and I'm not surprised at how large the room is. The shower is surrounded in glass so spotless I want to press my hand to it to see if it's actually present, but the bidet and toilet separated from the rest of the room by a smoky glass divider has me shaking my head. How much money was spent on this suite to offer guests such luxuries.

A walk-in closet beside the bathroom is almost the size of my bedroom at home. What house guest would bring so much stuff to fill this closet? If they did, I'd say they've moved in. Everything I own wouldn't fill this closet.

His voice lowers to keep our conversation from his family. "There's been no physical contact with the stalker?"

"No. There hasn't been an attempt. In a way, I wish they'd try. At the very least then I'd get a look at them, and if they got close enough, I could get my hands on the fucker."

Fixer's quiet for several breaths before I hear a door close. His voice no longer echoes. "All right. What's going on?" He knows me so well he can hear something in my tone I don't hear.

Hesitation will only prove his spidey senses are spot on, so I don't. "What do you mean?"

"You know what I mean. Something's going on." His throat clears before he sighs. "She's a beautiful woman, if the images I've seen aren't too modified. So, are you sleeping with her?"

Steadying my voice, I reply knowing it's not technically a lie. "I have not slept with her."

"Mhm. But have you fucked her?"
Well, shit!

My hesitation gives him the answer he wasn't hoping for.

"Dammit, Arrow… What the fuck are you doing, man? She's vulnerable. You're taking care of her. What are you going to do when she falls for you and you have to leave? You know you have to leave eventually; the sooner the better now that I know about your extracurriculars." It's obvious Fixer's pissed off even with his tone smooth and low because he sounds paternal.

"She's going to fall for you because you're her knight in shining armour. You're the man sent to rescue her from the bastard set on taking her out."

My snicker halts his words, and I can picture his head tilting while his scarred eyes squint.

"Jesus! You make it sound like we're in a fucking romance novel."

"If this were a romance novel, you'd marry her and live happily ever after. That option is impossible, and you know it. You live two different lives."

My thumb and forefinger pinch the crest of my nose to ease my growing stress headache. These are issues that plague my thoughts, and I can't see a way around it. Every scenario I come up with forces one of us to give up what we love; her the career she's built, and me the serenity I found in the forest.

"It's not a commitment thing. We know this isn't permanent. I like her. She likes me, but only for my tongue and my cock." I laugh, and he groans.

"Fuck off. You're a dick."

I chuckle as I make my way to my bag. "That's true, and yet you still call me brother."

Fixer laughs deep and breathy. "You'll always be my brother no matter how much I want to slap you for fucking your mark."

My smile dwindles. "Yeah. You're probably right."

I use my free hand to unpack the small bag and hang the two suit jackets, three dress shirts, and a pair of dress pants. I'm thankful the hotel offered laundry service, or I would've been doing laundry in the sink. They bear some wrinkles from being folded, so I'll need to iron them later.

My toiletries are set on the long bathroom counter bearing two sinks. Why two sinks? I never understood why rich people can't spit their toothpaste into the same damn sink?

My socks and underwear are set in the top drawer of the small dresser in the closet and my runners and dress shoes are set on one of many empty shelves. My bag is stuffed in the corner of the closet on the hardwood floor.

None of the floors groaned when I walked on. This makes me nervous. How will I hear anyone approaching? It'd be so easy to sneak up on me when I'm sleeping. Are the floors in Jade's room silent, too? Damn rich people and their perfectly sturdy homes.

"Did you find anything pertinent to this case?"

He grumbles making it obvious he's found something. "Listen, you'd better be careful with her. She's been through some shit and probably carries some heavy baggage."

"I know. She told me." Baggage doesn't even cover it with this woman. She has an 18-wheeler full of baggage.

"Just be careful. Okay? Don't let it get too deep; she's vulnerable even if she puts up a tough front."

"All right. You've said your peace, but I've got to go. I just wanted to touch base," I say and leave the guest room to make my rounds through the house.

He grumbles again. "I'll give you a call if I find out anything."

"Take care of those little angels of yours, Fixer."

"Not angels today. The little imps are riding my last nerve, but I love them. Talk soon."

I slide my phone in the back pocket of my jeans and decide to iron my clothes.

Afterward, I walk sock-footed—which Jade insists on—through the wide living room with a grand piano in one corner, a television larger than any I've ever seen hovering over a fireplace just as large, and several white leather sofas with numerous pillows in varying colours ranging from furry to silky. The entire room is painted in a desert sand including the tall ceiling.

A wide glass railed staircase arcs to follow the curve in the north facing wall. Almost every wall is made from thick panes of glass to allow the darkness of the night to shade the gardens and paths beyond them.

My feet pad silently over the cool cork floor. It's nice and I ponder getting some for the cabin.

A two-meter-tall picture on the south wall is of Jade staring directly into the camera lens with so much concentration in her eyes I wonder what she was thinking when the shutter closed. Her shadowy eye make-up is smeared below her eyes as if she had been crying. She's nude, sitting with her legs crossed in front of her chest as one arm loosely hugs them. Her fingers rest on her cheek with the exception of her the tip of her pinky resting on her bottom lip misshaping it. It's set on a white background which makes the wildly swashed, multi-colours of paint dried on her skin pop. Her hair is messed as if she'd just been through a sexual romp or an unrested sleep.

It's beautiful and tragic, and I can't tear my eyes away.

"I love that photo."

I spin to see Jade standing behind me, staring at the image, with her arms crossed over her chest while her serene smile warms her freshly washed face. She's so much prettier without all that black make-up obscuring her natural beauty.

My heart pounds in my chest. It's too damn silent in this house. "How long have you been standing there?"

Jade's eyes drop to me before she turns, letting her arms swing at her sides, and starts toward the fully stocked bar surrounded with mirrors of varying shapes and sizes.

"Care for a drink?"

"No, thank you," I say and follow as her ass sways beneath burgundy lounge pants. "It's a nice photo. What were you thinking when it was taken?"

My forearms rest on the cold, stainless steel bar top.

She pours herself a glass of red wine and takes a sip before recapping the bottle and resting it on the bar. Her eyes don't leave the image before a sigh eases from her.

"Are you hungry?" She's changing the subject.

My lips lift to one side as a breathy chuckle rides my words. "One day, you'll tell me about the photo."

She scoffs and flutters her eyelashes. "But isn't it more fun using your imagination?"

"Call me curious," I say and rest my ass on a tall black and stainless-steel barstool. "Come here."

Jade's face contorts. "Bossy much?"

Her eyes follow my tongue as it savours my bottom lip. "Yes, Jaybird, I'm very bossy. Now get your perfect ass over here."

To prove she's not my puppet and won't fall easily at my whim, she takes a long sip of wine before complying to my demand. Her hips exaggerate their natural sway as her teeth pinch her lip. She sets between my spread thighs and smooths her voice into a sensual whisper. "Yes, sir. You called for me? What can I do for you?"

Her tiny but strong fingers pull at my belt before releasing the buckle. Neither of us will blink or look away as she roughly undoes my pants, reaches in, and fists my aching cock. Her cool hand squeezes and eases her grip as she steps close enough to press her t-shirt covered breasts against my chest. Wine scented breath brushes my neck as her whisper has my cock throbbing in her grasp.

"Let me please you, master. I need to taste you."

If I didn't have such a strong desire to fuck her against this bar, I'd probably cum in her hand.

My palms hug her cheeks and force her mouth onto mine. She tastes like red wine. One hand skims down to her throat and grips around it with a tiny bit of squeeze to feel her out. I need to know if this will freak her out, or if she'll submit to it? Jade is someone I'll need to handle with kid gloves until I know her triggers and can avoid them.

My words growl from my chest as the thought of pushing my cock into her mouth has my blood racing. "Then get on your knees and open your mouth."

Without a sound, she takes a step back and lowers onto her knees. Her hands rest on her waist.

I have to adjust my cock to allow me to crouch without breaking my erection. My palms are up, so she places her hands in mine. I guide them to her thighs and lay them flat. "When I ask you to get on your knees, you'll sit on your heels and place your palms on your thighs."

"I didn't know there would be instructions," she says with a quirky grin.

I wink before I rise and walk around her. "Take off your shirt."

She turns her face to look over her shoulder at me before she complies, tossing the shirt aside and resuming her hand positions.

Next, I gently remove the fabric elastic from her hair and set it on the bar.

My words flow unrushed. "Tell me why I should allow you to suck my cock."

Her shoulders rise and drop before her head shakes. "Because I asked to."

"Good answer but that's not why I'll allow it." My palm strokes the top of her head to help her thick her hair to fall down over her ears. "You called me *master*. I like that."

Standing before her with my crotch inches from her face, I reach into my pants and sigh when my cock springs free. While she watches, my fist grips my length and my thumb glides over the globe of precum easing from the tip. It smears over the tip before I bring it to my mouth and lick it off.

She tries to lean in, but I step back.

"Patience, Jaybird."

My palm eases from the top of her head and down her cheek until my index finger brushes along her bottom lip. "Use only your mouth."

Jade nods as her glassy eyes catch the white led light beaming from below the bar. Her tongue coats her lips before she starts at the base and glides her tongue along the left side of my cock up to the tip, which she purposely avoids. Her face turns to repeat on the ride side to leave it slick with saliva.

She's so fucking beautiful as she looks up at me with a strong sense of confidence in her ability to drive me wild by her talent with fellatio.

I nearly spew my load on her cheek when her hot, wet tongue presses to the base of my testicles. Her lips hug my length as they agonizingly slowly ease up to the loose patch of tender flesh near the tip. She sucks it gently and teases it with her tongue.

Not wanting her to stop, the tips of my fingers brush over her head as my head tips back.

Holy fuck! My head's spinning.

She engulfs the head of my cock into her mouth as her lips form a seal.

A moan steals my breath. "Oh, fuck. Jaybird—"

In one fell swoop, my cock is buried down her throat while her nose presses to my belly. I'm not hung like a porn star, but I'm no schlump when it comes to penis size. Her taking me so deeply and holding me without choking nearly steals my sanity.

I watch her lips glide along my steely length. There's no set tempo to her pace, and I don't know if that's better or worse than when she pauses to make the longing for her to continue.

It's damn near impossible to resist spewing when she finally does take me down her throat and swallows.

"Slow down, Jaybird. If you make me cum, I can't fuck you."

Her mouth releases me as she reaches up, wraps her pretty fingers around my shaft, and slowly strokes me. "And what if I want you to cum down my throat?"

Lord have mercy!

My fingers weave into her hair and tip her head back. I can lean down and glare into her emerald eyes. My hand covers hers, stopping it mid-stroke. "What did I tell you about only using your mouth?"

Jade's eyes search mine for several seconds before she fights back a smile. "Oops!"

I chuckle despite my desire to remain in control of myself.

My fingers slip under her armpits to help her to her feet. In a blink, my fingers are wrapped in her hair and bend her over the stool I had been sitting in. She gasps and pants as if my speed startled her.

"I'm going to spank you for misbehaving. I told you not to do something and you did it anyway."

Two of my fingers slip beneath the waistband along her skin and slide left to right as

I inch her loose-fit pants down her thighs. She isn't wearing panties which has me wanting to bury my face in her ass.

"How many times should I spank you?" My palm strokes over each perfect ass cheek.

She's a bit sarcastic in her answer. "As many times as you think such an offense warrants, I suppose."

Jade stiffens when the heat of my palm leaves her right ass cheek. To prolong the anticipation, I wait until her breath leaves her.

Swat!

She gasps before she holds her breath.

"Is one enough?" I ask knowing full well one is definitely not enough.

Her head shakes even though I'm still fisting her hair. "No."

Swat! Swat! Swat!

"How about four?"

Her breaths come fast, short, and a bit nasally. "No."

I give her six more swats, alternating cheeks while she grips the legs of the stool.

"Is that enough?"

Believing she'll say she's had enough, I'm taken back by her whisper. "No."

Four more swats over the growing welts on her ass have her gasping and shaking. Two fingers plunge into her dripping wet vagina, and she cries out. Her hips thrust back against my digits as they arc inside her, pushing toward the front.

"More… Please," she murmurs.

I release her hair to pluck the condom from my back pocket. My fingers leave her pussy and dive into my mouth to suck them clean before rolling the condom over my length. I line up against her folds, and she looks over her shoulder but doesn't try to look at me.

"Fuck me, master. Fuck me too hard. Please."

Trust me, little bird, that's exactly what I'm going to do.

With one thrust, I bury balls deep inside her. My hearing grows hollow as if my brain has forgotten how to hear. My breath catches when her walls tighten around my shaft as if desperate to keep me connected to her.

I thrust--hard. So hard! Her hands brace her head from slamming into the bar as the stool slides beneath her. The outlines of the sculpted muscles in her back grow more prominent as her pussy tightens even more. She's close to coming. Can I withhold my own climax when she does? I intend to make her cum at least once more before I sit her on this stool and suck her clit until she comes apart. When she's done, I'll carry her to the sofa and sit her on my lap while I spoil her with kisses.

The doorbell chimes and we both jolt upright. My cock slides free of her and there's immediate regret in the loss of the strangulation.

I may have to kill whoever is at the door.

"They'll go away," Jade promises before resuming her position over the stool.

The chime rings about the room a second time just before the sing-song rings to alert the door's opening.

Fuck!

I bend forward and yank my pants from my knees, and we both pull at our clothes in a panic as we try to rush out of sight and around the mirrored wall beside the bar. She laughs as the elastic waistband of her pants slaps against her tummy. My underwear didn't come with my pants, so I have to battle to get them in place before whoever so rudely disturbed us sees me.

Jade's hair is messed from my grip, her lips are puffy and red, and her face glistens with a thin coat of sweat. Her cheeks are flushed, and her hands shake as she runs them over her disheveled locks.

She's the first to round the wall into sight which pisses me off. We don't know who came in or if they're friendly. The only calming factor is they used a key, which only a few select people hold.

I can't zip my pants because my erection is too fucking hard. The condom slips from my fingers as I'm aggressively pulling it off and it snaps against the tip of my cock. A rush of pain forces my lungs to empty with a huff. It hurt so much my erection is quickly subsiding, so it was worth it… I think.

A peppy woman's voice I've become familiar with echoes through the large room. "There you are! What's up, girlie?"

Jade's voice is higher than normal. "Oh, my god! What are you doing here? I thought you went home."

Kisses can be heard as I imagine the two are feigning kisses to each other's cheeks as I've witnessed them do.

"With everything going on, I didn't want you to be alone. I'm worried. If something happens to you, and I wasn't here, I'd never forgive myself. Besides, I can work from just about anywhere."

"Oh! Well—" Jade doesn't sound excited for Rachel's surprise visit. "Come on in."

What the fuck? In Vancouver, she said she had work to do in Windsor—a four-hour drive away.

My hope was to have Jade all to myself, but I know I have no right to claim her as mine.

My defiant cock has a mind of its own and aches for a release.

As much as I hate how quiet the floors are, at this moment, I'm grateful as I make my way down the hallway toward a bathroom. With my back leaning against the closed and locked door, I drop my pants to my knees, spit on my palm, and grip my shaft.

Jade's thick, dark hair wrapped in my fist.

The way she looked at me when my cock was down her throat.

Jade's incredible pussy.

My fist pounds over my length for merely a minute before my eyes squeeze so tightly, I see stars. Spasms ripple through me as I catch the spurting semen into my other hand. The last shot of ejaculation has my head falling back against the door with a thud.

After cleaning myself up, I take a soothing breath before opening the door and heading in the direction of the women's laughter. If I'm lucky enough, I can pass them without being noticed and hide in the guest quarters until… Until when? Rachel's probably staying here. There go all my plans for Jade.

CHAPTER TWENTY-THREE

Jade

"Do you want a drink?" Whether she says yes or no makes no difference. I need a drink—something very fucking strong. Instead of being relaxed after sex, I'm wound tighter than a jack-in-the-box. I imagine Rachel turning the silver handle while wearing a wicked grin and holding the top down to prevent the explosive fun. She doesn't notice my snicker.

Where the hell is Arrow? Rachel made a bad impression on him when she hit on him the first time she met him. How will he react if he reveals himself with an obvious hard-on bulging his jeans? The way her eyes scale men, she'll definitely notice. Hopefully he stays out of site until he's soft.

"Wine would be nice." Rachel slides the stool Arrow had me bent over closer to the bar and sits on it.

It takes all I have to restrain my laughter.

"Is white okay? I could use something cold." Before she agrees, I've poured some in the first crystal wine glass I bought in Switzerland from a couple who handmade them while I watched. It fascinated me how delicate they were during the process.

"Um, yeah. I had some shitty red on the plane. They were out of white. I chose to drink water after the first glass, but water didn't cut it after the day I had." Her head rests in her palm as her elbow meets the bar top.

The glass seems to hum as I slide it along the bar top toward her. She lifts it to her mouth and takes a big gulp. "Oh, that's good. I could use five more of these."

Her head tips back and side-to-side as she rolls her shoulders.

I should ask. A good friend would ask. "What's going on?"

We walk to the sofa, and she sits first. "I stopped in to see mom and she was in a mood. She can be such a bitch. Your parents were outside. They say hello, by the way. You should call them. They miss you."

My ass plops onto the sofa as my legs curl up and my arm rests on the back, so I can face her. My pussy is still so wet my labia are slipping together. It's a rude reminder that we have yet to see Arrow. Where the fuck is he?

She copies my position, so we can look at each other. Following a long blink, she takes a long look at my face. "Why are you so flushed?"

"Flushed?" The backs of my fingers press to my cheek and then my forehead while I feign confusion. If I can fake a convincing smile, I can do this, too. "I don't know. I was just in the music room when the doorbell rang, so I rushed to answer the door. Maybe that's why."

She seems satisfied with my response, but the sneaky smirk clouding her expression has my tummy feeling hollow because I know the next question. "So, your hot bodyguard… Do you miss him? Or should I say, do you miss his cock?"

Arrow still hasn't rounded the corner, so hopefully he can't hear our conversation. "I—I, um… It's not like that. I mean—" My breath won't leave me no matter how much I wish it would.

As if on cue, Arrow rounds the wall beside the bar.

Rachel follows my line of sight. With a gaped mouth, her face swings from him to me and back to him. She shifts so she can molest him with her eyes as he nears us.

"Oh, he's here. Is he living with you? Moving a little fast on my girl, is he?"

"It's not like that. This isn't permanent." I whisper so he won't hear. =

No way in hell is he going to live here forever. I'm not the type of woman who needs a man to feel safe or complete.

I can't blame her for staring since I'm hypnotized by the way his strong thighs and calves tighten with each step. His focus is on me as if Rachel isn't even here.

Before his eyes shift to her, he says, "Rachel, how long will you be staying?"

She ticks her tongue off the roof of her mouth. "Rude, much? I mean, if you think I'm a danger, you can frisk me. Better yet, I think you *should* frisk me. I could be hiding a dangerous weapon somewhere on my person. I'll give you five minutes to find it." When he doesn't react, Rachel stands and spreads her arms from her sides while they stare each other down. "Okay, ten minutes. Make sure you're thorough."

Arrow makes no move toward her. He doesn't even blink. Nearly a minute passes before she gives up and drops her arms.

"It's your loss." She shrugs, picks up her glass, and resumes her position on the sofa. "That could've been fun."

The way she winks at me makes my stomach tense, and I want to hit her.

What the fuck? Am I jealous? I'm not a jealous person. I've never cared enough about a partner to give a shit who they want to fuck or who wants to fuck them.

Arrow lifts his phone to open the screen as if she said nothing to him. "If you promise to stay inside the house, I'll let you be."

"What will you do in the meantime? I mean, you don't have to stay in your room."

His steely-gaze heats my blood. "I'm going downstairs to work off some tension."

Did he just smirk at me?

Picturing him shirtless in shorts while he punches the heavy bag and does sit-ups on the incline bench as sweat glistens over his skin, isn't helping with my vaginal wetness.

"Well, have a good workout." What else could I say? *I want you to do some push-ups over me while we both get in a good cardio workout?*

"Mhm."

Rachel's eyes follow his butt as he strides from the room. "He is sexy fucking man. I mean, come on now—that ass, those thighs? Tell me he fucks like he's seeking revenge or something even more wicked."

A glance over my shoulder proves he's not within earshot. "Yeah, he—he's good."

Why does my face feel hot? I can't blame the race from the music room this time.

"Oh, my God! You're blushing! The all-powerful Jade, AKA Phoebe Moore, is blushing like a high school girl after her first kiss. Wow! I never thought I'd see the day."

I scoff and toss a pillow at her, nearly knocking the glass from her hand.

What is it about Arrow? He's just a guy. A guy who knows how to twist me around his little finger. A man I allow to play with me for his pleasure. Actually, he seems to prefer to play with me for my pleasure. He makes me lose control of myself and temporarily forget who I am and all that entails. My tummy drops out like I'm soaring in a car over train tracks.

My head shakes far too much, but I can't seem to stop it. "Shut up and drink your wine. I need to get drunk."

Rachel puckers her lips and lifts her glass to cheers. "Let's make that happen."

We both tip our glasses back and empty them of every drop of wine. She hands me her glass, and I take them to the bar to refill them. Just as I open the fridge to retrieve the bottle, Arrow strolls from the hall leading from the guest suites. He paces through the main space while we watch his every step. His face is tilted down at his phone until he passes the sofa and struts nearer to me when he looks straight at me.

His loose-fit yellow and black shorts come to his knees and reveal calf muscles tense without effort. A towel droops over his shoulder partially covering his sleeveless black t-shirt snug enough where I could count his abs.

I swallow hard when he passes the bar as he winks and glides the tip of his tongue over his warm, inviting lips. Did it just get hot in here?

As I step over Rachel's discarded shoes, I hand her the filled glass, and she takes a gulp.

She leans in and whispers, "Can we go watch him work out?"

Can I punch you in the face?

"Oh, we have better things to do." I stand and stretch my arm before gesturing a huge wave. "Come with me."

"Like what?" she says as she stands to follow me. "What are we doing?"

"You'll see," I say and lead her to the spa room. Hanging on wall hooks are a dozen bikinis in varying colours and styles. "Pick one."

She picks a hot pink string bikini, and I choose my favourite suit with the red thong bikini. Why that one? Because it'll drive Arrow insane when he sees me in it. First, I'd better make sure I don't still have handprints on my ass.

We decided to bask under the heat of the early evening sun on floaties in the pool long enough to suck back several bottles of wine. I have a tolerance for alcohol, but Rachel is more of a lightweight and didn't finish her last glass. She swayed a bit the last time she got out to go into the pool-house to pee. I laughed, of course. What are friends for but to humiliate you at every turn?

Sitting upright on her floatie with her calves dangling in the water, she breaks the silence which had me lost in pleasant thoughts I can't recall.

"So, are you and Arrow a *thing*?"

Shrouding the sun from my eyes with my hand, I turn to look at her through the only eye daring enough to accept the brightness of the early evening sun reflecting off the water. "*Thing?*"

Her hand waves wildly. "*Relationship*; whatever you want to call it! What's up with it?"

What's up with our relationship… That's a head-scratcher. I have no idea where we stand. As soon as the stalker is exposed and dealt with, Arrow will get on a plane and soar out of my life forever. He'll go back to wherever it is he's from and live his best life—without me. It hurts to think about it. Eventually, everyone leaves me except for the people I pay to stick around because they're aiding my career. As long as the cash-cow is coughing up dough, they aren't going anywhere. But Arrow *will* leave; this I know to be true. It's the last thing I want to think about when I'm trying to enjoy a drunken buzz with my bestie.

"Nothing's *up* with it. We're fucking around, that's all." I lie back, close my eyes, and drop my arm to my side to allow my fingertips to dangle in the cool saltwater.

Rachel sentences start low and end in a higher-pitch. "I don't know. Seems like you two have a good thing going. I mean, bada-bing, baby!"

Please let it go.

"I think I have a sunburn." My finger brushes over the skin on my arm but I'm a bit too drunk to know if I am burnt. My hand dangles over the edge of the floaty and dips in the cool salt water. Rachel's back is to me and her skin is pink, so I scoop the water and fling it onto Rachel's back.

She jolts as if I've electrocuted her. "Jesus! Fuck, that's cold! You're mean!"

I laugh hard—likely an effect of the wine. "We should get out. Wait until you slide off the floatie. It's going to feel like we're dipping ourselves in water better suited for polar bears."

She groans and drops one leg up to her thigh in the water and whimpers. "I'm not going to like this."

As I slide into the water up to my waist, a shudder runs through me, stealing my breath. "Oh, my God!" I hop with my elbows raised as if not getting them wet will make me less cold.

Rachel is first to the stairs and rushes out creating waves that wash over my breasts and steal my breath once again.

I follow her up the steps, and she hands me a giant swim towel. We hug the towels to our bodies and laugh as our chins shiver.

"Do you want another glass?" I ask, and Rachel rolls her eyes.

"If I have another glass, I'll pass out right here." She points to the inviting bamboo lounger sprawled under the warm sun.

Quickly, we dry off and sink onto them. The sun does its duty to warm our flesh and my heart. I love the sun. I could sleep under it if I was sure I wouldn't burn crispy.

A shadow darkens the red behind my eyelids, and I open my eyes to give Rachel shit, but she's still on her lounger. Arrow stares down at me with his fists on her hips and skin glistening with sweat. He looks like a fucking god standing shirtless with the orange hue of the setting sun kissing him from his left side which deepens the valleys and brightens the mounds of muscle on his tummy.

If I had one wish, it'd be to have him drop his shorts and lower himself between my legs. Kiss me with enough passion to melt the sun and fill me full of everything he has to offer.

"Jade." He speaks with a drawl like a father does when he's about to question his child over something bad they did.

My tone is soft and reeks of innocence. "Yes, Arrow?"

"You're outside."

I sit up quickly and turn my head side-to-side while my jaw sags. "Oh, my God! You're right; we are outside. That's very observant of you. Quick, what colour is the sky?"

His nose twitches like he does when he's holding back from giving me shit. "I asked you to stay indoors. Do you remember that conversation?"

My head nods overdramatically. "Mhm. I do."

Rachel laughs so hard she snorts, which has me laughing, too. Arrow *isn't* laughing.

"Do you remember what you said when I asked you to stay indoors?" His chest expands and shrinks with deep breaths, and I want to run my fingers down it.

My finger presses to my chin as my eyes search the sky above his head. "Yes. I asked—and I'm paraphrasing—What will you be doing after you leave us alone, and that you didn't have to stay in your bedroom?"

The louder Rachel laughs the more difficult it is not to erupt into a childlike laughing fit.

Arrow snuffs his nose before his palm rubs the top of his head in frustration. "In the house; both of you. Now."

Rachel's laugh dies. "But it's so nice out here. Stay with us. A big, strong man like you could protect us from potential danger if it leaps over the tall cement wall."

"Yeah. Besides, you look like you could use a swim." I stand, press my hands to his pecs and give him a shove, but he doesn't fall into the pool. He barely even sways. I thought I was stronger than that. Damn wine!

My finger rises to point at him, but before I can tell him that he has no right to boss me around, the world spins, and I'm upside down looking at the small of his back. Upside down and wine doesn't bode well. To distract myself from the sudden desire to vomit, I tickle his sides with my fingernails.

"Coochie coochie coo!" I have no idea if Arrow laughs or not because Rachel's laughter dies when I hear a splash.

I push off his back to lift my face to see what happened, but Arrow spins so he can see.

Rachel's squeal drowns the loud swooshes of water as she swims to get out.

Arrow's voice is so deep it rumbles my entire body. "Stop fucking around. If you don't want to be locked out, get your ass in the house."

She sounds angry when she says, "I fell in. Don't be such a fucking asshole. Seriously, are you my father? *No!* You are *not!*" Rachel's words slur badly. "And Jade's not a doll you can toss over your shoulder and carry to your bed like a fucking neanderthal."

I laugh as the blood rushes to my head making my eyelids feel fat beneath my sagging cheeks. "He's not taking me to his bed. Wait! You aren't taking me to your bed, are you?"

A crack of his palm lands on my exposed ass cheek, and I squeal. Why did he do that? Rachel is here and there's no doubt she heard it. My butt cheek is going to have a red handprint which is impossible to hide behind a thong bikini.

"Stop it!" My complaint doesn't sound legit to anyone since my laugh broke through the attempted seriousness. "You can't spank me. Like Rachel said, you aren't my daddy."

Another swat has my back arching as my hand reaches around to cover my ass, which is impossible when each of his steps shifts me slightly. Rachel is still trying to get out of the pool with her glass filled with pool water and a heavy, drench towel dragging behind her in the water. She's laughing at herself as she stumbles about, trying to pull the towel out of the pool.

Arrow's voice rumbles. "If you behaved, Jaybird, I wouldn't have to spank you."

My whisper earns me his chuckle. "So, you're saying I should be a bad girl more often?"

Fingers slip beneath the thong and glide down the crack of my ass to discover I'm slick between my folds. I can't deny the way he's so domineering is getting me hot—the wine helps, too.

His finger dips into me before trailing down to my clitoris. My legs are closed which has my labia pressed together, but he has no difficulty in finding the sweet spot. His digit glides just right over my clit allowing the hood to pull back and forth over the tiny bundle of nerves.

Oh, hell yeah!

"Quiet." His chest rumbled despite the whisper.

Was I moaning? I don't even care right now. Just make me cum!

I grip his waist tightly and try to spread my legs to give him better access, but his other arm is wrapped around my knees, pinning them against his chest.

"Oh, god!" My lips pinch between my teeth to stop any more words from sneaking out. I'm so close. *So. Fucking. Close.*

His finger pulls away and my thong is snapped back into place.

"No! Please. Please, Arrow. Please, don't stop."

The garden door opens with a click, and he steps inside. I'm set on my feet and the world spins, weakening my legs. Before I can steady myself, Arrow has me wedding style in his arms. The door shuts with a thud and the metal on metal ensures the lock is set.

"Don't lock Rachel outside," I beg.

Rachel's voice is higher pitched when she's drunk. "I'm right here. I'm wet, but I'm here. I fucking fell in. It's goddamn cold!"

Arrow looks down at me with furrowed brows. "You shouldn't drink so much. Unstable people are vulnerable. Someone is targeting you. Don't you understand the gravity of the situation? You put yourself in danger by going outside. Fucking hell, Phoebe."

In an instant, my joyous drunken night goes to shit. "You don't call me that! Phoebe died a long time ago."

Pitying eyes lock onto mine. He knows my past is coming back to haunt me and the concern weighs heavily on his expression. I have enough self-pity to last me a lifetime and don't need to see it on someone else, so I look at his chest instead. If he thinks I'm going to smile to make him feel less concerned for me, he'll be waiting a long time. I'm not responsible for his feelings. If he wants to pity me, he can fucking do it somewhere else. I'm tired and want to go to bed.

Fuck him for ruining a perfectly wonderful evening!

CHAPTER TWENTY-FOUR

Arrow

Jade turns her back to me the moment I lie her on her bed. More than anything, I'd love to run my fingers through her lush hair strewn across the silky white pillowcase, but she'll only push me away.

Now I know calling her Phoebe when she's intoxicated is a horrible idea. It's something I should have thought about. There's nothing like a good drunkenness to rehash old traumas or reawaken anger. For this reason, I rarely have more than two drinks.

For some time after I was discharged, alcohol and pot were my vices. I'd go weeks without a drink or toke, but something would happen to set me off and I'd fall back over that edge. Intoxication was to a point; pushed past the happy, fluffy brain stage and I'd sink into the dark pit of sorrow. I'd rage and break things, fight in bars, or curl up in a corner of my house with my loaded gun at my chin while crying like a baby.

I was desperate to pull the trigger to end it all, but every time my finger would rest on the trigger, I'd see the love of my life smile. She looked beautiful with her wide smile, green eyes, and blonde hair piled high on her head in a loose bun that never seemed to contain her hair. Her singsong laugh convinced me to lower my gun. My love wouldn't allow me to join her in the afterlife—whatever that may consist of.

Jade's quiet and still, her breaths come in easy tempo. After pulling a blanket over her to keep her warm and to stop my attention from locking onto the thin strip of bathing suit material dipping into the folds of her ass cheeks. If she weren't drunk as fuck, my finger would follow the fabric, pull it aside, and dip into one of her holes.

But she's far too drunk, and that means she can't consent. I'm all about consent. Besides, she's unconscious and necrophilia isn't my thing.

With a glass of water, two aspirin, and the plastic garbage bin she kept in the bathroom beside her bed, I closed her door and returned to the living room. Rachel's sprawled on the sofa with one foot on the floor, the other bent and propped on the backrest. One arm is under her head while the other dangles over the edge of the cushion as if she were reaching for her phone on the coffee table and passed out.

If the woman didn't irritate me so much, I'd enjoy the view, but seeing her thong barely covering her vagina doesn't interest me in the slightest.

Do I not like Rachel because she's always getting in the way of my alone time with my Jaybird, or is it the way she looks at me like I'm an ice cream on a hot sunny day? She knows Jade is my interest, yet she offers herself up to me. It's wrong. What best friend does that? Fixer would never do that to me, and I'd never even consider his wife as more than a sister even though there's no blood relation. She's with Fixer, and I have no business trying to get between them.

Maybe Jade and Rachel have shared men in the past. Are they a regular tag team? If that's the case, they'll be sadly disappointed when I refuse that opportunity. I'm a one-woman man. If I'm with her, I'm with *her*, and she belongs to me.

Rachel can't stay on the damn sofa. If she throws up, I'm not fucking cleaning it!

She groans and curses at me when I pick her up wedding style. Her drunken attempt to slap me fails due to there being two of me. I jostle her to balance her dead weight, and I'm met with another slur. "You think you're all that. Well, you ain't shit. I mean, you have the whole *I'm dangerous as fuck so don't fuck with me* vibe perfected, and that's sexy as hell. But… If you think Jade's going to keep you around, you'll be sadly disappointed, mister. She loves 'em and leaves 'em all the time. It's how she is; you won't change her." Her skinny finger pokes my cheek.

"So don't think you can change her. She'll send you packing as soon as you catch her stalker. *If* you catch her stalker. They've eluded you pretty well so far."

"That's enough, Rachel."

"Fuck you, that's enough. Canada's a free country, and I can say whatever I want."

Her arms wrap around my neck and hold so tightly my face is filled with blood. For someone so drunk, she's quick to shuffle her tiny body until her legs are wrapped around my waist. I'm a strong guy, but even I can't contain this squiggly woman.

Puffy lips press to the nape of my neck, and I bounce her to make her stop.

"Stop that, Rachel."

She slurs with sexy intent. "Come on, baby. You can have me. I won't tell. Besides, Phoebe won't care. Take me to bed and sink into me."

"Never going to happen. Stop or I'll drop you on your ass." My menacing tone should have halted her, but she's relentless. She knows her grip is firm, and I can't pull her off me unless I hurt her. I won't do that.

Heat from her pussy over my crotch stirs my dick. It has a mind of its own and its nature is greedy. She moans as she rubs her clit against my Adonis belt. I have no choice but to grab her bare ass and hold her so tightly against me that she can't jerk herself off. Like fuck am I going to allow this woman an orgasm, even if I do nothing to contribute to her efforts.

My grip is so firm she's sure to bruise.

As quickly as I can, I walk her to her bedroom.

"Let go. Come on, baby, you know you want to fuck me. Your cock wants me."

"Shut the fuck up, Rachel."

She giggles. "Oh, a bossy man. I like that. Tell me what to do to please you, sir." Her laugh is ridiculously high-pitched. *Fucking drunk girls!*

"Shut the fuck up."

"That, I cannot do, but I'll gladly suck your cock." Glassy eyes with hooded lids gaze into mine. "Would you like to hold my hair and bury your cock in my throat?"

Grrrr! Yes, but no.

My cock is rigid as a pipe, betraying me like the prick it is.

"Your cock wants me." Her hands grip the back of my head, and she pulls it toward her, aiming for a kiss.

I try to push her off me when we reach her bed, but she will not release her hands from the back of my neck or her legs from around my waist with her feet locked at my back.

"Fuck, you're strong for a skinny little thing."

Rachel seems pleased with my comment and smiles despite her bottle lip nipped in her teeth. "My pussy is strong, too. I once made a guy cum without moving my body, just using my pussy muscles. Want to test it out?"

This fucking cunt has my cock desperately hoping I'll take her up on her offer. A hot pussy, deep and tight… *Fuck!*

My voice is hostile and deep. "Let go, Rachel."

Drunken eyes with slow blinks and heavy lids gaze into mine while she licks her lips. I don't want to hurt her but she's riding my last nerve. If I convince her I want her, maybe she'll release me.

My eyes grow dark and menacing and my voice drops to emphasize my advance. "If you let go and flip onto your hands and knees, I'll fuck you like I fucking hate you, because woman, I kind of do."

She debates with a twisted mouth as she searches my face to judge my truth. Her back arches as she leans back to rub her pussy on my crotch. Thankfully my shorts are able to contain my erection. *Treason!*

To gain her trust—still gripped on her ass—I pull her tighter to me and force her to rub against me. Her pussy's so hot it radiates through my thin fabric shorts. It would be so easy to pull my cock out and fuck her for my pleasure. I'd be cruel and not let her cum. Why? Because I'm a fucking asshole, and she's a backstabbing little cunt who doesn't deserve pleasure.

I lay her back on the bed, and she releases her arms to grip her B-cup breasts and pushes them together.

"Kiss me. and I'll let you fuck me." Her face is so close, her breath brushes over the scruff on my chin. "Make it good, motherfucker. Tell me you want me more than you want her. She has everything. She can share you. Don't you think so?"

Is she kidding me? She's supposed to be Jade's best friend, and she so easily will hurt her.

My head tilts away from her face and I stare her down with an evil leer. I can't help my lip from twitching as anger builds in my core. Before I realize what I'm doing, Rachel's staring up at me with wide eyes and my hand is around her throat. Nails dig into my forearm in her efforts to pull my hand away. It'd be so easy to crush her windpipe. Just one little squeeze in the right spot and her hyoid bone will crush. She's suffocating while I watch and nobody's here to save her.

A cold chill brushes up my spine and clarity has me blinking back from the edge. I wasn't here. I was back there—in the war—and it wasn't Rachel below me. The man who shot and killed a couple and their two young children was. How had I forgotten? That feeling of his hyoid crushing beneath my palm and the sounds he made as he smothered should haunt me always, and I'd suppressed it… Until now.

I'm a fuck psychopath!

I release her, and she gasps as she scampers up the bed to get away from me.

My head shakes as I slowly step backward hoping to erase what I've just done. I could've killed her. At that moment, I wanted to.

Maybe Fixer was right when he said I need therapy. He told me how it helped him get past the nightmares that had him burning in fire every night. The man he talked to was also a veteran who served overseas. The therapist lost an arm and a foot when he stepped on an IED, so he understands trauma. When this job is done, I'll make an appointment to see him—if I'm not in prison for assaulting Rachel.

"I'm sorry. *Fuck!* I'm so sorry, Rachel."

She stares at me in the darkness with her hand on her throat. Her voice is hoarse when she says, "It's okay. I deserved it. I—I'm a bitch." Her head shakes as she swallows before she retches and nothing comes out.

"Aw, fuck!"

As fast as my feet will carry me, I fetch the garbage bin from the bathroom and rush back to shove against her chest. If I'd been a second slower, her bed would be covered in vomit.

Her hair falls around her face as the alcohol she funnelled down her throat makes a reappearance with body stiffening force. Using a hair elastic on her nightstand, I breathe through my mouth while I pull her hair into a ponytail and twist the band enough to keep it back from her face. It's the least I can do for nearly killing her.

While she dry-heaves, I make my way through the house to Jade's room. Soft snores prove she's unconscious. The painkillers are in her bathroom, and Rachel is going to need them when she wakes with a head the size of New York jack-hammering inside her head.

With the pills and a glass of water from the bar, I return to see Rachel sitting on the cold tiled floor in her bathroom while she hugs the toilet seat. It's a good thing this bathroom is spotlessly clean. Otherwise, her cheek resting on the seat would be disgusting. She lifts onto her knees and vomits even more wine into the bowl. Her groan sounds hollow as it carries heavy regret.

I've never vomited from alcohol, but I've suffered from the ill effects of drinking more than my fill. There were days I wished vomiting was something my body was capable of. I can't remember ever puking my guts out, not even as a child. That's odd, isn't it?

"I'm leaving some pills and a glass of water on the sink. When you stop vomiting, take them with a few sips of water, and go to bed." After draping one of the bath towels over her back, I take my leave.

Once more, I check on Jade. The pills and water are untouched, and she's rolled onto her stomach. Moans that carry fear muffle into her pillow.

Knowing I shouldn't, I'm quiet as my runners cross the room until I'm standing at her bedside. Her face is mashed against the fabric as painful dreams invade her sleep. My finger brushes a stray lock of hair from her forehead.

My whisper is low so as not to wake her. "You're okay, Jade. You're safe. Nobody can hurt you. I won't let anyone hurt you."

Her moans stop but even with the shadows shrouding her face, a trail of tears dripping off her nose onto her pillow enrages my desire to beat the shit out of the motherfucker that hurt her.

Yes! That's what I can do. Maybe it's *him*. *He* could be the one. Please, let it be *him*. The many ways I can torture him have me grinning with excitement.

I stormed from her room, knowing she wouldn't wake from her drunken slumber, even if a high school band marched through her room playing off-key.

It's late, so I won't call Fixer, but I can email him.

Hey, Fixer. Do me a favour, please. Can you do your thing and get me an in-depth history on Phoebe Moore—AKA Jade? I know you've already searched for her, but I need to know everywhere she's lived when she was young, and if there are any claims against her foster families? Thanks in advance.

With a tap on the mouse pad, it sends. Now I wait. No—now I sleep. I'm fucking exhausted!

CHAPTER TWENTY-FIVE

Jade

My sleep was restless as suppressed memories awakened at the bottom of a bottle invaded my dreams. When sober, I'm better able to ignore them. I've had years of practice pretending my past never happened, but my sleeping hours break through my cold exterior.

Sunlight determined to scorch my retinas pours through the wall-to-wall windows. I usually close them using the remote before I go to bed, but I don't remember coming to bed. After some coffee and pills, it'll come back to me. It always does, even when I wish sometimes it didn't.

The room spills when I sit up. My fingers grip the blanket that was laid over me. It must have been Arrow because Rachel was too damn drunk to do much of anything other than pass out. Did she make it to her bed?

My bikini top is twisted around my body and no longer doing its job of covering my breasts. Instead of repositioning it, I yank it over my head and toss it to the floor. A glass of water and two tablets rest on my nightstand, and I'm quick to swallow them down.

Each sluggish step to the bathroom offers a welcomed coolness on the soles of my feet. I pee and shake my head at the dishevelled woman looking back at me. "We've got to stop drinking like this."

My bathing suit bottoms remain on the bathroom floor when I kick them into the corner by the shower. I turn on the shower knob and step in before the water sprays anything other than icy water. I shiver as it splashes over my face and down my chest. The chill has more power to yank me back to reality than ten cups of coffee. As the temperature rises, becoming too hot even for me, I spin the knob until it grows more bearable.

By the time I've shampooed and scrubbed the nightmares from my skin, the pills have eased the pipe bombs exploding in my head. With my hair wrapped in a towel-turban, I dry my body and head to the closest to pull an oversized blue t-shirt and yank it over my head, catching the turban and nearly yanking my hair out of my scalp. Still a bit dizzy, when I slip my leg into a pair of red spandex shorts, I lose my balance. Thankfully the grey and white striped bench in the middle of the oversized closet is close enough to rescue me.

My bare feet slap the cork floor as the hallway opens to the large living room. I continue to my left to the kitchen and pray to the universe

Arrow or Rachel woke before and made a pot of coffee. Waiting for it to brew may end me.

A half-empty pot rests on its heating plate and the aroma could wake even the comatose. It's strong—just how I like it!

I fill the cup and hold it beneath my nose to savour the familiar warmth as I breathe in Columbia's perfume. My lip presses to the cup's lip as the mug tilts.

"Good morning," Arrow says loud enough the neighbours may have heard him.

My entire being jolts, spilling the lava-hot java onto my chin. "Motherfucker! Goddamn that's hot!"

Arrow chuckles as he moseys past me to refill his travel mug. He pours as I continue to massage my bottom lip to ease the burn. After setting the pot on the burner, he screws a cap back on the mug.

"Are you going somewhere?" Before I attempt another sip of coffee, I look around to ensure Rachel won't spook me like Arrow did.

"Later." Arrow's head tilts back but his gaze remains locked on me. His snicker has me wondering if I said or did something last night I shouldn't have.

"What's wrong with your face?" I squint to emphasize my concern.

"Wrong?" he asks as his brows rise. "Nothing is wrong with my face. Perhaps you're still sloshed, and I'm blurry."

My eyes roll as I step back until my lower back presses to the edge of the granite countertop. "I might be hungover, but you're not blurry."

His eyes slowly climb my body. "Then, what's wrong with my face?"

My mouth twists as my eyes narrow to block out the brightness of the sunlit kitchen. "Nothing. Forget it."

Again, he snickers. "Headache?"

I mutter, "Don't be a dick about it." A gulp of hot coffee flows down my throat in the most delightful manner. "When's Kena coming to take over for you, or are you planning to be a permanent fixture in my guestroom?"

My lids pinch closed as weight shifts from one leg to the other. Every muscle ache is punishment for the consumption of copious amounts of alcohol.

The warmth radiating from his form alerts me to his near proximity. "I might stay on."

Being tall, it's easy for me to look him in the eyes without cranking my neck.

"Why are you so close to me?"

Arrow's finger lifts my chin before he leans in to kiss my cheek and stays his cheek pressed to mine. His voice rumbles, "You were a very bad girl last night."

I set my mug on the counter and match the sexual intensity carried in his whisper. "Was I? I don't remember."

"Oh, I think you do." Arrow's fingertips follow my esophagus before wrapping around my neck without applying pressure, sending a thrill of danger to ignite my fight or flight instinct. "You're mine: Red… or green?"

Bastard wants to play the dominant while I'm hung over? He really is a sadist.

"Green, but," My head shakes, and I groan, "not now; my head is still pounding."

Arrow snickers. "Good. This will be a lesson you won't soon forget."

With a hand on my shoulder and one on my neck, he offers no choice but to turn away from him. The heat of his strong chest presses to my back as his palm around my throat holds my head to his shoulder.

My ear heats beneath his whisper as he states his intentions. "Since you put yourself in danger by being outside—unprotected—and got drunk while doing so, I'm going to spank you."

My pussy is livelier than I am, and she's hungry. "Spank me? Why do you always threaten me with a spanking? You know I like it, right?"

His snicker carries cruel intentions. "Jaybird, you won't enjoy this one."

"No?" I ask and breathe in deeply to slow my hammering heart. Why does the thought of him spanking me excite me so much? I'm a twisted fuck!

Arrow's hand leaves my throat. But he's quick to fist my hair near the scalp. It hurts, but the thrill has my pussy damp. "There will be ten swats, and you'll tell me you're sorry between each one. Do you understand? If you forget, I'll add another."

After licking my lips, I nearly moaned and couldn't resist replying with sarcasm, "Yes, sir."

"Good Jaybird." He moans as me pushes his erection smothered in his jeans against my ass. A heated breath eases as he asks, "What are your safe words?"

"Red and green, but I won't need the first one." Why the fuck won't I shut up? The more I taunt him, the harder the punishment will be. Will he push me to my breaking point?

"Are you ready?"

"Yes, sir."

Arrow pushes my head forward until I'm bent as far as the island will allow.

The first slap is harsh and jolts my body. Even though I said I was ready, it came so fast I hadn't braced myself. The edge of the counter bit into my ribs, but the hurt felt good.

"What do you have to say, Jaybird?"

Seconds pass as I pull in two quick breaths. "I'm sorry, sir."

"I'll only allot you that one reminder."

Smack.

The other ass cheek feels the sting from his palm, and I can't help but giggle through my words. "I'm sorry, sir."

Four more times, he swats, and I tell him that I'm sorry. My nipples are pebbled against the cool countertop and my pussy is too hot in my shorts.

Arrow grips my ripened ass cheek and squeezes until I whimper.

His breaths are louder and quicker than when we started. He's thoroughly enjoying himself, as am I.

The vacancy of his palm when it lifts doesn't last as another, much harder slap makes it's mark.

"Fuck!" My moans and whimpers carry through the burn of his palm holding the slap against my heated flesh. "I'm sorry, sir."

Smack.

Pain rides heavily in my tone. "I'm sorry, sir."

Smack.

Fucking hell!

"Why do you have to hit the same spot? Christ, that fucking stings." I gasp as my back straightens, but he's quick to push my face back onto the granite using his grip in my hair.

"I'm sorry, sir. Fuck!" Not only is my ass scorching hot, but I'm so fucking aroused the crotch of my shorts must be soaked.

The last smack burns like fire singing my welted flesh. Tears drip onto the granite, and I'm gasping. "I'm sorry, sir. Please."

"Please *what*, Jaybird?" Arrow's voice is deep and sexy as sin.

My chin quivers but I can't form the words to reply. What do I want? I want to be filled. No, I want my clit sucked. No, I want— "I don't fucking know what I want."

Arrow spins me to face him and his mouth smashes onto mine. The scruff on his face hurts the soft skin around my lips as he assaults my mouth with his tongue. Hot hands glide up my sides until both of my breasts fill his palms. One is hotter than the other to remind me of how hot my ass is.

My head drops back as my elbows rest on the countertop to help balance me. Tingles from my nipples shock through my core to my clitoris as his fingers squeeze and roll.

"Tell me what you want, Jaybird." Arrow's teeth grip the base of my neck where it meets my shoulder, and he growls like a ravished beast.

The man plays my body so well it's possible I could orgasm just from nipple play.

He nips my chin, and my mouth opens wide to welcome his tongue, or whatever else he wants to put in it. "Tell me what you want, Jaybird."

My thoughts have scrambled, and words sound foreign. "I—I want y—you to make me c— cum."

Not a second passes and he's on his knees yanking my shorts off one leg. That thigh is lifted over his shoulder and his mouth encircles my needy clitoris.

My breath won't come as a wave of pleasure invades my sex. Arrow grips my burning ass as he skillfully sucks, flicks, laps, and grazes his teeth over my clitoris.

It isn't more than a minute before my mind is sinking into the painful pleasure of a mind altering, body quivering orgasm. If his strong grip on my ass fails to hold me up, I'd crumple to the floor. A deep breath rushes from my depths, ending with a final tremor.

My phone pings in the living room, drawing my attention. Someone has sent a message, but I'm fucking busy. It can wait. If it's urgent, they'll call.

He rises and presses his lips to mine as his palms hold my head. I can taste my orgasm on his hot, silky lips. My right hand grips his groin to rub his erection over his pants as I pull urgently on his belt with my left with the hope it'll give way.

Arrow's moans fill my mouth when the belt releases. My fingers make fast on his button and zipper to allow my hand to reach into his boxer briefs to free his erection to a more comfortable position. He spins my body to face away, grips my waist with one hand, and strokes his cock with the other.

I bend forward and push my ass toward him. The tip presses to my slick opening, and I want to scream to beg him to ram into me, but I swing my ass left to right to tease him. He swats my ass, so I laugh and continue to sway.

"Keep it up and I won't let you cum when I fuck you."

"That would be too cruel," I say and look over my shoulder at him. His chest expands as his brows lower over glaring eyes. "Okay. I'll behave."

I bend forward and jut my ass toward him, and giggle silently from the anticipation.

"Good morning," Rachel calls out as she staggers into the kitchen with her hand shading her eyes from the hard sunlight reflecting off the white surfaces.

What the fuck?

"You got to be fucking kidding me?" Arrow mumbles and pulls away from me. That's twice he hasn't been allowed to cum because of Rachel.

I hear his zipper and the clink of his belt as he refastens it. We're behind the island and she's approaching from the front. She can't see what we were doing, not that she can focus on anything through the blinding brightness. I'm quick to slip my foot into the leg-hole of my damp shorts and bend to pull them up my legs and into place before she drops her hand to look at me through only one slitted eye.

Did she hear us? How could she not? I'd be embarrassed, but it's Rachel and she's seen worse. If you hang around a rock band long enough, you see some shit.

"I think I threw up the gum I swallowed when I was ten." Rachel slides onto a stool and sinks her right temple onto the cool granite. "I fear my neck is too skinny to hold the weight of my gigantic head. Is my head bigger today than it was yesterday? I think it is. Is that possible?"

Arrow's jaw clenches below flared nostrils as he holds his mug so firm his fingertips have turned white. I can't imagine how sexually frustrated he must be. If I were a lesser woman,

I'd laugh out loud at him and tell him it's payback for the brutal spanking, but I fear the repercussions… Or do I?

He says, "I have to, ah—"

I cut him off as my fingers comb through my knotted hair. "Yeah. No, yeah. Um, go."

His wanton brown eyes shift to a harsh gaze when they leave me, and land on a suffering Rachel.

As he walks away, I pour her a mug of coffee and add a little cream from the fridge before sliding it in front of her face while her cheek still presses on the countertop.

"Oh, God. Thank you." Slowly, her head rises. Instead of gripping the mug, which was her intention, her palm grips her forehead. "Fuck. My heart is pounding too loudly this morning. How do I quiet it down?"

"You can't."

Arrow knew how to make my head stop swaying. He's sobered and cured me of my hangover. All it took was a naughty spanking and oral sex to cure me. But she can't have him.

She lowers her hand and glowers at me. "Why do you look fresh as a daisy? Aren't you hung over?"

My shoulders lift and don't drop for a beat. "I'm just okay. No reason. Maybe I don't get hangovers anymore."

"I call bullshit. I know you better than that, sister." Unconvinced, she huffs. "Out with it."

Her lips lower to the mug's rim and she slurps without lifting it. Perhaps it's too heavy in her weakened condition.

"All I'm going to say is that you have impeccable timing." I pull a sleeve of saltines from a box in the cupboard before sliding them in front of her in case she needs something in her stomach to accompany the sip of coffee.

"What does that mean?" Her brows furrow.

"Impeccable means—"

Her eyes roll and her voice rises. "I fucking know what impeccable means?"

I lean in closer to her. "It means, I was just about to get fucked by a really hot, horny guy until you showed up."

Rachel's gaze drifts past my shoulder but she stares at nothing in particular.

"What's the matter?"

"Hmm?" Her brows rise as her eyes widen to meet mine. "Oh, um. Nothing. I was just trying to remember what happened last night."

I laugh louder than she appreciates. "We got stinking, fucking drunk. That's what happened."

"Yes, indeed we did." Her eyelids flicker and she bobs slowly. "I puked so much. Did you?"

I shake my head and open the bag of crackers. "No. I wish I had. Maybe I wouldn't have felt so shitty when I first woke up."

I love having Rachel around because she brings me comfort. At the same time, she's a constant reminder of how powerful the nightmares were when I first met her. She helped me through them, but remembering her forehead against mine while we held hands floods back too often. Even though it hurts me, I'd never push her away because of it.

"So, I was thinking," I say and turn a saltine over in my fingers more than once. "Well, when I was on the road, there wasn't any time to spend with Arrow. People were always around. It was damn near impossible to be alone."

"Mhm." Rachel sips her coffee. "So, you want me to leave?"

Her wounded eyes are hard to look at. She's been my dedicated bestie for so damn long, and I'm about to shove her aside for some guy—a kiss, a fuck, and a lick.

Loser best friend of the year award goes to Phoebe Moore!

My lips pull tight in a plea. "Sorry, but yeah. I kind of do."

"I'll leave as soon as I'm done with my coffee."

346

With an open mouth, her jaw shifts as the tip of her tongue pokes at her back teeth; it's something she does when she gets upset or can't have her way.

"So, is he important to you? Like, is he sticking around even if you find the stalker?"

"I don't know." This subject needs to change. "What about you? Anyone special? You've been spending a lot of time at your parent's house lately."

Rachel bites her bottom lip and shrugs one shoulder. "Not really."

I lean toward her on my elbows with my coffee still clutched in both hands. "Out with it? Who is it? Anyone I know? Inquiring minds and all that."

"Maybe, but—"

My phone rings, interrupting us. With a groan, I leave my coffee and Rachel to answer the call from Lacey, and there's a text from an unknown number beneath the call alert.

"Hi, girlie. What's up?" I ask and smile because it's damn near impossible not to be happy when Lacey's in my head.

She excitedly tells me that she and Venus have a tune they think would make for a great song, but they need me to put the words together.

She pauses, so I cut in to beg for a reprieve from work. "Can I call you back in a bit? I'm in the middle of something."

"Oh, shit. Yeah, girl. No problem. If you give me a call around two, Venus will be home and we can work on it or whatever."

"I'll see what's happening then. I'm hoping to relax and not think about music for the next few days, Lacey."

Her petite voice rises higher than usual. "Nah, I get it. Chill and we'll chat later, babes."

Rachel's refilled her mug and is slowly walking backward toward her guest room so she can look at me. "I'm going to pack up and leave. You deserve some time for yourself after the month you've had."

I stand clutching my phone to my chest and feeling like a bag of shit for dissing both of my friends. "Sorry. It's just— Well, you know."

"Really, it's no problem as long as you call me when you get some free time, and you enjoy every second of that man." She raises her arm over her head to wave as she turns away, which lifts her short nightie to give me a partial view of her ass cheek.

"Wait a minute."

Rachel turns back to me.

I'm quick to walk around her and lift the hem of her nightie. "What the fuck is this?"

She turns and pulls away. "It's nothing. Well, not nothing, but it's—" Nervous energy has her rocking foot to foot.

Knowing how hard Arrow grabbed my ass when he picked me up has me wondering just what happened after I was put to bed. Did he do to her what he just did to me? Did he take advantage of her when she was too drunk to push him away? I'll fucking kill the bastard if he did.

My words are pointed and whispered, but my expression is stern. "Where did you get those bruises? They look like handprints."

"Um, yeah. That's the thing—" Rachel's tongue does that tongue on the back teeth thing. Whatever she's about to say, she's not happy to tell me. "I was very drunk, as you know. I may have passed out on the sofa. The big galoot picked me up and carried me to bed. There may have been a kiss or whatever."

Rage! Fire! Murder!

Her arms rise between us as she continues, "Don't get upset and scrunch your lips like that; it leaves wrinkles." She smiles hoping comedy will snuff the fire raging behind my eyes. "Listen, I hit on him. It's not like I could see well enough to know it was him. He was a guy, a fit guy, and I was a little… You know? So, I kind of pushed it a little. I'm sorry. I was so drunk. Do you forgive me?"

I scoff and shake my head and find myself pacing back and forth. "He took advantage of a drunk woman? Is that what you're saying?"

"It wasn't like that." Her head shakes as her shoulders lift, nearly meeting her crooked smile. "Seriously. It was nothing. Nothing happened."

"Nothing happened?"

Again, I lift the hem of her nightie and point to the finger bruises on her ass. He gripped her ass so tightly I could almost make out his fingerprints.

What kind of sick fuck can put his hands all over one woman and then another the very next morning? Is he fucking serious?

"He carried me to bed. That's all. I was a little squiggly, and he had to hold onto me."

"Yeah, but you must have been straddled around his waist for the bruises to be like that."

Rachel's face scrunches and her eyes close before she sighs and looks at me with her perfectly tweezed brows raised in their center. "It was my fault. He was a perfect gentleman. I was a fucking cunt. I'm sorry. I was so fucking drunk."

Who hasn't been so drunk they hit on someone they probably wouldn't have if they were sober? I can't condemn her for it when I've been just as guilty of such an offence once or twice. I've never hit on a friend's sexual partner, but that moral standing is embedded so deeply in me even my most intoxicated self won't go against it.

"It's okay. I'm not angry with you. Him, however—" My fingers comb through my hair to pull it away from my face. "Those bruises are too aggressive. You're too tiny for him to hold you that tightly. It's unnecessary and he's going to hear about it."

"Don't be too angry with him." Rachel rises on her tiptoes and kisses my cheek. "Call me soon. Promise?"

"Of course. We'll have another girl's night soon."

Rachel disappears down the hall and my focus aims at having it out with Arrow. First, I need to calm down.

CHAPTER TWENTY-SIX

Bare feet muffle sounds of someone approaching, so I startle when the door to my bedroom flings open and smashes against the wall. Red faced and flared nostrils alert me to the sour mood Jade's in. She's about to give me shit; how much shit and what it's about have me turning my chair away from the desk to face her. With my arms at rest on the armrest to seem less threatening, my head tilts slightly as I sigh in preparation for her to go off like a firework. She doesn't disappoint.

"What the fuck happened with Rachel last night? Did you fuck her?" Angry, spitting words fill the room as she stands in the doorway with her fists clenched at her sides. "She has bruises on her ass in the exact place your hands were when you fucked me. So, what's that about? Huh? What do you have to say about that?"

Slowly enough to irritate her, I rise and stretch before I reply. "Nothing happened. She passed out on the sofa. I picked her up and carried her to her bed. She spun around on me and tried to convince me it was okay to fuck her; said she wouldn't tell you. I had to hold onto her tightly to get her to stop grinding on me." With my hands on my waist, my chin rises to question her with my eyes. "What? Are you jealous?"

"*Jealous?*"

I saunter toward her with my gaze locked on hers. My lips quirks to the left as my thumb and forefinger hold my chin. She remains in place, shaking from anger and breathing heavily.

Jade's tone lowers as she hisses from behind her teeth. "I am not fucking jealous of Rachel. You hurt my friend. Your grubby paws bruised her. Tell me, did you enjoy feeling her up?"

Standing with merely a foot between us and letting my eyes drink in her body. This could go either way; she'll either hit or kiss me. And I sure as fuck hope it'll be the latter. "You're jealous."

"Fuck you!"

Jade swings for my face with an open palm, but I catch her wrist. Fury widens her eyes. She swings her left arm, and I grab that wrist, too. She screams when I pull her hands together behind her back which forces her chest against my chest, and I grip both wrists with one hand. Holding her tightly against my body as she thrashes to get free. I grab her throat with the free hand and squeeze just enough to get her attention. She stills as her eyes burn daggers into mine.

Calm and steady, I whisper, "That's enough, Jaybird. You got your point across. Now calm down."

She stiffens against me as a deep breath fills her lungs. Unable to restrain myself, my hand pulls her neck toward me as my lips mash to hers. At first, she kisses me back with as much fire as I'm giving.

Fuck, this is so hot! My cock is swelling in my jeans. Angry sex is my favourite passion.

Jade bites my lip hard enough where I feel her teeth tear through layers of skin.

Her head tips back and my blood drips from her sneer. "Fuck you, Arrow, and your bossy arrogance! Go to hell!"

"Only if you come with me, Jaybird."

Her lips are swollen and red from the aggressive kiss. I'd give anything to have them around my cock, but I'm sure she'd bite.

Distracted by my fucked-up thoughts gives Jade an opportunity to headbutt me. I don't see it coming and her forehead slams against my right eye socket. Stars dance through my vision before the immediate swelling throbs my heartbeat around my eye.

Son-of-a-bitch!

I grip her hair to stop the second blow from connecting with the bridge of my nose. She screams when I yank her head back. The grip I have isn't at the roots, so I know it hurts more than when I grip closer to her head during sex.

Her knee rises quickly and catches the inside of my thigh. A few centimeters, and I'd be on the floor with my balls jammed up into my stomach.

"That's it!" I release her hair, spin her to face away from me, and grip her throat hard enough to let her know I mean business.

She yells, "Get the fuck off me! Let me go! Get the fuck out of my house, you piece of shit!"

Her wrists are still in my grip and held against my stomach. I pull tighter on her throat until her head rests on my collarbone. She's arched and on her tiptoes. The only thing I need to be concerned with is if she kicks my shin with her heel, but she's too focused on getting air.

My teeth bite onto her shoulder through her t-shirt, and her scream grows from deep within her chest. I'm going to leave my mark on her to remind her of how *I* hold the control – how *I* set the pace – how *I* own her fucking ass!

Jade trembles in my hold as her breath comes short and quick.

Slow, methodical steps walk us to my unmade bed. The tan sheets are tousled from sleep. It's rare I don't make my bed the moment I leave it, but I'm glad I let the ritual slip this morning. We're about to shred this bed!

Jade's foot presses to the edge of the bed to prevent me from getting her too close to it. With a quick jerk, I yank her to the side to dislodge her foot and then rush her to the bed. I lift her and drop with her onto her face down on the sheets while I lie on her back. My hand leaves her throat to grip her hair and hold her cheek to the bedsheet.

My voice is low and deep as my mouth hovers over her ear. "What colour, Jaybird?"

Although enraged, her beautiful green eyes dance back and forth. In barely a whisper, she says, "Green."

Before she finishes the word, I grab her hips and flip her onto her back. I straddle her waist with her arms tucked down along her sides. She's pinned beneath me. A mix of fear and thrill has her gasping. She squirms to get free as adrenaline has her parted lips quivering.

Her eyes follow the movements of my fingers as I undo each button on my black dress shirt. It falls open and my hand glides down my abs. Deliberate and slow, I unfasten my belt, pop the button to my jeans, and lower the zipper.

"Do you want me, Jaybird?"

She swallows and watches my hand reach into my pants.

My breathy chuckle quickly fades into a moan when I free my cock. It stands at attention as I lazily stroke up and down the shaft. A droplet of precum gathers at the tip. Jade licks her lips when my thumb glides over the sticky lubricant. I raise my digit to my mouth and let my lips surround my thumb as I suck it clean.

"Do you want to taste me?"

No longer squirming to get free, both of her lush lips are pulled inward and held between her teeth. Her head shakes defiantly, but we both know she's playing a game of consensual non-consent.

My bent index finger rests beneath her chin as my saliva dampened thumb presses firmly to her bottom lip until she gives in and opens her mouth wide.

I whisper but expect no reply. "My feisty little Jaybird. What am I going to do with you?"

She's surprisingly quiet as she stares up at me with wide eyes. Her hurried breaths carry a tremble that's sexy enough to have me biting my bottom lip, and yet I want to cradle her until she finds serenity. Is she afraid or aroused? Perhaps both.

"You're going to suck my cock like the little slut you are, then I'm going to fuck you until you beg me to stop." My finger dips into her gaping mouth, and I study how my index finger brushes over her hot, wet, soft tongue. I nearly cum just thinking about how incredible it'll feel to brush the tip of my cock over it.

To ensure she won't bite my cock off, I ask, "What colour are you, Jaybird?"

Jade lifts her head until she can engulf my entire finger and sucks like it were a straw in a thick milkshake. She watches me admire her mouth from beneath heavily hooded eyes. I nearly melt when her tongue dances over the tip before she slides her tongue underneath as if teasing a small cock.

Keeping her arms pinned at her sides, my hand weaves into her hair. "If you want me to stop, kick your feet. Do you understand?"

Cattiness burns in her tone as she snaps, "*Yes, sir.*"

Oh, goody! Jade wants to continue this anger game. And yes, it's a game—a game I intend to win. She may battle all she wishes as long as her colour remains green. Who doesn't love a good resistance fuck when both parties welcome it?

I rise higher on my knees and slip my ankles over her arms to pin them to the mattress, so she can't free her arms. My thighs hover above her tits. The goal is to allow her to breathe comfortably but with a sense of having no control.

She can say green or kick her legs at any time and this will end, but no matter how nervous or afraid Jade is, she's too stubborn to give in. As a responsible dominant, it's up to me to judge where to draw the line because she won't. Going too far in the moment can be a rush, but afterward she may drown in regret or emotional issues.

Jade doesn't like to be restrained as I discovered not long ago, so holding her down like this is teetering her on her edge.

Hesitation has her eyes wide and shifty.

"What colour are you, Jaybird?"

A gasp seems to pull her from her thoughts. Her whisper is barely audible. "Green, sir."

"Are you sure?"

She nods and forces a smile I recognize as fake.

To test her resolve, I cover her mouth and pinch her nose to restrict her breath. "What do you do if you want me to stop?"

A whimper sticks in her throat. She pulls, hoping to free her arms, but fails.

"If you're choking on my cock, and you need me to stop, what do you do, Jaybird?"

Another groan fails as her head jerks side to side hoping to remove my hand from her face, so I press her head firmly onto the mattress and bend forward to glare into her terrified eyes.

"Eyes on me." I speak slowly and calmly to ease the panic attack she's about to embark on. "Think. What did I tell you to do?"

Her upper body stills, and she kicks her legs. She gasps upon the immediate release of her mouth. "You're a fucking asshole."

"You're goddamn right I am. And you're about to discover just how much of an asshole I can be."

Using her hair, I lift her head and brush the tip of my cock over her pillowy lips. She opens wide as I push forward enough to fill her mouth. In this position, it would be damn near impossible to go down her throat without hurting her or me.

Looking down at her, I'm in awe of my Jaybird's natural beauty. Her strong cheekbones, sharp nose, and puffy lips are divine. Her beauty shines through without all that goopy make-up covering her up to make her look like a devilish vixen. Her hair is a mess and half of my cock buried in her mouth is an image I hope never to forget. My knuckle brushes over her flushed cheek as I study the way she eagerly sucks and teases the tip of my cock like she did with my finger.

I'm a visual lover. To see how un-fucking-believably erotic this scene is from my view is enough to push me over the edge. Coming in her mouth won't be the endgame this time no matter how desperately I want to let myself fall into the abyss of my pleasure.

Even though the sensations waving through me each time my cock slides in and out of her mouth is enough to do me in, I have to keep in mind this isn't about me. It's about her and how she needs to find forgiveness in whatever causes her so much anger. "Suck my cock. Just like that. Good girl."

She stiffens and her eyes dart to mine. The reaction is subtle, but I take notice. Was it the instruction or the affectionate *good girl* that threw her out of the moment?

"Suck my cock." No reaction, so I moan and repeat, "Good girl."

She stills and her eyes pinch tightly closed as she takes a deep breath.

"Eyes on me, Jaybird."

She looks up at me and her eyes soften. Several quick blinks bring her back from whatever hell she was about to slip into, and she begins to suck the tip of my cock with vigor.

I pull free of her mouth and bounce the tip on her parted lips. Her tongue pokes free to taste but quickly retreats when I refuse to tap my cock on it.

Her breath huffs with amusement when one of my eyebrows rises and I grow a smirk. As I slide down her body using my hands to continue holding her arms pinned at her sides, I straddle her hips, lean forward, and brush my lips over hers.

"Very good, Jaybird. Now I'm aching to fuck you until you can't breathe." I press my erection against the soft fabric covering her mound. "What colour?"

Jade's effort to tilt her hips to savour the pressure of my cock on her clit is thwarted under my weight. Her breathy response, "Please," earns my lips on hers with a harsh, urgent neediness.

Each time my lips pull back, she pleads that one little word that drives me fucking wild, like I'm a goddamn porn star. "Please."

"Please, what, Jaybird? Tell me what you want?" The saltiness of her neck and collarbone, and down between her breasts is an aphrodisiac, and I need more.

"You. I want you. Please?" Her chest rises to meet my mouth, urging me to take her jutting nipples. "Fuck me."

My deep voice is savage as I growl, "I'm going to fuck you like I hate you."

In a well-orchestrated move, I lift off my left knee, grip her hips, and flip her face down on the tan sheet. With one hand pressed to the small of her back, I grip the waistband of her shorts and yank unforgivingly until they're down her thighs enough to expose her pussy and her heart-shaped ass.

She thinks I'm going to pull it off her while I lift it, but as soon as her arms are free, I twist until the shirt is snug around her neck and gently pull her into a back arch. Jade lifts onto her arms to support herself, but I pull the makeshift choker a little more.

My free arm crosses over her breasts to tighten my hold on her. Jade's fingers pull at the fabric, but it doesn't give.

"Calm down. You can breathe."

"I know," she says and swallows before she pants twice and whispers, "but I don't want to."

My mouth presses to her ear. "What colour, Jaybird?"

CHAPTER TWENTY-SEVEN

Fear holds me still. Arrow has wrapped my t-shirt around my neck making it difficult to breathe, and I teeter on the edge of panic. I'm barely able to suppress my fight-or-flight reaction, yet I'm so fucking turned on.

"Calm down, Jaybird." His words are clear and loud against my ear, but the desire to disappear from my reality has me wishing he'd pull tighter. I don't want to die, but vacating my bullshit thoughts for a while sounds great, even if it means passing out and falling into the emptiness of serenity, even if it's only momentarily.

"Make me disappear," I whisper, unsure if he heard me or if he understands what I'm suggesting if he did.

Arrow pushes my face to the sheet, and I know what's coming. I grip a handful of tan coloured sheets to brace myself for him to slam into me and fill me to my core.

I hate the colour of these sheets. In fact, I detest the earthy theme of this room. After Arrow leaves, I'll hire someone to redecorate.

Wait… *After he leaves? Fuck.*

A hot palm slaps my left ass cheek, but I only feel an ache in my chest. My eyes pinch tightly closed to eradicate the burn of tears edging nearer. Why do I care so much if he leaves?

From behind me, strong fingers glide through the slick between my labia until they pause against my clitoris. All thoughts of anything but the pleasures his fingers could bring me fade into the dark recesses of my mind.

My body will feel; my emotions will not.

My back arches as my hips swivel, intent on finding relief from the sexual tension. The tightness from my clitoris to my bellybutton grows hotter with each brush of his digits.

Without thought, I beg, "Please."

Did he just snicker?

"Please, *what*, Jaybird?"

Please don't make me beg!

"I need to cum—to," hiccup, "fade away." I'm fucking crying. When did the tears start?

"I'm going to fuck you now. It'll be vicious and unrelenting. What colour, Jaybird?" The sure strength in his tone leaves no denial that he's dominant. He owns me, but I'm given a choice.

I don't want to make decisions.

I don't want to think.

I just want—

Fucking end me, dammit!

My tone borders on primal. "Lime fucking green. Now, will you please fuck me like you hate me?"

Arrow's thick cock punches into me like an MMA fighter's fist to his opponent's face. Shockwaves of pain and pleasure thrill my body, but an empty fullness I can't fully comprehend lingers in my mind.

A scream shreds my throat as he pulls the t-shirt to add more strain on my neck.

One of his hands grips my shoulder for leverage to pull me back as he fucks forward. His thrusts are violent, each one accompanies his gruff guttural grunts. He's barbaric, and I fucking love it!

The restriction on my neck slows the blood from flowing to and from my brain. He's strangling away any thoughts determined to torture me. My entire being is light and airy. The pressure of his thrusts pushes me closer and closer to my death. Is it death? I can't be sure, but I want it.

Arrow shifts his stance but remains on one knee with his other leg steadying himself with his foot on the bed. He holds firmly enough to bruise me as he forces me to move how he desires. The t-shirt remains taut, but his other hand leaves my shoulder and glides down my body until the heat of his palm flattens high over my mound. His ring and index finger pinch the top of my labia together around his middle finger and finds my swollen button. Something vibrates my clit, dropping me into a euphoric darkness where there is no up, no down, no anything.

Choke me harder. I want to float away.

His cock presses toward the front with each brutally hard and rapid assault.

My pussy grips his thickness as if wishing him to sink deeper where it'll remain imprisoned forever. My breaths fail to come and bright stars behind my eyelids melt into darkness as my body erupts into another climax

Have I vaporized into nothing?

All too soon, the room grows brighter as I gasp for each breath. My cheek brushes up and down on the soft sheet. Although too weak to lift my head, my pussy continues to throb and twitch around his cock.

Arrow's thrusts ease as the t-shirt drops loosely around my neck. His consistent breaths pause, and I hear him swallow, A moan precedes his deep words. "Fucking hell, Jaybird. You feel too fucking good."

The instant he pulls free of my vagina, the emptiness feels deeper than physical. His thumb presses into me several times before it pulls free, and I'm thrust into with enough force to expel my breath.

Plunge after powerful plunge continues to steal the air from my lungs. The constant quickness of my breaths affords me a dizzying light-headedness I savour.

Arrow's thumb sinks into my asshole, and I cry out. Although this isn't the first time that cavity has been invaded, the immediate stretch is shocking. I love the taboo associated with anal play. A sense of complete fullness has me bucking back against his digit.

"You like your ass filled?" Arrow groans more questioning than in a statement. "What colour, Jaybird?"

I try to look over my shoulder but can't see more than his knee. "I like it."

He stills inside my pussy, but his thumb pulls and stretches my asshole. "I asked you, what colour?"

I enjoyed the discomfort better when he was fucking my pussy. "Green. Stop asking. I'll tell you if I need you to stop."

A warm palm glides up my back and brushes strands of hair off my neck with a tenderness unsuited of the situation. "I will ask you whatever and whenever I want. I'll fuck you, or spank you, or choke you, if I want. I'll do amazing things to you, but I won't stop asking your colour. Do you understand?"

When I grunt instead of speaking, his palm slaps hard on my hot ass cheek.

My words rush from me. "*Fuck!* Yes, I understand."

His voice is calm and undeniable. "Sir. You'll call me *sir*."

"Yes, *sir*!" Sarcasm won't fare well with him when I'm supposed to be submitting to his dominance, but it's fun to see how he'll react.

Another crack to the welt has me yelping and squirming to get away, but he grips my hip to keep me in place. "Jeez! Fuck!"

The bed sinks to the right and the squeal of a nightstand drawer fills the room. Things rustle inside before Arrow's weight returns behind me.

"Colour?" he asks as cold liquid dribbles over my super-heated asshole.

My lubricated fingers press into the pucker and scissor as they pull back.

"Neon fucking green!" I moan and arch my back before remembering to say something. "Sir."

The head of his cock pushed past the outer rim of loosened muscle, and I want more of the painful discomfort. I crave penetration. Give it all to me and make it hurt.

Unwilling to do this the slow and responsible way, I push back and take his entire cock in one thrust. My breath is stolen as the immediate stretch has me wishing I hadn't done that. And yet, it's fucking glorious. I need this.

"Jaybird, slow down." Arrow whispers but he sounds like he spoke from a mile away.

"Punish me."

What did I just say?

Arrow doesn't respond. Instead, his hips begin to sway, and his girth makes my walls feel like they're going to rip apart. I need this. It's what I deserve. It's my pain, and I'm in control of it. I can stop it whenever I want or let him continue to abuse me in a way *he* never did.

Tears flow down my cheeks as I push back to match the motion of his hips.

Something vibrates over my clitoris and my body ceases to move.

I swallow a moan, and it singes my throat. It returns through a wail unlike my own. I need more.

"Harder. Fuck me harder! Please," I beg through gasps.

Arrow humps me slightly harder and faster. He moans and grumbles something I wasn't meant to hear. Desperation rides the tone, urging me onward.

My scream rips through the room echoing back to haunt me. "Hurt me! Fu-Fucking hur-hurt me! Hurt me. Plea-please?"

Arrow grips my throat and arches me back until the back of my head presses to his collarbone.

I don't want his cock to dislodge from my ass, so I arch my back to keep him inside me. His pace has slowed but he continues to slide in with the tempo of a ticking clock, allowing me to focus on my clitoris. The vibration increases, much to my favour.

"Don't cum, Jaybird." His dangerous whispers flow gently into my ear with so much heat he could melt my flesh.

Don't cum?

"You're a dirty little slut. I'm so fucking deep in your tight ass you won't shit for a week. Tell me you like my cock in your ass."

"Please?" I beg.

"Don't cum." He snickers wickedly before his teeth sink into the base of my neck.

It fucking hurts. *Yes!*

The vibrator slides up and down alongside my clitoris. It's thin and hard, but powerful. My pussy and tummy muscles flex each time it slides over the tiny bundle of nerves hidden beneath the swollen hood. The physical reaction must do something to his cock because he groans each time it happens.

I'm so fucking close to tumbling over the edge. This feels so fucking good! His body is warm and hard—manly in every sense of the word. We smell like sex and our moans blend together in a sensual song.

I grip firmly to his forearm to hold his hand in place, thus keeping the vibration where I need it most. My free arm reaches around to his ass or waist—I can't be sure at this point. My nails dig into his skin. Arrow's teeth clench tighter urging my scream to weave between our moans.

"Oh, God. Please—"

"Not yet, Jaybird."

The vibrator lifts from my clit. Disappointment has my head shaking and tears soaking my face. I'm crying again. *Why?*

"Breathe slowly, Jaybird."

This feels so fucking good—absolute perfection in its taboo nature.

He continues to hold my neck, growing tighter over my arteries to slow the blood flow to my brain. I'm beginning to float. My breaths have slowed, but my heart continues to pound behind my ribs.

"Now, Jaybird. Give me your pleasure." The vibrator presses to my sweet spot, and Arrow bites my shoulder hard enough where the skin may have given way. *It's perfect.*

Nothing exists but my clitoris. An imaginary balloon in my tummy is painfully full. It's about to burst, and I may literally explode when the pleasure releases. I want it to happen, yet I'd love to remain on this fantastical brink of utter bliss eternally. This is as close to the sweetness of death as one can be without a reaper. If death is coming for me, I welcome it.

I'm not sure who's wails are whose. My physical existence is no longer dense but fluid. How is he holding onto me when I'm draining away?

Nothing. Black. Floating. Ecstasy.

A roar from somewhere inside me wrenches me from sure death as my body convulses from the agonizing taunting of my hyper-sensation clitoris. I scream again, unsure if the gratification forces air from my body or pure anguish that it's over.

Arrow's cock swells inside my ass, firing me into another less powerful orgasm. He thrusts twice more before he pulls out, drops the vibrator, and pumps his cock with his fist.

My neck is freed, and I wither forward until my face and chest melt into the sheet.

A manly wail is cut short as strong thighs press against the back of mine and his testicles rest on my asshole. Hot splatters slap to the small of my back—one, two, three, four. As Arrow's lungs empty, so does his strength. He sags forward resting along my back. Hot breaths waft over my left shoulder blade lifting prickles on my skin.

Neither of us can find the strength to move. It could be a day or a minute that passes before Arrow slides off me onto his back. With his palm starting on his forehead, it slowly glides down his face taking with it some beads of sweat and comes to rest below his neck.

My legs slide out from under me, and I remain face down on the sweaty sheet. His eyes are closed, jaw clenched, and his Adam's apple bobs.

His face slowly turns to meet my lazy stare. His cheeks are flushed, and his lips are swollen and pinker than I know them to be.

What is he thinking as he studies my features? His eyebrows twitch to lift in their center and his lips move as if he's about to say something but closes them. His face turns to look at the ceiling before he whispers, "I'll get a towel. Don't move."

My arms slide up the bed until they're tucked under my cheekbone. I feel utterly used and physically elated, but I remain broken. I'm damaged so deeply inside that no amount of self-punishing sex can erase it.

My eyes sting with the threat of tears. I cried plenty during sex, so I refuse to allow another tear to fall. But it's too late to pull them back. To hide my shame, I turn my face away, so we can't meet eyes upon his return.

Arrow tenderly wipes his seed from my back. There's a pause when my snuff catches his attention. He lies on his back and pulls my arm, not allowing me to refuse. I snuggle against him with my arm over his chest, a leg over his waist, and my saturated face pressed to the base of his neck.

He says nothing as his warm palm strokes the arm I've laid over his chest. He isn't judging me or pushing me to explain my tears. I couldn't even ask.

CHAPTER TWENTY-EIGHT

Brightness burns my retinas, and I try to blink the pain away. A sense of desperation haunts me. Where am I, and what happened?

Jade.

She isn't on my chest where I swear she was a second ago when I blinked. It must have been a very long blink. I'll admit, that's the best rest I've had in… I can't recall.

I sit up and the sheet sags onto my lap, tenting around my erection and I instinctually fist it. My cock may not be huge, but what good is a massive cock if it can't be rammed into a hole to bring pleasure to both parties? A vagina is only so deep, and hand-to-heart I love to be balls deep in a pussy!

The memory of this morning creeps into my thoughts. That may have been the best orgasm I've ever had. I couldn't breathe but that didn't stop my heart from threatening to shatter my ribs to escape. Everything hurt, but a magnificent hurt it was. My world went black around me. Even my mind fell into a state of numbness. Jade shudders beneath me when my withered cock slithering from her body snapped me back like a slap to the face.

And she cried during and maybe after. For a woman who shows the world she's impenetrable, she sure isn't. The way she looked at me; what was that? There was a softness to her eyes she had no intention of explaining, so I stopped myself from asking.

Jade's typical glare is always incisive to prove to all how hard and strong she is. It's a defence to keep people at a distance. That snappy mouth of hers isn't anything to cozy up with either, but I'm breaking through and earning her trust. Has anyone before me accomplished this feat?

Falling asleep so easily afterward isn't something I've ever done, yet that's exactly what happened. Perhaps she's forcing my demons to leave me alone when I sleep, and I'm helping her to conquer hers.

After a quick trip to the bathroom to pee and brush my teeth, I skip the underwear and slip on my grey jogging pants. My feet slap the chilly floor as I follow the gurgling sound of a coffee maker. The scent draws me to the kitchen like a moth to a flame.

Jade's back is to me. She's wearing the same shirt and shorts I peeled off her earlier. The shirt bears more wrinkles than it had before I twisted it around her neck.

Her palms press to the counter as her hips press to the cupboard while she stares blankly through the wide window. Trees sway in their battle to defy the whipping wind as thick rain clouds loom above with the threat of releasing.

She doesn't see me approach or even flinch when I stand beside her. She may be looking out the window, but she only sees what her thoughts reveal. What could they be?

"Is there coffee?" I ask as softly as my voice will allow.

She jolts as her head jerks to look at me. "Jeez, fuck! You scared the shit out of me."

Laughing is probably not the best idea, but I can't resist.

"You have to stop doing that. It's not funny," she says as her hand presses to her chest. "Did you enjoy that?"

Still amused, I reply, "Actually, yes. That was funny."

"Ha-ha. Asshole." She punches my arm not hard enough to hurt me in the slightest.

"Where's Rachel, by the way?"

Jade's arms cross over her chest as her weight leans on one leg. "She's gone. I checked her room and she's gone. I asked her to leave, so— Anyway, I'm waiting for the coffee to finish brewing. Are you hungry?"

Rachel's gone? I thought that bitch would never leave. Maybe she got sick of hearing us have sex in the kitchen. Hopefully she left beforehand. The thought of her getting off on watching us makes my stomach turn. But she's gone!

While smiling like the Cheshire cat, I round the island and pull out a stool to sit. "Why? Are you going to cook?"

Her hands slap to her rounded hips as her head tilts. "Ouch! I'm so offended. Yes, I can cook. It's one of my favourite pastimes. I don't often get a chance to cook for someone else and rarely see the point in going through the effort for myself."

She takes two mugs from the cupboard.

"Why?"

She sets them in front of the nearly finished brew coffee maker and frowns at me. "Why, what?"

"Why don't you cook for yourself? Aren't you worth the effort?"

Her head shakes and she scoffs. "Why would I cook a gourmet meal for myself when I can just as easily eat a tray of prepared veggies and fruit, or heat up a bowl of canned soup? I like to make life easier and use my time more productively."

I see her point, but she *is* worth the effort, and I wish she could see it herself.

As she fills the two mugs with the steaming black java, she asks, "What do you take in your coffee?"

"Black is fine. I wouldn't want you to go through the effort."

She turns to glare at me, and my entire face lifts into a *gotcha* expression. My wink has her rolling her eyes before turning back to her task. "Since you don't want me to go through the effort, you're getting fiber cereal."

Her expectant gaze brings a smile to my face. There's no way I'm going to show my disappointment. "I like fiber cereal. The more fiber, the better."

"Twigs and straw it is!" Jade snickers as she reaches into the cupboard to pull out a box of what I assume will be awful tasting cereal. She slams it on the island in front of me while her tongue tastes her lips.

Does she like this horrible cereal that'll likely have me able to shit through a straw later?

My lips press together as my eyes widen. "Mm, yum!"

She puts a bowl in front of me along with a carton of milk. "You're all set. Do you want to add some sugar to it? Your stodgy ass could use a little sweetening."

My scoff is unintentional. "Jaybird, in that case you need to gnaw on some sugarcane all damn day just so you don't bite someone's head off."

Her face swings away to hide her amusement. She says nothing as she claims a tray of fruit from the fridge and sets it on the island. She sits kiddie-corner to me and chooses a piece of mango and pops it into her mouth.

She watches as I pour milk over the cereal. I should pour the contents of the bowl directly into the toilet instead of allowing it to scream its way through my body first. Hopefully, we don't have anywhere to go today; I'd hate to shit my pants.

"You don't have to eat that... I mean, you'll lose some clout with me, but I'll offer you the out." Her defiant snicker is enough to make my cock hard.

"Jaybird, be careful."

She leans forward on her arms and her hair falls over her face. She's quick to swoop it behind her ear. "Careful? Is that a threat, tough guy?"

My spoon clinks as it comes to rest in the bowl. My fingers whip any possible residue of the gross cereal from my lips. "What's your safe word, Jaybird?"

Jade's spine straightens and she swallows. A defiant glare crosses her face. "Fuck you. That's my safe word."

"*Fuck you* is how you get me to go harder." My cock is tenting my grey joggers, and she's noticed it. "What. Is. Your. Safe word?"

Her breath quickens and her cheeks flush a light pink. "Red."

Before she can react, my hand is fisted in her hair and my mouth opens over hers as my tongue digs inside. Using her hair, I force her to stand. My free hand grips her cheeks, and she stares at me with wide eyes. Was she not expecting me to react?

"You—my little Jaybird—are going to suck my cock. You're going to choke on me. If you can't use your safe word, tap me anywhere three times. Tell me you understand?"

She tries to speak calmly but her words come too quickly. "I understand, sir."

"Good Jaybird."

Her hair makes for a good handle to force her onto her knees. She whimpers but doesn't protest. I tilt her head back and lightly slap her face. "When I tell you to, you'll take a deep breath and hold it. This is going to be intense, and you aren't going to like it."

My sweatpants drop to my ankles and my cock juts toward her face as if it were a dowsing rod seeking water and her mouth is a lake. Slowly, I stroke my shaft. Her eyes drop to my cock, so I shake her head and tell her, "Look at me. Don't look away. I want to watch your eyes fill with tears."

"Yes, sir," she says without hesitation and doesn't bother to quash a genuine smile.

My feet separate to rest on either side of her knees. "Open."

Her smile is quickly lost when her mouth widens to accept my cock.

"Now that is a pretty image."

The tip of my cock meets her lips, and she closes them around the head to suck. Although it feels fucking amazing, it's not what I asked her to do.

I pull back and lightly slap her cheek, again. "I didn't tell you to suck."

Jade's eyes are wide with faux fear, but the way she's licked her lips twice proves her eagerness to continue.

"Open," I say and direct her mouth toward my cock. This time, I push in until the head of my cock hits the back of her throat.

Her body jerks with a retch, so I pull back until the head of my cock rests on the roof of her mouth. She nods.

My head shakes. "You don't need to tell me when you're ready. I'll decide that."

As my hips lean closer toward her face, my cock disappears down her throat. She tries to shift herself but my hold on her hair and my feet keeping her knees together make it difficult.

I pull back and stroke my knuckles down her cheek. "You're such a good little bird."

Her smile reaches her eyes which are so glassy the threat of tears looms.

"Wrap your lips around my cock and take all of me." She does, and I buck a few times deep into her throat. An unintended moan slips from me. If I didn't want to make this last, the sight of her on her knees, looking up at me with tears leaking from her eyes while my dick slides in and out of her mouth would be enough to push me over the edge.

She breathes quickly when I step back but leave the head of my cock just inside her lips. Her tongue attempts to push into the slit and my cock jerks. My head tilts back and my jaw clenches. That feels fucking amazing! *Too amazing!*

I pull free and bend down to smash my lips on hers. Not only am I desperate to taste her mouth, I need a few seconds to put my body's desire to orgasm in check. This scene isn't done yet, not even close.

"This mouth… I could kiss this mouth all fucking day." I stand tall with her hair still clutched under my control. "Open."

I push my cock half inside her cavernous mouth and stop. Her pretty green eyes stare up at me, sheen and clear.

"Take a deep breath and hold it."

Jade breathes in. I push my cock down her throat, and she retches, but I hold still. The second retch has me pulling back.

"Relax your throat."

Her eyes roll as if to silently say, *I don't need instruction on how to suck a cock.*

"Roll your eyes at me again, and I'll make you sit in the corner, on raw macaroni noodles, for an hour."

Her eyelids twitch as she considers the irritation that would cause. She could steal me away with those eyes. Does she have any idea of how captivatingly beautiful she is? The softness they carry right now could make me fall in lo—.

Fuck!

"Open wide. Take a deep breath. You will not choke this time."

Two breaths fill her before she opens wide to accept me.

I push all the way into her throat until her nose presses against my Adonis belt. Seconds pass and I don't pull back. She blinks away tears and they stream from the outer edges of her eyes into her hair. Finally, her body jerks as her throat constricts around my cock. I pull back and frown.

"You need more practice. Perhaps I'll make you do this every hour until you get it right."

There's no reaction from her as she breathes quicker than she had been.

"We'll try again. Take a deep breath."

As soon as she does, I slide all the way in. Her eyes close which forces another river of tears to slide from their outer edges.

"No. Open your eyes. I want you to look at me."

She complies and my nod seems to please her because she tries to force her mouth further onto my cock, which I didn't think possible until her chin touches my balls. All the air in my lungs leaves me.

I've had my cock sucked on many occasions, but I don't remember it feeling this good. It must have, right?

Her hand rests on my thigh, and I take that as a signal she's coming to her edge, so I pull back. She gasps as a string of saliva stretches from her bottom lip to my cock hung inches away.

Again, I lean forward and force her mouth into a brutal kiss. She whimpers, and I'm not sure if it's because my kiss is too rough or she wants more than just this from me.

"Breathe deeply and hold it," I whisper as my lips brush over hers with feather-like tenderness.

Jade inhales and I quickly push inside her mouth, deep into her throat. My finger and thumb press on either side of her nose to add another layer of fear. Tears flow and her cheeks flush deeper pink by the second, but she doesn't look away.

"You are never more beautiful than you are right now when you're messy because I've used you. I should take a picture, but it wouldn't do this moment justice."

Both of her hands press to my thighs, and I know she's close to her limit. She's quick to blink away the tears but still doesn't tap. Her face is almost purple, but she doesn't tap. How far should I push her? She won't tap; I know she won't. It's like she wants to punish herself to the point of self-destruction. She has some emotional issues she needs to work through, and I want to help her do that, but not like this.

My fingers release her nose, and I yank my cock from her mouth.

Jade gasps but she's determined not to look away from me. "I can take more, sir."

My hands—free from her hair—cup her jaw, hold her shoulders, and gently lift her until she's on her feet. My thumbs brush the tears from her face.

She says nothing. She doesn't need to. Her stare reflects mine and it's terrifying. We've developed feelings for each other.

CHAPTER TWENTY-NINE

Despite the wrinkles wedged in his face from years of inner torment, his features seem to soften. I'm suddenly nauseous but not because I didn't tap for a reprieve. No, it's something else.

My cheeks rest in his hands for what seems like minutes, but likely only a few seconds. My fingertips brushing over his forearm snaps him back from wherever he was, and his features harden.

He spins me away from him and pushes me forward until I have to grip the edge of the counter, so my ribs don't mash against it.

His palm comes down hard on my ass cheek, startling a yelp from me. The jerk from the impact presses me against the bar. Another swat to the same cheek nearly yanks a sob from me. Two swats to the other cheek and tears drip down my cheeks. His superheated palm brushes over each ass cheek and the heat seems molten.

"More," I whisper and jut my ass out for his access.

Why do I want more? Why? Because the pain mixed with sexual desire takes me out of my head. I think too much. I overthink everything and it becomes too much. The only way to make it stop was alcohol, until Arrow showed up. He so easily demands all of my attention there's no room for evil thoughts to take over. He owns me, and what's worse is I like it. No, I need it.

What's happening to me?

Five more swats to each ass cheek have me sobbing. The heat ignites pins and needles on my welted ass and has me forgetting my connection to the man spanking me. So, why the torrential tears?

Before I can over-analyze, his hand spans over my throat and pulls me upright until the back of my head holds against his collarbone.

His cheek rests above my ear. The heat and rumble from his words radiate through every cell of my body. "You're my needy little Jaybird."

His free hand glides down my tummy and into my shorts and doesn't stop until his middle finger presses against my clitoris and the two fingers on either side pinch outside my labia like a taco around his finger. My body instinctually squirms, and I whimper as he brushes lightly back and forth, pulling my labia with his strokes.

Being owned like this feels too good! My strong female independence tells me it shouldn't, but my body savours his attention too much to be denied.

"Your cunt is fucking soaked. Should I make you cum or let you sit unsatisfied in your wet shorts all day? How eager would you be to please me, so I'd agree to give you an orgasm?"

Moans flow from my core with each rushed breath. I'm close, but I don't want to cum yet.

His movements slow and then stop. Desperate for movement, I try to buck my hips to no avail. He presses tighter over the arteries running alongside my throat. It's not enough to make me black out, but I feel a bit floaty.

"Tsk, tsk, tsk, horny bird. Don't move. Stay completely still, and I'll consider letting you cum. Can you do that for me, Jaybird? Can you follow that simple command or are you too stubborn to give yourself to me? Don't bother answering."

There's no point in trying to speak even if I wanted to defy him, which I don't. Forming words seems an impossible task. Instead, I hold still, but my rapid breaths balloon my chest so wildly my body shakes.

His fingers continue their manipulation over my clitoris. My kneecaps quiver and I fear they'll let me fall, so I tense my legs to lock my knees. More than anything, I want to buck against his fingers or jut my hips forward to give him better access, but I don't dare move.

Even my moan seems to vibrate throughout my body, thus adding to my torment. I want to cum. He has me so close. So. Fucking. Close.

Arrow's hand leaves my throat and covers my mouth and nose, preventing me from breathing. He snickers when I instinctually wrap my fingers around his forearm. I don't pull him away. Instead, I slide my hand up his arm until it covers his hand.

I will not panic. The situation is different from when I was a little girl. Arrow isn't going to hurt me in the ways the monster did because I'm an adult now, and I can stop it if I choose to.

My free hand hugs his other forearm to my body because there's no way in hell I'll let him stop masturbating me when I'm this close.

My lungs burn but I don't care. The assault on my clit is absolutely delicious. Bliss is within reach, but I don't want to succumb. The pleasure is beyond anything non-sexual life has to offer. My mind and body are captivated by one thing—his fingers.

His growl vibrates me from head to toe. "You're *mine* little bird."

Arrow's fingers plunge into my vagina while his knuckle somehow continues the pressure and stroking over my clitoris. His fingertips push forward and thrust short, hard thumps toward the front and it sets me adrift over the clouds and into a dark abyss.

I know my body requires air to survive. My heart pounds and my lungs burn. I'm slipping further and further away. My orgasm rolls through me like a slow-moving wave, enveloping me as it grows more dire. I'm coming and blackness overwhelms my existence.

Let me die.

A sudden gasp of air cools my lungs, but the rush of oxygen sets my brain on high alert which intensifies my orgasm. My body jerks and twitches as animalistic grunts not suiting a lady shred from my core. Warmth soaks my shorts and continues to flow down my thighs until it tickles my calves.

My legs can hold me no more, but I don't fall. He has me safe in his arms; protected from anything wishing me harm. I have no fear as his soothing words anchor me until clarity brings reality back to me.

"You're mine, Jaybird. You're beautiful, smart, and the sexiest damn woman I've ever met, and I own you."

Still holding my back against his chest, he lifts me off my wobbly legs and carries me to the sofa. He doesn't lay me on it; he pushes my thighs against the back. With his hand around the back of my neck, he shoves me forward until my face rests on the cushion.

My soaked shorts are aggressively yanked down and pulled off my feet. He's harsh when he fills me with his cock. The sudden invasion didn't hurt since I'm soaking wet, but the stretching of my spasming walls after such an all-enveloping orgasm is fucking blissful.

Each word follows a thrust. "Yes. Fuck. Me. Yes. Please. Please. *Fuck!* Arrow."

He pounds into me as if he's trying to get to the other side of me. I love it!

The pressure in my tummy from lying over the back of the sofa makes his cock seem massive, as if each thrust pokes deep into my body. The thudding against my cervix has me screaming through another orgasm. It's not a match to the first climax, but delicious nonetheless.

"Squeeze my cock. Ah, fuck! Cum on my cock." A deep guttural groan threatens to blast from his chest against his will, and it's more than he can restrain. "That's it. I'm done. Fuck!"

Five thrusts hard enough to leave bruises on my thighs from the sofa's frame end leave him buried as deep into me as his body will allow. Fingers dig into my waist, and he stiffens. My bottom lip pinches so hard between my teeth it may bleed. The swelling just before I feel his semen rush to escape his cock is a new sensation to me. I've never felt that before, and I'll consider it my reward for good behaviour.

Arrow swallows loudly before his breath seeps from his lungs. His forehead comes to rest against my back. Gasping breaths that could scald me bring prickles to my skin.

At the moment, I hadn't considered a condom. Hot panic rushes through my veins, and I launch upward and push him away. My eyes darted to his cock.

Relief.

"When did you put on a condom?"

Arrow's breaths have slowed but the flush in his cheeks and the droplets of sweat on his brow are enough to prove how hard he worked to enjoy himself. "I'll never go bareback unless we've both been tested and are in agreement of it. I like pushing boundaries and tempting fate, but no condom is a line I have yet to cross."

"You've *never* fucked without a condom? Never?"

Arrow's head shakes. "No, *never*. I almost did with—" His eyes stare fixedly on the floor by my feet, but he quickly blinks back to reality. "It doesn't matter. I won't cross that line with you unless we've discussed it first."

"Wait." I cup his cheeks to direct his attention back to me. "With whom?"

"It doesn't matter," he says and pulls away from me.

Oh, no you don't!

My voice rises as anger that I'm not good enough for him to bear his soul to take over. "You want me to open up to you, but you won't tell me anything about yourself? What the fuck, Arrow?"

He grips the waistband of his sweats clinging to his hips and rushes toward the hallway. After yanking up my shorts, I follow with an angry curiosity bringing life back to my weakened legs. Every footfall lands with force. The bathroom door shuts and locks before I can grip the handle to twist it. The resistance has me seething.

"Fine. You want to play this game where I'm expected to tell you all about my past, but you don't have to say a fucking word about yours? Our deal is *off*. I am no longer going to be your plaything to entertain you." My arm rises above my head and my finger juts toward the door even though he can't see me. "Fuck you and your twisted little fucking games!"

My feet slap the floor as I rush to my room to the nightstand to collect my phone. I hold it up for facial recognition and finger my phone to open my texts. I skip the unseen messages and find my conversations with Alex. Before I can tap the screen, I'm flying through the air.

A sharp huff forces from my chest as I land on the bed looking up at the ceiling. I can't react quick enough, and Arrow straddles over my hips with my wrists pinned beside my head. My phone remains clutched in my palm ready for me to send a text to Alex to fire Arrow immediately. It's not what I want—not really—but it's what I must do.

Arrow's lips pull into a thin line, nostrils flared, and his cheeks are flush from anger. Brown eyes burdened with anguish lock onto my throat, but they don't see me.

A swallow bobs his Adam's apple before his tongue wets his lips. In a voice low and gritty carry impactful words. "I lost her; it was my fault." His wide eyes dart back and forth as if he sees her and not me. "I sent her in first. I should've been the one to lead; it was my job to know it was a trap. I—"

Arrow's jaw clenches and his nostrils flare. His breaths are deep to stop his glassy eyes from filling with tears. They squeeze so tightly that the lines leading away from them intensify.

My anger instantly shifts to sorrow and pity. I won't offer him pity; he's not the type of man to welcome it.

My voice is calm to soothe him. "Arrow."

His head shakes slowly to signify he's done discussing it. He's off me and walking away before I can say or do anything. Should I follow him and make him explain? Normally, I would, but pushing this man will force him to toughen up and lock me out. I know, because we are very much alike.

But I want to know who he's talking about? Who is the woman he claims to have lost? What does he mean he sent her in first, and where did he send her?

I sit up and stare at the doorway.

The war. It's plainly obvious to anyone who knows he went to war to see that he's burdened with PTSD. He often loses himself in a stare and, when startled, rage fills his expression. And his nightmares haunt him by forcing him to relive whatever horrific trauma he experienced.

But I want to know more; I need to know more if I'm to help him. Can I help him?

The lighted screen on my phone falls dim, drawing my attention, so I pick it up and go back to the message I received when Arrow had me in the kitchen before Rachel interrupted.

My palm scrapes over my face as I scroll through and open the screen.

A dim photo of Arrow with his hand in the air about to swat my reddened ass fills my screen, only Arrow has a large red X over him. The words, "You're mine. He'll pay," have me gasping and dropping my phone on the bed.

With my hand on my chest, I rush back to look at the photo again. Is my face distinguishable? Can this person use the photo to blackmail me, or will they sell it to make a fortune? But the side view of my face is too blurry to know it's me.

A moment of relief calms me, but I know something more threatening looms. They can't get in the house because everything's locked. Did Rachel reset the alarm before she left? I race to the front door and see it's locked and the alarm is activated. Arrow must have reset it, but when?

I collect my coffee from the kitchen and take a long drink. Arrow's mug is gone. He must've taken it to his room. Like an idiot, I was hoping he'd be sitting here waiting to explain further. Of course, he's hiding away. I would too, but he needs to see this.

He's not in his room and the only other place he might be is the gym downstairs. The sound of grunts slows my approach to the open door. I peer in and see Arrow slam his fists repeatedly into the heavy bag. It swings slightly with each blow. Every muscle on his bare back and thick arms tightens from the shock of the blows. Sweat drips down his tanned flesh as his chest rises and falls with a fury.

I take one step toward him when he pauses and hugs the bag as whimpers ride his gasps. With his cheek against the leather, facing away from me, a sob and snuff catch my attention. More than anything, I want to go to him and let him use me to comfort himself instead of an inanimate object, but it's not what I'd like him to do for me, so I back away. As much as I don't want to admit it, he's changing me.

Leaving him to work out his emotions, I decide to leave my phone on the counter in the kitchen with a note to view the photo. He has my password, so he can take a look when he brings his mug back.

I rush to my room and shower quickly. Dressed in a spandex outfit and a baseball hat, I set off to punish myself with a hardcore run to clear my head. Whoever was looking in the window is likely gone by now. Besides, this neighbourhood is lined with houses and people outside to enjoy the weather. I've always felt safe here.

CHAPTER THIRTY

Soggy from sweat and tears, I wipe my face and chest with a towel left for this purpose. There's no sign of Jade as I make my way through the house to my room for a shower. She's probably in her recording studio in the basement or somewhere else away from my path.

It surprises me that she hasn't chased me down to ask for more information. Maybe she sensed I needed time for myself. We're the opposite in that she accepted my hold while she worked through her issues, even if she wouldn't admit it today. I, however, would not.

I'd better find her and smooth everything out so we can be friends again. And by smooth everything out, I mean kiss her ass and beg her to forgive me for being a fucking asshole. She's right; I can't expect her to tell me her haunting secrets if I won't do the same. The only people I felt comfortable talking to were the psychologist and Fixer.

Fixer understood well because he was there. He doesn't remember much about the explosion, or that he was on fire when I pulled him out.

That's probably a good thing. I'll never forget the stench of his burning flesh.

Jade isn't in her room. She isn't in the recording studio or the media room either. As I rush from room to room searching the silent house, anger has my jaw clenched. If she fucking left unescorted because I flipped out, or she's suddenly afraid of me because I got a woman killed, I'll… I don't know what I'll do, but the punishment will suit her offense. She's not to leave without an escort. She knows this, but where the fuck is she?

"Jade!" My roaring voice in the main room of the house should be heard throughout it, but there's no reply. "Fucking hell!"

How did I not notice her phone on the bar? No wonder she isn't answering. Atop the screen is a small sticky paper.

There's a photo in my texts you need to see. Gone for a run. Back soon. J

I scoop up the phone and punch in the lock code. The screen lights up with a picture of Jade and me in a precarious situation. They took the photo from right outside the window. The asshole watched us.

I send the photo to my phone and immediately send it to Fixer and ask him to tell me all he can about it. My time would be better spent outside searching for her.

If something happens to her, I'll never forgive myself.

Panic has my fingers shaking as they tap the screen of my phone to call Alex. My feet carry me outside and around the entire house on the cement path just in case she hasn't left or is already back.

"Arrow? What's wrong?" Alex's voice is heavy with concern because I never call him when a text will do.

"She's not here. She said she left a note that she was going for a run." My breaths come quickly from the efforts of my sprint around the house. "She left while I was working out. Can you access the cameras; see the direction she headed?"

His voice is distant before it booms louder. "Yeah, I'll just, ah… Okay, how long ago?"

"Maybe an hour." I can't tell him more than that because he'll see the video of me forcing her to suck my cock and then fucking her in the main area. The camera's record there. I should have fucking had her erase that part of the video, but who knew I'd need Alex to review the feeds. "I'll need access to the feed. What's the password?"

"Just hang on. Okay, here we go—" There's a lengthy pause, and I know he went back too far.

I quickly suggest, "Just check the outside cameras."

His throat clears before his lips smack. "Mhm. I think we need to have a discussion after we have her back in our custody, Mr. Silas."

Mr. Silas? Oh yeah, he's livid.

"If you think we need to." I'm careful to not sound regretful of my actions, because I'm not. What I regret is having him be witness to them. The cameras are there for her safety, and I'm a fucking idiot for not taking her to another room. "Did she leave on her own?"

Alex's voice is monotone. "Yes. It seems she left thirty-seven minutes ago heading east. She's wearing workout wear, so I assume she's going for a run." He clears his throat again and his voice grows louder as the phone returns to his cheek. "Mr. Silas, you'd better find her and bring her home safely. I'll call the band. If anything comes of it, I'll call. Mr. Silas, find her."

I call Elsa first, but she's just as shocked to hear Jade's missing and promises to call Jade's phone to see if she'll answer and call me if she does. Next, I call the person I don't care for, Rachel.

"Hey, have you seen Jade?"

"Ever?" she asks, and I know she's trying to be funny, but now is not the time.

I can barely form words since the run has me panting. "This is not the time for joking. She left for a run without an escort, and I can't find her anywhere."

"She called about twenty minutes ago. Said she was pissed at you because you're a hardcore asshole."

That can't be denied; I was a complete fucking asshole. Telling Jade the whole story would have broken me. I'm supposed to be her protector—her dominant—so crying like a fucking toddler in her presence is incredibly inappropriate. I'm a fucking marine. We don't fucking cry!

"She isn't wrong, but I have to find her. What if her stalker's watching? She's in danger, Rachel. If you know where she went, tell me."

The woman sighs as if bored. "She didn't say where she was going."

My intuition has me tingling. "Do you know where she is?"

"Listen, if I knew where she wanted to go, don't you think I'd tell you?"

My voice drops an octave as I pointedly ask, "Is she with you?"

"Oh, my God! Question asked and answered. Go fuck yourself, *Arrow*. You don't deserve her." The line goes dead. *Bitch!*

My feet hit the pavement in rapid succession as I sprint in the direction she headed. I can't stop my skin from crawling about my conversation with the bitch. She's some kind of special. Why Jade keeps her in her life when all she does is cling to her baffles me. Does she feel obligated to keep Rachel close because they share a lengthy past?

I've run several blocks but Jade's nowhere to be seen. Maybe she's back at the house. I call the house phone and hope the maid has arrived and will answer the call.

"Hello," she says in a thick Italian accent.

I keep my voice free of concern. "Hello, Maria. Have you seen Jade? Is she at home?"

"I don't think so, Mr. Silas, but I just arrived, so I can't be sure. Is everything okay?"

"There's nothing to worry about. Thank you, Maria. If she returns, can you have her call me?"

Concern continues to ride her tone. "Of course. Goodbye."

"Bye." I hang up and rush back to the house.

My phone rings as I arrive back at Jade's house. "Hello."

It's Fixer. "Hey. We'll discuss the contents of this image at a later date, but the first thing I noticed is that I'm almost certain a woman took the photo. If you look at the shadow around the reflection, light transfers through either a thin fabric hood or long hair."

With the phone on speaker, I open the photo and blow it up. How did I overlook the reflection? If I weren't in a haze of worry, I'd have taken a moment to examine the photo more thoroughly.

He continues, "Had they stood back, their shape could tell us more. Let me know if you need me, and call when you find her."

"Thanks, Fixer. I will."

I hang up and stare at the photo and run the conversation with Rachel from start to finish. She worded her replies oddly as if she didn't know Jade's intentions. If she's with her and Jade said not to tell me, she wouldn't. She's hiding something; I can feel it.

Could the stalker be Rachel?

With my keys in hand and gun holster strapped around my chest, I rush to my car and speed down the lock-brick driveway and onto the street, heading in Rachel's direction. At a stoplight, I scroll through the documents on my phone to find her exact address and punch it into the GPS. The twenty-five-minute drive takes less than ten minutes.

It's a nice neighbourhood with houses reaching in the millions. There's no way Rachel paid for it. What does she do for a living? I never did ask.

I park a few houses down from hers and take a moment to observe. Can I get in her house unnoticed? Does she have a camera system where she could be watching me or get a notification of human presence? I see no *beware of dog* signs on any neighboring homes. There isn't a soul in sight. This type of neighbourhood has people minding their own business and often indoors or in their private backyards.

Casually, as if I belong here, I walk toward the red-brick house. The drapes are drawn, so I can't see inside. The benefit is that she can't see me coming. Should I ring the doorbell to announce that I'm here or listen to my hunch and not announce myself? With little effort, I fling myself over her six-foot wooden plank fence into her backyard. It's well decorated with lots of foliage, a decorative fire pit, and an inground pool with a waterfall pond flowing over heavy boulders. The sitting area is made to be an extension of her kitchen, but the sliding glass panels aren't open.

I pull the latch, but the panel doesn't budge. My lock-picking kit is never not with me, so I use the tines to jimmy the lock free. Gun in hand, I open the doors wide enough to slip through and close them behind me. The kitchen is in perfect order aside from two wine glasses with tiny puddles or red wine remaining.

Each step is methodical and silent as I make my way through the house, watching and listening for any activity, but the main floor and upper are vacant. A stair creaks under my weight, and I still. Silence.

The basement is decorated like a movie theatre with ten leather recliners that look pillowy soft. The television gives me pause from its massive size. I've never seen one that large.

A noise catches my attention and flattens my back against the wall. I hear it again but can't determine if it's a voice. With my gun safety off, I make my way down the hall checking through each open door. The sound grows louder as I approach the third door. It's wide open and dimly lit.

A deep breath fills my lungs before I peek inside. Rachel is sitting cross-legged on a four-poster canopy bed with pink frilly lace draped over the top and hanging beneath. It's a child's bed. Posters of rockstars popular twenty-years-ago line the walls. A dresser with a wide mirror bears photos of little girls resembling Rachel and Phoebe making funny faces or smiling.

This is a teenager's room, so why is it in Rachel's house?

Rachel's eyes lock onto mine and she smiles, but it's not a welcoming smile. "I figured you'd come." Her eyes take in the room, and she sighs.

"This is exactly how my room looked when Phoebe and I were young teens. She'd come here to hide when the nightmares took over. She was safe here. I kept her safe, not you. She's the person she is because of me. I created Jade. It was me who first called her Jade."

Her eyes drop to the mattress beneath her, and it draws my attention to the lace hanging oddly below the bed. Something is under the bed—something human sized.

"Did she tell you I got her into singing? I did. She was good; way better than me. We learned to play the guitar and wrote songs together. Her first single was written in a bedroom just like this one. She didn't want to sing, but I signed her up for the school talent contest and she won."

Even though the barrel of my gun's aimed in Rachel's direction, it doesn't even phase her.

She continues, "This was her sanctuary, and mine. This is where I fell in love with Phoebe. She hadn't yet turned into the Jade the world knows. She was quiet, reserved, and scared. I protected her, and she loved me for it."

"Where is she?" I ask and tilt my head hoping for a better angle to see the hidden form beneath the bed. As I step into the room and slowly make my way around the perimeter and nearer the bed, I notice a needle jutting from the crook of Rachel's elbow.

She's holding the plunger with her other hand. "She belongs with me. I'm her savior, not you. I was there for her—*me*! I love her! I've always loved her!" Rachel takes two deep breaths and calms her tone. "But she didn't see me. She was always looking past me in search of something bigger and better. Regular life bored her. The more she moved around the less time she spent with her demons. She thought if she could just get famous, nobody could hurt her and get away with it. But the stronger she became, the more she felt trapped and violated. So, I had to save her from it. Don't you see, Phoebe was dying. Fame was replacing Phoebe with Jade. I don't like Jade. That woman was mean and selfish. She pushed Phoebe into a dark corner so nobody would see her."

"Where is Phoebe now?" I ask in a stern but undemanding voice. It's best to soothe the subject to earn her trust.

Rachel snickers and looks down at the needle as she pushes the plunger halfway down to inject something into her vein. Her head rests against the wall and she smiles weakly. "Phoebe's in her safe place, but you're too late. I've saved her from the cruelty that is her life. She's suffered, but no more." She slowly pushes the plunger completely in and moans. "I'm going to join her now. We'll be together again, as we were always meant to be."

I slowly step forward as Rachel's head drops to the side and gradually sags along the wall until the shoulder meets the pink duvet. Her eyes roll back, proving she's drugged herself with something.

As I rush toward the bed, I secure my weapon and drop to my knees. I fist the lace and yank it from the bed, revealing Jade's back. She's curled in a fetal position facing the wall. Her arm is out of reach, so I grip her ankle above her running shoe and pull her out.

She's blue. This colour is familiar to me— too familiar. Phoebe's face isn't Phoebe's. I see Kayla Jamieson; the woman I loved with all of my heart.

A flash back to the war reveals the bodies of the recently deceased. They all wore the same hue. Pain shreds through me, and I scream like I did that day. I see Fixer, and he's on fire.

The memory of dragging myself through the dusty ground toward the burning hut while screaming from panic and terror rushes before me in fast motion.

There was nothing I could do then, but I can now. I dial 911 and begin CPR as I explain the situation and where to send help.

I shove down on her chest, stopping only to force breath into her body. Her eyes remain fixed, but I don't look into them, promising myself I won't look until they can see me again.

"Come back to me, baby. Don't leave me. Don't fucking leave me." Tears blur my vision. Breathing air into her proves more difficult as my lungs burn from my efforts.

It seems like an hour before I hear the sirens, and forever before they rush into the room.

"Step back, sir. Let us help her."

I fall back against the wall, gasping, and watch the tall woman sort through her bag as the smaller man checks her vitals.

She's lifeless. My beautiful, broken Jade is gone. I can't do this again.

My plea is a whisper, "Please, don't take her from me. I'll do anything. Just don't take her."

CHAPTER THIRTY-ONE

Blinding brightness pulls me from a deep sleep. I don't remember dreaming, which is odd. The bed is hard beneath me and something tickles my face. Cold air blasts up my nose and my mouth is so dry.

My arm is so heavy my effort to lift my arm to pull the tube away is in vain.

"Jaybird, you're in the hospital. You're going to be okay."

My eyelids feel like balloons when they ease open. "What?"

A distant man's voice softer than the first rushes to say, "I'll go get the doctor."

Deep vibrations warm my body as Arrow's voice hovers above me. "Jaybird, open your eyes. Look at me, baby. Let me see those beautiful green eyes."

Again, I pull open the balloons and try to focus on the face above me. "Arrow?"

"Yeah, it's me." He lifts my hand to his lips and kisses my fingers. "You're okay. Nobody's ever going to hurt you again."

Confused, my words slur. "Hurt me?"

It all floods back like a sped-up television show. Rachel and I had a glass of wine. She brought me downstairs promising to show me something I'd love. My head started to spin, and walking was difficult. She held me up and brought me to a room that looked exactly like her childhood bedroom. It was pretty and the perfect room for a happy girl, but it only brought back every painful memory that led me to hide beneath her bed.

My scream sounded distant and enraged Rachel. She was so upset that I didn't want to be in that room. I fell to the floor and hit my head because my arms couldn't prevent it.

She was screaming at me, but the ringing in my head had the words sounding muffled. She kicked my thigh. I tried to crawl away and headed toward the bed where I used to hide beneath it just like when I was a little girl and had a terrible nightmare. I'd make myself as small as I could behind the lacy pink sham. The gap between the fuzzy blue rug and the hem of the lace terrified me. If he came for me, he'd see me through that tiny gap. The promises that the man would never hurt me again were only words and didn't stop the fear.

But it wasn't him hurting me this time.

I was desperate to get away, but I'm so much bigger now that hiding as well as I could when I was a tiny girl was impossible.

Something stabbed my arm before a cold rushed through my vein. Rachel was speaking as she brushed my hair from my face, but she may as well have been speaking German for all I knew. Limp and barely able to move, she pushed me beneath the bed. The space is much tighter now, so I struggled with weak limbs to pull myself to the wall, and then nothing.

Speaking burns my dry throat. "Rachel."

Arrow's warm palm glides up and down my forearm. "She can't hurt you anymore."

Why not? Where is she?

"Water."

A straw is set on my bottom lip, so I suck in the icy liquid, swish it in my mouth, and swallow before taking another sip. It's all I can manage even though I want more.

His whisper carries pity, and I don't like it. "You're okay, Jaybird. You're going to be okay."

A feminine voice is near my face as a light flashes over my eyes. "Ms. Moore, can you open your eyes and look at me?"

Not with that bright light shining in them! My arm feels too heavy to lift to slap her away. The room spins, and I'm falling asleep.

The next two days are spent in the hospital as I'm given one test after another at the insistence of Alex. Arrow's anxious to get me back home where I can recuperate with peace and quiet.

I've heard them arguing in the hall despite their attempts to keep their voices down. Nobody has ever fought over me—nobody who legitimately cared for me without gaining something for themselves in return. It makes me feel small and fragile.

Since I became an adult, I've taken care of myself and needed nobody. Relying on someone to make me happy would only lead to disappointment, so I kept everyone at arm's length, even Rachel. She said she loved me, but her jealousy that I became the famous singer and not her was obvious despite her effort to pretend otherwise.

Although my foster family tried to make me feel like their child, there was always something missing. Alex is the closest thing to family, and I pay him to be with me. Therefore, he isn't family.

But here I am looking into the pale brown eyes of a man promising he'll never leave me, but promises can be easily broken. I'm scared to let him love me. I can't give myself to a man who won't let me in. If only he'd tell me his story.

He sits on the chair beside the hospital bed with his arms crossed over his chest, and staring at nothing. Pain riddles his face.

My hip aches as I sit up on the bed. Arrow stands and offers his hand. I manage on my own to sit up and dangle my legs over the edge.

"You fell asleep."

"I'm so damn tired." My fingers try to comb through my hair but it's a mess from days without a brush. "Can I go home, yet?"

Arrow's voice is low, but the steadiness proves he's in control. "In a little while; paperwork. The doctor needs to discharge you and then they'll bring a wheelchair to take you down." When I grimace, he adds, "It's hospital policy."

We wait in silence for the wheelchair to bring me downstairs. Arrow stands against the wall with his gaze lost through the window. He's a million miles away.

"What haunts you?" My voice startled him.

He stands taller and pulls his hands from his pants pockets to cross his arms over his chest.

"No, don't shut down," I say and glance at his arms. He nods and lowers them to his sides. "Tell me what haunts you."

"Now?" he asks as he sits in the plastic and metal chair beside the bed.

"Yes. Tell me now."

Sadness pools in his eyes as they see into the past. After a deep breath and long exhale, his voice lowers to just above a whisper. "I was in love with Kayla Jamieson. When our tour was over, we were going to get married. She wanted to settle down and have three kids. She wanted two boys and a girl, and I would tease her that we'd have two girls and a boy." Arrow's smile grew but quickly faded. "We were on a scout. A tip came in that a family was hoarding weapons, so we were sent to find them. We'd searched this village twice before and nothing ever came of it. They were friendlies, as far as we knew."

I remain silent as my palms rest on my thighs.

Arrow's hand surrounds his face and glides down over his chin before joining the other on his lap. "I gave the order for Kayla to lead and Fixer to follow. I was going to stand outside to keep watch. There was silence just before the explosion. It was short but eternal—if that makes any sense. The next thing I remember, I was face down with a mouth full of dirt. Awful pain in my legs made standing impossible. I knew better than to look at my legs to see if they were still there. I'd seen too many soldiers go into shock when they'd seen their bodies mangled. So, I didn't look, and I didn't try to stand. The shack was on fire, but I crawled inside anyway. Somehow, I pulled Fixer away from the devastation. He was burned very badly but alive. I went back in to find Kayla. She got the worst of the impact. There was no way she was coming back to me. I held onto her until someone physically pulled me away."

Arrow falls silent as the painful memories drip from his staring eyes.

"I'm sorry," is all I can think to say.

His eyes dart to mine before he blinks rapidly as his palms wipe away the evidence of his weakness. "It was a long time ago."

"But the pain is still fresh."

Arrow looks at me as if understanding that we both suffer from distant memories that will never not resurface in our nightmares. He's slow to stand and his heavy black boots shuffle the blue and white checkered floor as he nears me. His palms cut my cheeks as his slight smile warms me.

I whisper, "But I am sorry you lost her. Maybe one day you can tell me more about her."

His blink lingers as a breath fills him. "I'd love that. You know, I think you and she would have gotten along very well."

"Oh? Why's that?" My mouth twists as I examine his crooked grin.

The orderly pushes a rickety wheelchair through the door. "Your ride has arrived. Want to take it for a spin?" He's far too cheery, but I welcome him with a smile and a shrug.

Arrow offers his arm for me to hold when I slide off the bed. "Because she was just as stubborn and pushy as you are."

"I am not!" I pause when his wide eyes question the validity of that statement. "Yeah. All right. You win."

"Let's go home, Jaybird."

EPILOGUE

Two Years Later

The promotional tour for my new album has ended, and I'm more exhausted than I've ever been. Who knew being six months pregnant would be so tiring? Arrow and I are a week away from celebrating our one-year wedding anniversary.

The sunlight shining through the swaying trees catches the diamonds on my wedding band. When Arrow slid it on my finger, he explained that the single ruby in the center signifies his heart, and I now own it. Little does he know how sacred this gem is to me.

No matter how often I remember the way Rachel tried to kill me, the memories of her helping me when I was young pull at my heart. I loved her, but not in the way she wanted. I wasn't hers. The threat of losing me to my career or a man was simply too much for her. I miss her every day, even though she tried to kill me.

I will never feel complete in the sense of being safe and free from struggling through my burdens alone. When the ghosts from my past haunt me, Arrow's there to pull me back from their reach, and I do the same for him. We've got each other's back.

Twice a week I speak to a psychologist who helps me to open up. She's been a great source of strength for me. She's taught me some great managing skills to help with my anxiety, so I no longer drink alcohol to drown my fears from my history that plagues me. I feel about as normal as anyone can be. Well, normal and the size of an elephant with ankles to match.

"Hey, what are you thinking about?" Arrow asks as he reaches for my hand.

I reach for him and our fingers weave together between our wooden Adirondack chairs. The sun reflects off his sunglasses until his free hand shades his face.

"Nothing much. Just… I'm happy."

Arrow squeezes my hand slightly. "Me too."

"But I never thought I could be."

"Same." He sits up and lowers himself to his knees beside me and rests his free hand on my swollen belly. "Here we are, two happy souls about to give life to a tiny human. It'll be our responsibility to raise this wee boy into a mentally, emotionally, and physically strong person before we send him off to make his mark on the world."

"Hang on a minute," I say, and cup his cheeks in my palms. "I haven't even given birth yet and you're already shoving him off to make his mark on the world? Slow the fuck down. I want to hang onto this tiny human for as long as possible, if that's all right with you."

Arrow's sunglasses do nothing to suppress the full force of his salacious glare. He grins as he takes my wrists in one of his hands and holds them firmly at my chest.

With a tilt of my head, I whimper before I play the victim in a deep southern belle accent. "What ever will you do with me, Mr. Silas?"

When he grabs me like this, I know he wants to own me, and I love to play along.

My husband growls his sexy deep voice as he helps me to my feet. "I have plans for you, my bad little Jaybird."

Still carrying the accent while feigning innocence, I say, "But, sir, there's no reason to punish me since I haven't done anything to purposely irritate you. And, I'm pregnant, so you can't bind me in rope and suspend me from the tree. You can't affix me to our St. Andrew's Cross and paddle my ass until it's red hot. You can't pu—"

My breath rushes from me when he pulls me against him until only my round belly prevents us from getting closer and grips my hair in his palm to control my head for a deep, lingering kiss.

"Jaybird, don't taunt me. One day you won't be pregnant, and I'll punish you for all your indiscretions."

"Threaten all you want, sir. I'll just get pregnant again, and you'll be shit out of luck."

He laughs heartily and takes my hand in his to guide me to the bedroom. "Good. Let's make it an even dozen. We'll start now."

Confused, I reminded him, "I'm already pregnant, in case you've overlooked the mountain under my shirt."

Standing beside the bed, Arrow's fingers brush my hair off my shoulders before cupping the back of my neck. "You and your mountain are absolutely beautiful. You're the ice cream on my pie. Let me worship you, and then we'll practice making the next baby. Practice makes perfect, in case you hadn't heard "

"Oh, I've heard," I whisper as my eyebrows slowly climb, widening my eyes. "Give your head a shake if you think I want to be pregnant twelve times. How about we shoot for three?"

"You never know what the future holds, Jaybird. But for now, lie back and let me worship the love of my life."

Who am I to deny him his just desserts?

~ The End ~

Thank you for reading The Rockstar's Bodyguard: Rule Breakers, book three.

Please take a moment to leave a review or recommend this book to a friend or book club.

Scan for a universal purchase link to Amazon

If you have social media and love to boast books, tag #PebblesLacasse. She loves to read what her readers have to say, and often rewards those who boast her books with random surprise gifts.

Thank you,

Pebbles Lacasse

ABOUT THE AUTHOR

Pebbles Lacasse is a contemporary romance and erotica author. She leans toward writing bad boys desiring women who didn't know they have a kinky side. However, she's also known for her women with a dominant nature, and a secret yearning to be loved. Her books and short stories often take her readers into the BDSM lifestyle while revolving around real-life issues, and there's always a happy ending. The captivating stories of romance, love, and tender moments keep her readers coming back for more.

As someone living with Porphyria, Pebbles stays indoors to avoid UV light which gives her plenty of time to write. That's not to say she doesn't love "glamping," fishing, kayaking, and swimming, she just has to do it with protective clothing. If there's something she wants to do, she'll find a way to make it happen.

Pebbles is very family oriented. She and her husband of 34+ years raised their children in southern Ontario where she was born, and remains to this day. A 150+ lbs Mastiff takes up a lot of room in their home and in their hearts. His best friends are the two rescue cats that think they rule the home. The chickens couldn't care less about the dog until he chases them when they come too close to his outdoor toys.

Discover more about Pebbles on her website:

https://www.pebbleslacasse.com

Free ebook with newsletter subscription:
https://bit.ly/pebbleskinkynews

Connect with Pebbles Lacasse via Linktr.ee

Join Pebbles' ARC Team

YOU MAY ALSO ENJOY:

Full Novels & Series

My Wife and Master Jake
Broken Charm
Snowman's Burden

Rule Breakers Series
The Complete My JoeSmith Collection Boxed Set
The Coaching Rayna Two Book Series
The Naughty Goldie Series

Short Stories

Little Miss Muffet
Hello Officer
Mistress Rabbit
A Run with Charley
Carter's Mistress
Still Waters Burn Deep
Dominatrix for Hire

Anthologies

Quarantined: A Boxed Set of Pandemic Proportions –
Still Waters Burn Deep

Scan for Ebook Catalogue